BLUE NORTHER

SILVER RIDGE RANCH

BOOK ONE

TILLY H. COLSON

GOLDFINCH & KEYS PRESS

AUTHOR'S NOTE

Colt and Violet's story is one of heartbreak and healing. Of lifelong love and the power of second chances.

While I myself love an angst-filled read where the MMC yearns *hard* for the FMC, and their second chance at a happily-ever-after feels written in the stars, I truly believe that above all else, your mental health matters. Please read through the following content warning list. I've tried to be as thorough as possible, but always know you are welcome to reach out to me if you feel something has been missed.

In this story, you'll find: main characters dealing with infertility and mentions of fertility treatments, mentions of pregnancy loss, pregnancy after pregnancy loss and infertility, anxiety in pregnancy, full-term pregnancy complications including unplanned c-section and maternal complications following delivery, divorce (between MCs, they were not intimate with other people during that time), parental death (off page for FMC), mentions of a family member with cancer, stalking (not between MCs), assault with a weapon, mental health struggles for a secondary character/family member, discussion on page surrounding depression, mature language, and open door spice between the main couple.

*For everyone who believes in
the power of soulmates, and the immense courage
held within a second chance...*

Blue Norther:

A fast moving cold front that ushers in a rapid drop in
temperature, strong winds,
and dark blue skies.

Violet

Nine years ago...

The sun was so damn hot it felt like I'd rubbed the jalapeños I was growing on our back porch right across my skin. But I wouldn't move. I couldn't. This chair, this singular spot on our property, had become the one place I could turn off my mind and just... ignore the pain. Ignore the heartbreaking numbness of going through another loss.

My husband, Colt, had been a rock through everything. Of course he was; I married the best man in the world. Which was why I knew he was inside, but not working on finishing the drywall in the laundry room like he said. No. He was cleaning the bathroom so that I could sit in our shower. He'd pretend not to hear me crying for ten or fifteen minutes, and then he'd come in and hold me. Just like the first time I'd lost a pregnancy. And the second. And the third.

No one could give us any answers. No one could figure

out why things just weren't happening for us. We were young. Active. Colt's mom and dad had five kids. And while my parents only had me, that was a personal choice, not one forced onto them by flawed biology.

No. I was the problem. Something was wrong inside of *me*. Inside the eggs my body made, or maybe something in my womb. Even science and IVF hadn't been able to help us. That's what hurt the most. This hope I held in my heart that I was finally going to be able to tell Colt he was going to be a dad, and actually get to keep that promise.

Our first egg retrieval was a nightmare, and recovery had been more painful than I thought it was going to be. Not to mention the side effects from all the hormones I had to take. But again, Colt had been so understanding, never once getting mad at my outbursts. Never once downplaying my fears.

I wiped away the tear that escaped, finally tipping my face down and out of the sun, letting it fall into my open hands. My head felt like it was stuffed full of cotton. My body wasn't my own. I hated it. I hated the way it had failed me, time and time again. The way it had failed my husband. Our families. Our friends. The way I had failed everyone.

Eight weeks ago, we'd transferred one of our two embryos. We chose it because the other wasn't graded that well, and our doctor had higher hopes this one would be our golden ticket.

And for eight weeks, we were cautiously optimistic. Until I started spotting.

I knew what people would say.

Don't give up! It's only been a few years.

You and Colt just need to go on vacation and pretend you're still newlyweds.

Just stop putting so much pressure on yourself. It'll happen when it's meant to happen.

But what those well-meaning people didn't know was that we were once newlyweds who didn't try to prevent pregnancy.

What they didn't have any understanding of was the number of times Colt held me while whispering reassurances that our time to be parents would come, all while I could feel our chances slipping away.

I just can't do it anymore. I don't want to walk past my husband every day and see the longing in his eyes. I can't go into the nursery, the first room in the house we renovated, now sitting empty with boxes of furniture to build that I just can't find the energy to assemble. I want space, distance, from this pain I'm inflicting on everyone.

The porch door opened and I quickly ran my hands over my cheeks. It wasn't the right time for him to see me crying. I wasn't supposed to fall apart until I was safely hidden in the shower.

"Hey," he said as he cleared his throat, placing his hand on my shoulder. "The bathroom is all cleaned up if you feel like taking a shower."

My hand reached back and I wrapped my fingers around his wrist, turning my head to kiss his thumb.

"Thank you," I managed to choke out. While I went inside, Colt stayed on the porch. From our bedroom window, I watched him—hands tucked in his jeans, his eyes sliding closed as he tipped his face towards the sun, just like I'd done. I watched his lips move, gentle words of prayers sent towards Heaven that I knew would never be answered.

I made my way into the bathroom, the shower already running and steam filling up the space. As soon as I stepped in, I turned up the heat. I wanted to feel it searing into my skin. Not to ease the painful cramps. Not to take away the way my back ached and my legs shook. But to warm the numbness that had taken hold of me. If I could wash some of it away, maybe I could convince myself to stay.

But as I sank to the floor, my tears mixing with the water

pouring down over me, the numbness stayed. And I had my answer. I couldn't. I *wouldn't.*

The shower door opened, taking some of the warmth I was so desperate to feel deep in my bones and flinging it out into the room. Colt's body loomed over me, the normal safety and security I felt from his presence dwarfed by the weight of what I needed to tell him.

"It hurts." I broke down, my entire body shaking.

"I wish I could take away the pain, baby. I wish I could carry it for you."

"I can't keep doing this," I cried as he sat in the shower behind me. My husband's arms wrapped tightly around me, his legs bracketing my own. With a shuddering breath, I melted into him. "I mean it. I-I can't."

"I know, darlin'. I know."

"You don't." I couldn't face him. This would break his heart. Break him. But only temporarily. He'd be okay in the end. He had his family. He had his job. And once he moved on from...well, me...he could find someone who would give him the one thing I'd never be able to.

"You deserve to be a dad," I sobbed. "I'm taking that away from you. My body is stealing the chance you have for that."

Colt's hand lifted off me, gathering my hair and pushing it off my shoulder. He pressed a kiss to the freshly exposed skin. "I don't *need* to be a dad. You're enough for me. This life we have together is enough." His voice was heavy. Gravel-filled and tear stained. I felt his lips near the shell of my ear as he spoke to me, barely above a whisper. Soft, full of comfort—and fear.

Fear of adding to my pain. Fear of pushing me off the edge into the dark abyss biting at my ankles, threatening to pull me under.

He didn't know there was no reason for that worry. Because I wasn't going to be pushed.

I was going to jump.

"It's not. I'm not. I'm broken. You shouldn't have to put up with this."

"Put up with what? Supporting you? Loving you? It's the fucking honor of my life to get to do those things, Vi."

"No. I can't...I can't breathe. The way you look at me, scared I might fracture and fall apart all day, every day. The way you stopped talking to my belly when I'm awake and only talked to it when you thought I was asleep. I need a break."

"Then we'll take a break. I'll call the clinic right now and tell them we're taking a few cycles off. They'll understand."

"I don't mean a break from IVF," I whispered.

"What kind of break, then?" Colt asked.

I bit down on my bottom lip, hating the words that were about to come out of my mouth, but knowing the bitter taste of them would be worth swallowing down if it saved Colt from a lifetime of regret. "From here. From us."

"From us? No. Absolutely not. We've been a team since we were twelve-years-old. We're not...this is something we can work through. This is something we can survive."

"It's something you can survive, because I'm setting you free."

"What the fuck are you talking about?" he growled, no real bite behind the words. "You want us to separate?"

"No, Colt. I want a divorce."

COLT

TWO YEARS LATER...

I saw her the second I walked into the funeral home. She sat at the front, her blazing-red hair tied back with a black satin ribbon. My wife's...my *ex*-wife's...shoulders were tight, her neck turned as she spoke to a woman who had paused at the end of the aisle.

Jennie Murphy had been like a second mom to me growing up. She loved me for who I was, and she loved me for loving her daughter. It broke my heart that the first place I was going to see Vi in the two years since our divorce was at her mother's funeral.

Hell, I didn't even know if I should come. If I was welcome. If I was wanted.

What if I saw her here with another man? Someone who her mother also approved of?

I shoved the nauseating thought down. It didn't matter.

Paying my last respects to a wonderful woman and checking on Violet, making sure she was okay, was the only thing that did.

"Colton Ford."

I turned, Violet's father walking along the back wall towards me. I checked to see if she'd heard him, but if she had, she didn't turn to face me.

"Pete. I'm so sorry for your loss."

"Thank you, son. I'm so grateful for the time we had together, and that the cancer took her quickly. She didn't suffer like my mother did."

I nodded. "I'm sorry I wasn't able to come say goodbye before now. I loved her."

His hand landed on my shoulder. Although I was nearly half a foot taller than Violet's dad, the sweet gesture of a father and widower comforting me like I was truly his son hit me square in the heart.

"Jennie knew how much you loved her. She loved you the same." He dropped his gaze, looking across the church to his daughter. "Are you going to go talk to her?"

"I'm not sure what the right thing to do is. I want her to know I'm still here for her, that I want to make sure she's alright. But if she doesn't want to hear that from me..."

"She does. She *needs* to hear it. Violet's been working so hard, taking care of her mother. Taking care of me. She didn't have time to heal before she was rushing to be with us after Jennie's diagnosis. And she doesn't know how I spend time each night down the hall, listening to her cry for you."

That admission stole my breath. There was nothing I could do except nod, because if I tried to speak, I knew my voice would break.

"Go. I know it will mean so much to her that you came today."

I turned and headed down the aisle. My heart was thundering loudly in my ears, and I had to shove my hands into my pockets to stop them from shaking. Christ, it felt like the first time I tried to tell her I wanted to be more than friends.

"Is this seat taken?" I asked, watching her cheeks and the tip of her nose turn the most precious cherry-red color. God, out of the millions of little things I missed about her, that response to my voice was right at the top of the list.

"What are you doing here?" she asked, wiping at her nose with a tissue. Her question wasn't harsh, or angry, but rather filled with awe. And that broke even more of my heart.

"I wanted to say goodbye to Jennie. And I wanted to be here for you, too."

She reached over and grabbed her purse, moving it from the spot I'd asked to occupy and setting it on the other side of the bench.

"You can sit."

I wasn't going to be told twice. Bowing my head, I slid down next to her. Was there enough room that I didn't need to be so close that our legs touched? Yes. Was I a bastard for wanting that contact and making sure it happened anyway? Of course.

But then she shocked me. Because my beautiful wife—fuck saying *ex*—held open her hand. My fingers slid along her palm, until they were intertwined with hers.

Lord, I missed her so damn much, I was fighting back tears over holding her hand. I was also probably on the fast track to Hell for how many cuss words I'd said in my head in the last five minutes in a place of reverence.

We sat just like that, silent, for what felt like an eternity.

"How are you?" she asked, finally breaking the silence.

"Miserable. You?"

Vi choked out a laugh. "Yeah. About the same."

I turned, still holding onto her hand, but enough so I could face her. "I'm so sorry about your mom."

"Thanks."

"Pete told me you took care of her. That you've been taking care of them both."

"Someone had to...my dad was falling apart. You obviously know they live in Arizona now, since you're here."

I nodded, not sure how to tell her that I'd been the one looking after her parents' place back in Silver Springs. That I still talked to them regularly.

If she expected me to fill that information in for her, she didn't pause long enough for me to. "Living with them again was a gift I hadn't been expecting. I wish my mom had beat it, you know? I'm mad that she wasn't one of the people who ever got to ring the bell, or have the party. I'm furious I only had thirty-two years with her. But I don't think I would have had that much concentrated, truly connected time with her at the end of her life if things had worked out any other way."

"That's a beautiful way to look at it."

"You know me, ever the optimist." I knew she was joking. I knew the sarcasm was meant to protect her like thick armor.

"Who was taking care of you during all of this?" My thumb circled over the back of her hand.

Her eyebrow raised, the tissue in her free hand coming up to wipe at her nose again.

"Is that your not so subtle way of asking me...?" I watched as she struggled to get the words out.

"No, Violet. I wasn't trying to pry."

"There's nothing to pry," she whispered. "I know everything was so raw and painful two years ago, and I know you already know this, but I didn't leave you because I wanted to love someone else. I left because I love you so much that this pain in my heart is worth it if it gives you even the smallest chance at happiness."

"Still not ready to listen to me?"

Her head shook.

"Okay. Tell me about work. Are you still ghostwriting?"

We fell into easy conversation after that. Violet slowly opened up, talking about the summer she spent in Colorado right after our divorce was finalized. About the manuscript she finished while living in a tiny cabin in the woods. It was all hers, and she beamed while talking about it. I tried my hardest not to panic when I heard just how remote the cabin was. After all, she wasn't living there anymore, and she seemed to be in one physical piece in front of me.

We talked about my family, about how things were going in Clarence County. I told her about some of the renovations I'd worked on—but not all of them. I knew that hearing I was still checking projects off her honey-do list wouldn't make things better. So I skipped over those things.

I couldn't tell how many hours had passed as we sat there talking. Everyone just let us be until the sun grew hazy outside the windows. People milled about and dwindled away, until we were almost the last people left.

"Honey?" Pete walked towards us from the altar, where he'd just taken the last of Jennie's pictures down. His arms were wrapped around the frame, pressing it against his chest like he was giving her one last hug goodbye. "We should...we should think about heading home."

Violet nodded, her hand slipping off my arm.

"Colt, would you like to—"

"He has a long trip home, Dad. We should let him go." Violet's eyes dropped to the floor, her open body language shutting down in an instant.

"I don't have to go," I offered, my hand reaching out to rest on her arm. "I'd actually love to stay."

But the Violet I'd just been talking to was gone, and in her place, the wife I'd held in the shower as she broke down in my arms was back. And I knew the door had closed once more.

Still, I opened my arms, praying she would give me this

one last moment to hold her. One last moment to wrap my arms around her. She hesitated, but only for a second.

Her body still fit against mine perfectly, but of course it did. Because even if she didn't want to remember, the universe made her for me. Just like it made me for her.

My head fell against hers. I heard her father walking away, the door to the room creaking open, then clanging shut as he allowed us to have this last moment together.

"I love you, Vi. I know you think there's a day when I'll move on, but there isn't. The door will always be open. You'll always own every piece of my heart."

"Don't say that."

I lifted my head, tipping her face to meet mine with my thumb under her chin.

"Darlin', it's the truth. Just because I set you free, doesn't mean I don't pray every damn day that you'll return to me."

COLT

S EVEN YEARS LATER, PRESENT DAY...

I was a grumpy bastard. Was officially diagnosed by my family long before my own friends fucking agreed. Not that I cared. I'd known it my whole goddamn life, and I wasn't shy about showing people just how grumpy I could be. But as the first-born son of a ranching family in Texas, yeah, you better believe that hard ass attitude was drilled into me every waking moment of my entire childhood.

Now, that childhood was well over thirty years behind me, but as a deputy with the Clarence County Sheriff's Department, it still served me well.

"You're a dick, Colt." Lucas Mandarano thrashed back and forth in my hands as I led him towards the cell he'd be spending the weekend in.

"I'm not the idiot who got drunk at noon and started a fight at Davney's, now am I? You're lucky Gunner and Gage stepped in when they did. Heard you were fixin' to throw a stool through a window—and I hate to be the bearer of bad news, but that could have easily caught you a third degree felony charge."

"Fuck them, and fuck you, too."

"Mm. Enjoy your stay at Casa Clarence County. It's going to be a lovely weekend outside, fall's really setting in. Too bad you'll be stuck in here with a fucking terrible hangover."

I slammed the cell door a little louder than necessary, chuckling at the grumbles coming from Lucas. It made up for the fact that my shift was meant to be over an hour ago.

"Colt, you got a minute?" My boss, Hank Porter, stood with his arms across his chest. Hank wasn't the warmest person, either, but ever since his wife Daisy came into his life, he smiled from time to time. It still was eerie as shit when it happened. I no longer had my wife, so smiling wasn't something I had to worry about anymore.

"Yeah, of course. What's going on?"

"I figured we could do our turnover brief now. I know you're on your way out the door, but since you have to be back here bright eyed and bushy tailed tomorrow at 7:00 AM, I figure it's now or never."

Right. Turnover. Hank was leaving for two weeks…a family vacation with his wife and kids. And as the chief deputy, that meant I was taking over in his absence. I tried not to groan.

Sure, each promotion was nice. But I hated dealing with bureaucracy. Put me in the field. Let me investigate. Let me break up bar fights. Hell, let me write speeding tickets. Just get me out of the damn office.

"You look like I'm about to put you in front of a firing squad," Hank laughed.

"Nah. Just a long shift. I'm looking forward to sleep."

"Aright, let's get this briefing underway so you can get outta here as fast as possible."

———

Two hours later, my mid-shift was finally over. I'd have a few hours to flip my body back to day shift mode, instead of the weird hours I'd been working over the last week. Because in the morning, I'd be expected to report back to the department to attend to everything Hank normally took care of.

I groaned, my feet pounding against the pavement as I walked towards my truck. My phone buzzed in my pocket. *Hank couldn't have something to fill me in on already, could he?*

No. It wasn't Hank. Pete Murphy was calling me. Weird, because it was the middle of the month. My stomach soured for a second, thinking something bad might have happened to Violet. Her dad and I still talk to each other about once a month when I go check on his old place right down the road from my family's ranch, but there was no reason he should be calling me today.

"Pete. Everything okay?" I asked as I answered the call.

"Colt! I hope I'm not catching you at a bad time?"

"No, not at all. I'm just heading home from work."

"Oh good. Good. Look, I was hoping maybe you could swing by the cabin today. You know, the Logans called me last week and said there had been some break-ins recently on our road. I've got someone who wants to use the place for a while and just want to make sure they'll be safe there."

"Someone?" My heart rate doubled as I hopped into the cab of my truck. *Please tell me she's coming home. Tell me she's finally coming back to me.*

"Yeah, you know how it is. I barely ever get down there anymore. Figured someone else might as well get some use out of it. Let me know if there's any damage, okay, son?"

I loved that he still called me that, even as I crossed over into my forties and hadn't technically been a part of his family in years.

"Of course, I'll let you know what I find. There is a great security firm here in Silver Springs that I can recommend if you are looking for a security system. Could remotely monitor things from your favorite golf course in Arizona."

He laughed. "That sounds awesome. I'll have to look them up when I figure out how to use my tablet. Got that damn thing for Christmas last year, and I still can't work it. Anyway, thanks, Colt."

"Any time, Pete."

Damn. It wasn't Violet. I shook my head, trying to clear away a lifetime of memories as I headed out to her parents' place. She hadn't grown up in Silver Springs like I did. My whole life was spent out on the Silver Ridge Ranch. As the eldest son of the town's founding family, I think everyone was shocked when I went into law enforcement. My family knew I loved living on the ranch, but I wouldn't be happy ranching my days away.

No. That was something my brother Beau enjoyed. And sometimes my sister Jessie—the baby of our family—would help out, too, with all the misfit animals she collected over the years.

I drove past my mom's diner. Yes, Dolly's was the best place to eat at in Silver Springs, and no, I wasn't biased because she's my mom. And nine out of ten people in town would agree with me. My family's legacy was all over this town. Hell, it wasn't just the diner—the main street through Silver Springs was named Ford Avenue after my family: the Fords. My brother, Lachlan, owned an auto body shop, though it had been closed for years since his accident. My other brother Hayes was a firefighter. Our grandparents had once run the mercantile in town, and they'd be rolling in their graves if they knew it was now a shared office space.

Even with the reminders of my family all throughout this town, every time I drove through, I still saw the reminders of *her*.

Reminders of her at the middle school, where we met the first day after she transferred into my seventh grade class—*also known as the best day of my life*—until our first kiss later in high school that happened in the hay loft of my family's barn.

Christ. *Vi wasn't back.* I didn't need this goddamn trip down memory lane. I turned the radio up, but completely tuned it out the closer I got to the cabin.

We were lucky; being best friends who lived only two miles down the road from each other had its perks. It really became fun when we were teens and could sneak out to meet up at the springs my family kept just for swimming in. They were separate from the spring that everyone came to get drinking water from, and Vi and I would go skinny dipping under the moonlight.

Yes. The very springs the town of Silver Springs were named after were on the Silver Ridge Ranch. Most people in town stopped into the well house that was down the road, across the street from the twenty or so acres all our houses were spread across.

The springs fed cold, crystal clear water to the well house, and the water had been a nickel a gallon for almost a hundred years. My great-great grandpa had sworn that the water was healing. And I'd believed the legend myself.

Right up until the water hadn't helped Vi. I hadn't had a drop of the stuff since.

My fingers gripped the steering wheel so tightly I felt the ache in my teeth. Christ. Why the hell was I getting myself so worked up on memories?

I flipped on the turn signal, jostling down the driveway faster than I probably should have. Pete was right. There were a string of break-ins recently, and I should have come and checked out here myself before he had to call me.

Parking my truck next to the line of trees surrounding the driveway, I hopped down. A quick walk around the cabin showed everything still secured from when I was here two weeks before. The wind picked up, cold enough that I tightened my jacket around myself.

Novembers in East Texas really were a mixed bag, but this year, it felt colder than normal.

My phone buzzed in my pocket.

"Ford," I answered.

"Hey, you got plans tonight?" my brother Hayes asked.

"Other than getting my old ass to bed for a few hours so I can flip to days, nope. Not a thing. Thought you'd be heading into the firehouse."

"Nah. Finally got a night off. Beau was thinking about bunking with the guys out at the bunkhouse, but I convinced him we'd be fun company, too. I'm gonna grab a couple of steaks and some beer from my place, and then I figured we could head to Lach's."

"Yeah. Okay. Did you ask Jessie and Hawk?"

"It's kind of a brothers only event."

"You're almost forty. It's just a family dinner at this point. Don't you want to see Beckett?"

"Of course I do. But Jessie's on a tear about not swearing around him. I can't deal with it tonight. We got shit we need to address with Lach, anyway. You're going to see Jessie this week for your dinner with them. What's the difference?"

That was true. My sister, her husband, and my nephew came to dinner once a week at my place. It was a tradition Jessie had started after Violet left, and now that they were all living on the ranch, it was something I looked forward to every week.

"Yeah, shit. Fine. But I'm telling Jess I wanted to include her, and that *you* froze her out."

I closed the cabin door behind me, setting my hat on the counter before I marched over to the thermostat and turned the furnace on. The house was at sixty-three degrees, which wasn't terrible, but that probably wasn't going to be comfortable for whoever was coming.

The low battery alarm started flashing.

"Cold. That's just mean, Colt. You're in a pissy mood today, aren't you?"

I opened the first drawer in the kitchen, trying to remember where I stored the batteries from the last time I changed them out.

"Damn it."

"What's the matter?"

"Nothing. Look, I gotta go. But I'll see you at your house later, okay?"

"Alright."

I pulled the phone away from my ear and tucked it back in my pocket. The first drawer was a bust, but I hit the jackpot with the second drawer. It only took a minute to swap out the batteries, and I could already feel the cabin warming up as I walked around, checking on the rooms. Everything was exactly how I'd left it at the beginning of the month.

I grabbed my hat off the counter and a flash of silver out the window caught my eyes. Perfect. Whoever was staying looked like they made it, just in time for me to have to say hi.

I stepped out onto the porch, and time stood still. My throat closed up and I shoved down the urge to cough. My mind must've been playing tricks on me, because there, standing with her eyes closed and her face tilted towards the sun, her beautiful red hair cascading down her back so far it disappeared behind the car between us, was the one person I'd been dying to see every day for the last seven years.

"Violet?"

VIOLET

"Ouch," I groaned as I rubbed the tiny foot pressing against the skin of my belly. "Keep it down in there, would you?"

It was ridiculous to be arguing with my stomach, but I still took every chance I could to talk to it. My belly was so large at this point in my pregnancy, it sat on my lap. And the sweet baby boy rolling around in there would just not listen to me. *Typical.* Was there a part of me that feared I might struggle parenting on my own in the future? Oh, absolutely. But I also knew there was more than enough love in my heart to get us through.

My son's butt pressed out against my hand, and I couldn't help but laugh. This was the third—and final—day of our drive from New York to Texas. Leaving my apartment, my life, behind was unexpected and I was still numb from how quickly everything had happened. A quick call to my OB, and it was clear they weren't happy I needed to travel this far into my pregnancy. But I had no other choice. Since flying this far along was out of the question, the only choice I had was to drive.

So I did. And we were finally, *finally,* in Texas. My GPS was happily counting down the hours, and we were just about to cross the one-hour-left line.

"I promise, sweetheart, we're almost there."

God. *We're almost there.* What a perfect metaphor for every facet of my life at the moment. I was almost to my hometown, almost back to the cabin I'd grown up in. And at thirty-six weeks into my miracle pregnancy at forty, I was nearly to the finish line where I'd hold my son in my arms. For the first time in my life, I'd kept my baby safe in my body for more than twelve weeks.

Safe. That was my job as his mom. So many other babies had been failed by my body, but not this one. Which is why I had to get out of the city. I had to leave my apartment, my favorite bagel shop, and my friends...I had to keep my baby safe.

My eyes drifted to the folder in the passenger seat. It wasn't going to be enough. To find who was out there...to keep me safe. But I had to try.

Another kick reminded me I wasn't just parked at the gas station for no reason. My tank was sitting below half-full, but with just over an hour until I made it to Silver Springs, I didn't want to end up arriving and leaving myself on empty. Aside from a quick stop at any open grocery store to fill up the cupboards, I had no plan to head into town any time soon. No real need to announce my return.

I huffed as I hauled myself out of the driver's seat. Luckily, I'd already been in touch with the OB at St. Clare's, the small hospital I'd deliver the baby at in Bell Ridge. It was at least a thirty minute drive from my parents' house, but first time babies were often slow to arrive, and I was planning on an induction at thirty nine weeks, anyway. I liked having a predictable schedule and sticking to it.

"Hey, pretty mama. You need some help over there?"

My hand immediately left my belly. I squared my shoulders and forced myself not to shrink back. There were good men in the world, and I probably looked ridiculous trying to fiddle with the pump.

I turned and gave a quick wave to the man walking towards me. Tall. Slender. White tank top under a flannel jacket with jeans slung low across his hips. He flicked the cigarette in his hand before bringing it back up to his lips. If I wasn't careful, and he got to close, I was pretty sure I'd throw up all over him. The baby hated the smell of smoke.

"I'm all set. It was just a tricky handle."

"Why don't you let me help you with that? Where's your man? He has you out pumping your own gas while you're cooking his baby. Now, that's just not right."

My skin pebbled. "I'm perfectly fine. That's twice now I've said it. Are you going to take the hint or do I need to get loud?"

"I wouldn't mind hearing you scream out my name."

The older I got, the more I hated men. Truly. They didn't exist in the real world like they did in the novels I wrote. When I was writing a male lead, there were so many female-centered characteristics that made him likable. But not these real world assholes. They just wanted to take from women. And take, and take, and take. It's why once I'd found the love of my life in seventh grade, I didn't let him go.

Until keeping him, depriving him of true happiness, would have killed me.

But there hadn't been a man in my life since. And this asshole in front of me was exactly why. Because no one would ever be Colt.

"What a disgusting thing to say to a woman."

I wasn't sure how the hell I was going to play things as the creep continued to walk closer to me. Thankfully, and honestly not a minute too soon, a state trooper squad car pulled up to the pump behind mine.

"Ma'am, everything alright?" he asked, probably because I was staring a hole through him. I looked back in front of me, but the jerk who was just standing there was nowhere to be found.

"Everything's fine. Thank you." I waved.

After filling my tank, I didn't dare walk inside to use the restroom. No. I was back in the car and spent another hour praying I wouldn't pee myself on the way to Silver Springs.

Right as my audio book finished playing, I was greeted with the familiar roads of Clarence County. My heart picked up as I pulled into the cabin's driveway. There was a big black truck sitting off to the side, and the lights were on in the cabin. The sight made me want to cry. My dad warned me there might be someone here opening the house up for me. It was nice that he wanted to make sure everything was working, and I knew he was worried about me being on my own with just weeks left in my pregnancy, but I also just wanted to get out of these clothes, soak in the big tub I knew was waiting for me upstairs, and crawl into bed for the next week.

Grabbing my phone from the cup holder, I sent off a text to my dad.

> I'm here. Looks like the person you hired to open the cabin for me is here, too. I'll let you know how they did.

Before slipping it into my jacket, I looked at the message that came in from my business manager.

RYAN:

> Did you make it to Smallville, USA yet?
> Population's what? You and a raccoon?

He'd sent it an hour ago, just after I'd gotten back on the

road from that nightmare of a gas station. Served him right, having to wait for my reply.

> Very funny. I did in fact just make it. The raccoon says hi, and they can't wait to meet you when you come to visit me and the baby.

Stepping out of the car was, as always, an extra hard task. I gripped the *oh-shit* handle and the door frame, hoisting myself unceremoniously from the driver's seat.

And then, as my heart slowed and the breeze greeted me, I let my eyes drift shut, the sun warming my skin as it filtered through the tall trees surrounding the place I once called home.

"Violet?"

I must be hearing things. The wind shook the leaves overhead. A bird chirped from somewhere in the distance. And I certainly didn't hear a—

"Vi?"

Shit. My head spun as I faced the source of the voice I hadn't heard in almost a decade. And as much as I wanted to believe there wasn't a single way in this world that my ex-husband would be there, standing on my parents' porch the very minute I made it back to my hometown, my ears hadn't failed me.

He was there. And his eyes were locked on mine, the same disbelief I felt staring right back at me.

My breath caught in the back of my throat, my eyes stinging at the sight of him. As much as I wanted to play it off as if they were aching from the long drive or sensitive to the sunlight, I knew the truth. And it made me want to let every tear I was holding back fall to the earth.

Because my husband was still the love of my life. My *ex-*husband. Even after all the loss. Even after all the heartbreak.

Just because I had to walk away to survive didn't mean it wasn't the toughest decision I ever had to make in my life.

The baby rolled as I straightened my back, tugging my jacket tightly around my chest. I fought the urge to groan. There was no way Colt wouldn't notice my belly. I was going to have to tell him the truth before I'd even thought of a way to soften the blow.

"What are you doing here?" he asked, his eyes wide and not blinking, as if I would disappear if he did.

"I should be asking you that. You make it a habit of trespassing on my property?"

He chuckled, bouncing as he came down the steps. God, he looked good. Colton Ford had always been a solid man, but even with his Deputy's jacket wrapped around him, I could see he'd bulked up in the time since I'd said goodbye to Silver Springs. That cowboy hat on his head made my legs feel all sorts of wobbly that had nothing to do with being in the car for too long.

"It's not trespassing when your dad asks me to check in on the place. I thought it was strange, seeing as how I normally come on the first of the month to make sure everything is still okay. Should have known you were coming down to use it when he mentioned someone visiting."

"Yup. I'm here," I laughed, trying not to wince as the baby rolled again. I needed to use the bathroom, and it was close to being an emergency.

His feet hit the gravel of the driveway, his eyes narrowing on my face. *Shit.* He was about ten steps away from making it around the car. And then he'd see all of me. He'd see my belly.

"You okay?" he asked, pulling me from my panic. This was good. It was okay. Better to get it out in the open now first thing. We could talk. I could explain.

"Sorry. It's been a long day. A long week, actually. What did you say?"

"Are your bags in the trunk? Pop it for me and I'll bring them inside for you."

"I can handle it on my own."

Colt's right eyebrow jumped. "Are you? On your own?"

"Smooth."

He shrugged, walking towards the trunk. Maybe I could just stand here until he had my bags inside? Maybe I could move around the car as he walked back to his truck? Maybe...I should press the button on my fob to pop the trunk for him so he would stop staring at me.

Come on, Violet. Pull it together.

"There," I sighed as the trunk popped open, "and thank you."

Colt nodded as he reached in, setting the two small suitcases I had packed in my hurry to leave New York on the ground.

"Not planning on staying long?" His voice held a note of sadness as he asked.

"Actually, I'm planning on staying for a while. Just figured I could get whatever I really needed in town."

Colt's eyes locked on mine, but he simply nodded before shutting the trunk.

"We've been having some trouble with a group of kids the last few months breaking into places. Just want to make sure you're okay, that you'll be safe out here."

"Oh..." What Colt had just said scared me. Not about the rowdy kids, not really. I had something else to be worried about—and his words reminded me of that. "I guess I should think about getting some security cameras or something."

Colt nodded. "We've got a company in town now. The guys at Montgomery Defense are great. Jessie's husband Hawk actually works there. I'll ask—"

I thought he'd reach down for the bags, bring them to the house. But instead, Colt took two steps towards me. And then two more. My stomach swooped as I watched his eyes rake over my body, from my hair, to my lips, down to my chest—and then right to my belly.

Colt's jaw dropped.

"Holy fuck. You're *pregnant.*" I watched as every emotion cycled through him. "Oh my God, Violet. You're pregnant!"

"I am."

My stomach kept rolling, twisting itself into knots, and I couldn't honestly tell whether it was from the butterflies exploding at the way his eyes mapped out every inch of my belly, or the way his face was beaming out pure excitement...or the nausea bubbling up to the surface because I was about to drop the biggest bomb right in his lap the literal minute I got back to town. I was supposed to have more time.

Time to decide when to see him again.

Time to see if he'd moved on.

Time to have this baby and get settled in my new life here.

But most importantly, I was supposed to have time to figure out how to tell the man I still loved what I had done.

He closed the distance between us in what seemed like a mere second. Colt's legs have always been one of my favorite features, but the way they moved his body towards mine, all power and determination, made my own legs feel weak.

"I'm so happy for you," he whispered. And then I found myself wrapped in the arms of the only man I've ever loved. The man whose baby was doing somersaults in my belly.

COLT

i was pregnant.
My Violet.
She was standing there, right in front of me, all big, beautiful belly. Every emotion simmering under the surface of my skin since I saw her get out of her car slammed into me like a freight train. Because how many years had we spent waiting for that? How many positive tests ended in tears? As far as I knew, Violet had never even made it out of the first trimester before. I never got to feel our babies kick. I never pushed my head against her belly to see if I could hear the heartbeat.

It was the coward's way out, but I bolted as fast as I could. I set her luggage inside, said goodbye faster than I'd ever said anything else in my life, and fucking ran to my truck. And not a second too soon. Because seeing her like that, it rattled me right down to my goddamn core.

How many nights had I fallen asleep to the thought of her carrying my baby? Even after our damn divorce, it was my favorite brand of torture. Imagining what life would have been like if I was able to give her the one thing she wanted more than life itself.

For a second, just as I rounded her car and saw her—really saw her for the first time in seven God-forsaken years—I thought that baby was mine. My brain flashed through every emotion in the span of a single second, and my heart nearly burst through my chest.

But the reality of everything hit me so fucking hard.

I wasn't the man who put that baby in her belly.

I wasn't about to be a dad.

I wasn't anything to either of them.

The first tear fell, and fuck...I managed to swipe it away as I cleared my throat. If there was ever a time I needed to get a grip, it was right goddamn now. She wasn't carrying my baby. It was some other man's. Some fucking joke of a man, if he was sending her off to a cabin thousands of miles away from him as pregnant as she was. What was she thinking, traveling so far along into her pregnancy? I couldn't be sure—because I didn't stay long enough to ask—but she looked far enough along that it was alarming to think about her making the trip down to Texas from New York City.

Yeah, I knew that's where she lived now. Her dad had told me she moved there a few months after I last saw her. Chasing her dreams of publishing her manuscript while living a life completely different from Small Town, Texas. And she had. She'd chased her dreams so far and so well, that she was coming home pregnant with another man's baby.

I didn't even fucking know *her due date.* I didn't stop to ask. Just hugged her like she was telling me it was my baby, and then ran to my truck when I remembered there was no way in hell it could be. Because the last time we'd been together—one night before the divorce was final, when emotions were so goddamn high I thought my heart might crumble in my chest —*fuck.* No baby waited for that long. After a lifetime of thinking it would be me, I was forced to stare down the cold, sobering truth.

I wasn't ever going to be the father of Violet's children.

Dammit, these tears needed to fucking stop. My hands twisted against the steering wheel, trying to fight off the tightness in my chest. *Pull over.* The rate at which I was blinking away tears was fucking pathetic, but the last thing I'd do was put someone else on the road in danger because I couldn't get a fucking grip.

I drove back onto the ranch as the ache in my chest spread through my body, my shoulder, my arm...*fuck, what the hell was happening?* Hayes was a firefighter. I needed to get to him. I was about to fucking die.

Trying my best to breathe against the pressure sitting on my chest, I threw the gearshift into park and scrubbed my hands over my face. *Get a grip, Colt!* My fingers sat against the spot over my heart that was tattooed with a violet. I'd gotten it done the day of our divorce. For her. Because I knew, even as I set her free, even as I signed away my right to be her protector, her provider, that Violet Ford would never be replaced.

With my body in absolute agony, I dragged myself down from the cab of my truck and forced myself towards my brother's front door.

"Hey, Colt. Decided to skip the nap?" Hayes called out from over my shoulder. The world tilted as my body turned around. Nothing I tried helped to get the words out of my mouth. I couldn't say it. I couldn't admit how hung up on her I still was. As soon as I turned, I saw Beau walking alongside him.

"What the fuck is wrong?" Beau asked, his eyes scanning over my face. "You look like you've seen a fucking ghost."

They kept coming closer, but no matter how hard I tried to speak, the mounting pressure on my chest stopped me. My hand found its way above my heart and I grasped at my shirt.

Hayes got the message.

"Are you having a fucking heart attack right now?"

I almost wanted to laugh at how pissed he sounded.

"Sit down." Both Hayes and Beau hooked their arms through mine and walked me to the porch. I was unceremoniously shoved to the steps by Beau, who mumbled something about getting some aspirin while Hayes got down on his haunches and looked me dead in the eyes.

"Tell me what's happening," he demanded.

"You'd think I was your kid brother with that tone..." I finally got out.

"You look ready to fall over, and you want me to apologize for the tone in which I'm speaking to you? Fuck all the way off. I'll leave you here for Beau to deal with. That dipshit will kill you, for sure."

I wished I was in the head space to laugh, because Hayes was right. Beau would try to help, and I'd be gone before I knew what happened.

"My chest. It's tight. And it's aching in my shoulder and my arm."

"Fuck." Hayes looked up over my shoulder and whispered something about Beau before looking back at me. "Alright. Looks like I'm playing wee-woo driver today. You know I've always wanted to turn the lights and sirens on in your truck."

"Ain't fucking happening," I groaned as I flexed my left hand. The pain was getting better, but the pressure was still there.

"You want to tell me what the hell you were doing when this came on?"

"No." I snapped. The damn ache behind my ribs was suddenly nothing compared to the burning behind my eyes. The last time Hayes or Beau had seen me cry, we were sure our brother Lachlan was going to die after a horrible accident in his mechanic's garage left him with a crushed leg. He lived— thank God—but all of us had broken down in the hospital as we waited to hear his fate.

A large hand clamped down on my shoulder. "Is this a heart thing? Or is something else going on?"

I looked into my younger brother's eyes. "Vi's back," I whispered.

His eyes went wide as his head slowly nodded with understanding. "Fuck. You just saw her?"

"She's at her parents' place. That's not..." My fucking voice caught in my chest again. "That's not all."

"She brought someone with her?" Hayes asked. It wasn't a secret I never wanted to let Violet go. That I wanted to fight for our marriage. That I wanted to fight for the twelve-year-old version of me who promised to always be there for her. But I walked away, knowing it was what she needed more than anything at that time. She needed space to heal, and I was the idiot who thought she would come back to me.

"No. She was by herself." I sucked in a harsh breath and spoke the words that were causing all the pain out loud. "She's pregnant."

"She's *what?!*"

"She's pregnant. Very pregnant. And it's not—" My vision went blurry, and then before I could blink back the first tear, Hayes' arms were wrapped around me.

"I found the—what the hell happened?" Beau's voice demanded from behind us.

"Not a heart attack. A broken heart. Violet's back—and she's pregnant."

I didn't have to see my brother to know that his face would be emotionless as he listened to the news. Beau never forgave Vi for leaving, even though it wasn't his place to hold a grudge.

"Fuck. Well, I finally found your fucking aspirin. Here." I heard the bottle rattle behind me before Beau's hand was waving wildly in front of my face. "Better to be safe than sorry."

"Get him out a dose, dipshit. Does it look like he can fucking manage it on his own right now?"

"Right. Christ. This is so fucking weird. Violet's back, after all this time." Beau's laugh held no emotion. "And pregnant. Why the fuck is she back? To rub it in your face?"

"She wouldn't do that. She was shocked to see me. And she was..."

"What?" Hayes asked.

"She looked sad."

"You said she's here alone?" Beau handed me a glass of water, and I drank it down after chucking the aspirin to the back of my throat, nodding.

"Where the fuck is the guy who knocked her up?"

That was the million dollar question.

I growled at the thought. The vibration ricocheted through my body, and I winced from the pain that lingered in my bones.

VIOLET

Bread. Eggs. Milk. Toilet paper. Chocolate. Chocolate. Hot sauce. More chocolate.

I sighed as I looked down at the pathetic shopping list I'd managed to put together at the last minute. My hands were still shaking from seeing Colt, the scent of him lingering in my memories from the hug he'd surprised me with.

I was *not* ready to think or confront my feelings about all that, so chocolate—copious amounts of it—were in order.

A shiver rolled through my body. *That was weird.* The feeling of being watched raised the hairs on the back of my neck. No. I'd just gotten here. Everything inside of me was hyper-aware because of what happened in New York. But there was a tall man, standing next to the oranges, who kept looking over his shoulder at me. I had to be overreacting. I just needed to take a breath and—

Shit. I bumped my cart into the display of Granny Smith apples. As if that loud clang wasn't bad enough, I watched as apple after apple came off the precisely stacked pyramid display. Why would anyone think that was a good idea...I looked around desperately for help, but Tall Man was nowhere to be seen.

Knowing I couldn't just leave my apple disaster to some poor, unsuspecting teenager working late hours after school, I slowly got down, using the edge of my cart for some stability, and started rolling apples back towards the display. I grimaced, holding my belly as the baby moved, who apparently was not appreciating the way I was twisting.

"Whoa," a deep voice boomed over me, chuckling. "What happened here?"

Heat filled my face as the stranger got down, slowly rolling apples the same way I was.

"My clumsiness got the better of me," I said as I leaned back, stretching so the baby would settle. It gave me a chance to look at the person working beside me. Clean shaven. Kind eyes that kept glancing my way, but didn't give off the same creepy vibes as the man who couldn't stop looking at my belly. No. There was something almost like concern in this man's eyes.

"Gotcha. Texas isn't known for snow, so I guess this apple-anche is the closest thing to winter excitement we're going to see around here."

God, he was charming. I could feel my face flooding with heat. The stranger got up, stacking the apples back onto the display. "All better," he said as the last one went into place. He turned towards me. I was useless, still down on the floor, contemplating just how ungraceful I was about to look when I hefted myself up.

"Do you need a hand?" he asked.

"Oh no. Just taking a minute to run a calculation about the mass, volume, and velocity needed to escape one's own gravitational pull," I joked.

"Those were a lot of fancy words. Are you a physicist?"

"Nope. Just a pregnant lady who sometimes has to decide if it's worth the hassle of getting off the couch," I laughed.

"Well, I'm *definitely* not a physicist, or an expectant mom, but two masses have to be better than one, in these situations. Can I help you?" The kind man held out his hand to me. I nodded, pretty sure I was only accepting because I could not, for the life of me, think of any other way I was going to be able to get back up.

He did most of the work, pulling me up like it was nothing.

"Thank you." I laughed softly as I let go of his hands, brushing my own over my belly before turning towards my cart. "And thank you for helping me clean up the runaway apples. I fear this is a story I'll tell my little one every time he comes shopping with me."

"It was no problem. You have a good rest of your shopping trip. Maybe just skip the canned soup aisle, though. I saw a display of baked beans that was already teetering precariously the other day."

"Noted. Thank you again." I waved as I pushed my cart as fast as I could manage. I was about to skip everything and just run to my car, but I was genuinely hungry and knew, for my sake and the baby's, that I needed to get actual food to eat.

Turning the cart down the cereal aisle, I stopped. Tall Man was there, his hands around a box of Bran Flakes. It took one second for him to turn and face me, his eyes raking down my body again. I squared my shoulders.

Just get to the oatmeal. You'll be fine.

He was staring at me, and I just stared right back. I wasn't about to let a stranger make me feel uncomfortable. It was almost as if he was waiting to see if I'd back down first, but as I got closer, he simply went back to looking at the box of cereal in his hands.

Maybe I looked like someone he knew. Maybe he just had

no manners. Whatever the reason was, I didn't care. Grabbing the first box of maple brown sugar oatmeal I could get my hands on, I hightailed it out of the aisle.

It took me another ten minutes of wandering the store to feel like I had an okay selection of groceries. After I stopped into the Sheriff's department tomorrow—the one in Bell Ridge, and not here in Silver Springs where I knew I was likely to run into Colt—my plans were to hide out at the house until I could gather up enough courage to talk to him. Now that I was back, he deserved to know the truth.

"Ma'am." I turned, looking at the guy behind me in line. My apple-disaster rescuer was behind me in line.

"Sorry. I don't have any apples with me," I joked. "I hear there's a lovely selection in the fruit department, though some may be a little bruised for an unknown reason."

He laughed as his eyes dropped to my belly, where I was rubbing my hand over what I was almost certain was the baby's foot pushing out at me.

"Can I help you to your car?" he asked.

"Oh, I...uh. No, that's so kind of you, but I've got everything under control."

"That'll be $112.85, dear," the cashier announced as she placed the last of my ice cream into a bag and handed them over the partition to me.

"Sure thing." I placed the ice cream into my cart and held my credit card over the receiver, waiting for the all clear from her side. As soon as I saw the receipt start to print, I began to push my cart out of the way.

"My mama would actually throttle me if I didn't help," the man behind me offered. "Besides, it's getting dark. Our town is pretty sleepy, but it's always better to be safe than sorry."

Sweat pricked on the small of my back. *He was just being friendly. He was just trying to look after a woman who was clearly very pregnant. One who had admitted to being clumsy earlier, and that he'd seen first-hand. I didn't need to fear him...*

"That's very sweet, but I'm okay."

"Oh, honey." The cashier smiled at me, clearly understanding my hesitancy wasn't just about being polite or independent. "You're safe with him, he's a deputy. And I know his mama—she would actually throttle him."

"Thanks, Ms. Carolyn." She scanned his Coke and a sub from the deli.

The tips of his ears turned red as he smiled at me. A deputy. He worked with Colt. The apprehension in my muscles drained away.

"Well, I can't be responsible for your mom being mad at you. I'd actually love the help. Thank you."

"I'm Nate, by the way. Nate Jones. Or Jonesy, if you're my friend," he informed me as we walked out of the store.

I smiled, a little hesitant to relinquish control of my shopping cart to him. He swooped in very smoothly and smiled as he took over. Probably a good thing as I felt my belly tighten. Braxton Hicks contractions were becoming a part of my nighttime routine lately. They were completely normal—at least that's what my midwife had said when I asked about the risks of traveling so far this late in my pregnancy.

"It's nice to meet you, Nate. Thank you again for helping me out to my car. It does make me feel a little bit like I'm eighty, but I'll let it slide because I am actually very tired and appreciate the help."

"Dang. I was hoping you'd call me Jonesy. I feel like helping someone through an apple containment breach and subsequent cleanup at least puts us in the friends category."

"Friends, then," I agreed.

"So..." He raised his eyebrows as I pulled my keys out,

clicking the little button that released the back hatch on my car.

"Oh," I laughed, "I'm Violet."

"Well, it's *very* nice to meet you, Violet, even if you did put me straight to work from the very first minute of our friendship." He winked at me. Oh God. I could feel the heat flooding my face. He had to be *at least* ten years younger than me, not to mention the fact that he kept looking at my very, *very* pregnant belly.

We got to my car and Nate made quick work of transferring my groceries for me. I stood like an awkward potato, just watching until he was all done.

"Thank you again so much for the save with the apples and the grocery bags." I held out my hand to him.

Nate smiled, looking down at my hand with a chuckle before he shook it. "No problem, Violet. Get home safe, okay?"

"You got it."

He pushed the cart away from my car and I got in the driver's seat, locking the door behind me quickly. I watched as he kept an eye on my car until I backed out and left.

With the last of the groceries put away, I made my way to the kitchen table where I'd left my laptop sitting open. God, I was exhausted. But Ryan was meant to email me about the contract extension I was on and a potential new project. There was no way my mind would let me rest until I checked to see if that had come in.

There was one unread email in my inbox, but it wasn't from my business manager. My throat ached and I tried to swallow past the pain as I clicked into the message.

Callie,
I know you think you can run and I won't be able to find you.
That's why you haven't been back to your apartment in days.
That's why you left behind your cell phone on the table in the
kitchen, isn't it? You think this will stop me? You think you'll just
go away, and I'll stop trying to make you see that it's always been
you and me? I'd cover the whole world to find you again. For just
one more chance at making you mine. Because you are mine.
And one day, you'll see that. I'll make you see that.
Stay safe. I'm coming for you, baby girl.

I slammed my laptop shut. The nausea crashed into me so hard I nearly fell out of my chair as I tried to scramble to the sink. The baby rolled as I dry heaved over and over. Thankfully, nothing came up.

Why had I thought it would stop just because I'd left?

I would close down that email account. Ryan could handle all my correspondence from now on, or he would just hire someone else to. My only priority was getting that sick person out of my life.

And he could be anyone. He could be anywhere.

He was in my apartment.

Grabbing a glass from the cupboard above the sink, I filled it with tap water, watching the bubbles swirl as it filled higher and higher. It's true, I left my last cell phone in my apartment on the table before I left, because I thought that would be safe. If he'd been tracking me through it, watching my movements somehow, I didn't want to lead him straight here to Texas.

No. The only people who knew I was here would never hurt me. I got away. What someone sent to me on the internet couldn't hurt me. He couldn't hurt me. *I'd gotten away.*

COLT

*V*iolet's pregnant.

"You listening to me, Ford?"

Violet was back in Silver Springs. I saw her with my own eyes three days ago.

Deputy Nate Jones crossed his arms as he leaned on the door frame to Hank's office. Which, of course, was officially mine for the next few weeks.

"Yeah, you want to swap out your three night shifts next week with Hamilton, who has some family event he wants to be on days for?"

Violet's pregnant. She was just standing there, so goddamn beautiful. Pregnant.

"Right. You sure you're okay?"

"I'm fine." I pulled my readers down, tossing them on the pile of paperwork in front of me. "Consider the scheduling matter handled. Now leave me alone."

Jonesy left, muttering something under his breath that I absolutely didn't have time to worry about. *Jesus.* These reports were making my eyes bleed. I knew it was a fucking painful, but necessary, part of my job to fill them out, but I didn't know how Hank sat here, hour after hour, running through all of them. A great reminder why I wanted this position to only be *temporary*. I had enough bureaucracy to deal with in my chief deputy position.

I shook my head, the burning in my eyes returning as I focused on the computer screen in front of me.

"Hey, apple-anche. What's going on? Everything alright?" My ears picked up on the greeting that came from the front desk. God, that was awfully familiar for greeting someone at the station. Jonesy needed to watch himself. Most days, one of us had to slap him on the back of the head for being such an outrageous flirt.

"Nate! I guess you were telling the truth about working here. If it's not too much trouble, I was hoping to speak with a deputy today."

The second her voice hit my ears, I was out of my—er, Hank's—chair. I forced myself to slow down, taking a breath as I crossed my arms and leaned against the door frame.

"Yeah, of course, Violet. I can direct you to someone back in our offices, or I could even help you if you wanted to explain why you're here and what you need help with?"

I watched as Vi shifted the large legal sized envelope in her arms, holding whatever was inside closer to her chest. Her cheeks turned a rosy red as she shook her head. Stubborn, like always.

"Jones." My voice boomed across the office as I pushed off the wall, walking towards the locked door. "Buzz her in."

He spun around to look at me, but I just nodded. "Uh, sure thing, Ford."

Violet's eyes went wide, her lips opened like she was about to tell me off and run right out of the station. But then her eyes dropped down to the envelope again, and she squared her shoulders, taking a step towards me. *Interesting.* Whatever was in there was bad enough that she'd set aside everything between us.

And honestly, that terrified me.

"You two know each other?" I asked as she got closer.

"What?" she hissed.

"You and Deputy Jones. He called you 'apple-anche'. What the hell does that mean?"

"Oh." She smiled. "I caused a bit of a scene at the Shop and Save the other night. He helped me with my groceries. The day...the day I got into town."

Fuck. I hated that. I should have known she'd need to get things once she got settled. Why hadn't I offered to take her? Oh, yeah. I was too busy thinking I was having a heart attack...

"What's going on?" I asked as my hand slipped to the small of her back. Violet stopped walking, pulling away from my touch.

"I'm just here to speak to a deputy. My dad...Well, he thought it might be a good idea. But it seems like you all are busy, so I'll just set up an appointment and come back at a better time."

"Nope. Not so fast. My office. Let's go."

Violet's bottom lip was immediately assaulted by her teeth, but that frustrated pout had lost its power on me years ago. I just chuckled as I turned, leading her back to Hank's office. Her eyes went wide as she read the plaque on the wall just outside the door.

"I drove to Bell Ridge because I thought you still worked out of the Silver Springs satellite office. You're the sheriff now?"

"No. Hell no. I'm just filling in. Come on and sit. You want to take off your jacket?"

"Um. Maybe? It's warmer in here than I was thinking it was going to be."

"I imagine carrying the baby makes you warm, too."

Her eyes dropped to her hands, then looked back at me. "Colt...I...I don't want to make you uncomfortable."

I stopped, sinking into the chair before pointing from my wife to the chair in front of the desk. Really fucking wished there was a sofa or something more comfortable for her to sit on, but Violet just sighed and rolled her eyes as she sat down across from me. She slipped her arms out of her blazer, and I had to fight every damn desire in my body to look her over.

Instead, I cleared my throat and distracted myself with logging onto the ancient laptop I'd just been reading reports on.

"Why would I be uncomfortable?" I asked, raising my eyebrow. I knew what she was going to say. I'd been fucking avoiding her every chance I got. But part of me wanted to hear her say it. To admit that the circumstances of her return to Silver Springs, so far into a pregnancy and without the baby's father anywhere to be seen, was suspicious.

"You just sort of ran away right after you saw me. And I wouldn't expect you to stay. It's just that..." Her eyes dropped to that damn envelope again. "I want to talk to you about all this, but not when anyone else is around. I need to explain. I didn't think you'd be *there* when I pulled up the other day, and I got flustered. I should have said something then."

I crossed my arms, pressing back into my chair. "So say it now."

"I can't. I shouldn't have come down here. I thought you'd be out on patrol in town somewhere. I'm sorry."

"Don't even think about getting out of that chair." My voice dropped low, the vibrations of a growl rumbling through my chest as my eyes snapped to her emerald green ones. Her hand came up to twist the gold bracelet she was wearing, one I didn't recognize. I wanted to smack myself. *Why would I?* She's been gone so long, away from me and from Texas, there was no doubt in my mind nearly everything about my wife would be unrecognizable to me now. "Tell me why you're here, and we can go from there."

"I wanted to know if the road my parents' house is on is frequently patrolled."

Ice filled my veins.

"Why, Violet?"

"Because I'm about to be a mom, and I'd like to know that the baby and I are in a safe place."

Alarm bells blared in my mind as she looked at everything in the fucking office except for me.

"Look at me."

Her eyes closed for half a second before she sighed, looking directly in my eyes. "Are you in danger?" I asked.

"Don't be ridiculous. I just want to know we're safe. I'm thinking about having a security system installed, but that felt like overkill for a quiet place like Silver Springs." Her lip slipped between her top and bottom teeth.

"You're lying to me." It wasn't a question. I knew that was one of her tells. Apparently *that* hadn't changed.

"No, I'm not."

I sat back, my arms folding across my chest. When it came to pulling a confession from someone, I was stubborn. I could wait. I could watch Vi squirm a little.

She cracked faster than I ever thought she would. "Fine. There was someone in New York."

"Someone?" *The baby's father? Just say it, Violet. Tell me about him.*

"I'm writing now."

She didn't know I knew all about her novels. That every single one she'd ever published sat on my bookshelf at home. That I'd read through them like a madman hoping to catch a glimpse, a nod, to something that we once shared.

"We think it's a reader. A fan. God, I hate saying it like that. I don't know who they are. At first, they reached out and were so sweet. Commenting on all the little clues I hid throughout my stories. It wasn't anything out of the ordinary. Just someone who seemed to like my writing."

She was beating around the bush. Something had spooked her. "Until?"

"Until they asked me how my pregnancy was going."

My skin pebbled. *Fuck. They were watching her.*

"I haven't announced that I'm pregnant, and I won't be. So my readers wouldn't—shouldn't—know. And I know what you're thinking...someone probably saw me out and about, but I've been seeing a midwife, and she comes to my apartment for my visits. I wasn't ever at an OB office. I just couldn't after everything." Her voice caught and I nodded, shoving down my own emotions that were pushing up to the surface.

"Someone could have seen you shopping in the city, or running an errand? Hell, a book signing? What about getting an ultrasound for the baby?"

"No, no, and no. I had my meal plan delivered to my apartment. I haven't had a book signing in over a year, and because I was on deadline, there was no time to run errands. I'm behind schedule, and writing is all I have time for. I did have an ultrasound. One. That was the only time I went to a hospital and I wore baggy clothes. I hid my belly. It was the first appointment of the day, and I was the only one there."

Had she found out what she was having that morning? I knew it wouldn't matter to her. It wouldn't have mattered to me, either.

"Okay, so this person asked you about your pregnancy, and you said what?"

"I didn't say anything. I deleted the message and blocked the person on social media. I was so freaked out that I told my business manager, but he thought it was just some spillover anxiety from the pregnancy."

I already hated him, and I didn't even know his name. "No. You were right to trust your gut."

"I know. You taught me that the day Mary Lucas cut my bangs, pretending to be my friend, and then everyone laughed at me in gym class."

"I don't know why they laughed. I always like you with bangs."

She smiled at that, but her hand moved to her belly, and I saw her face fall. "I am scared, Colt. I thought it would fade away, but more messages came. And they've become more... intimate."

"What do you mean, *intimate?*" I bark at her so hard I have to clear my throat and cough.

That's when she opened the envelope she'd been holding onto.

"These all went to my business manager's office. It's the only address on file for my pen name."

She slid the packet across my desk, her eyes instantly dropping back down to her hand resting on her belly.

I saw the first page, and I wanted to vomit. Someone had been sending Violet the most violating messages. A predator watching over their prey. No wonder Vi looked exhausted— she was.

Fuck that. Normally, if a citizen of Clarence County came in with this, we'd set them up with a twice daily patrol, then someone in the tech department might dig a little deeper to see if they could get something off the person's computer or device. But like hell was I about to leave Violet to the hope that someone so depraved wouldn't follow her here.

I picked up the papers, shoved them back into the envelope, and pushed back from the desk.

"Let's go."

Violet's eyes went wide. "Go where? Do we need to speak to another deputy?"

"No. We're going home. You're moving back home."

"Colt." She rubbed her temples, not moving to get to her feet. "I'm not moving in with you. I just told you I'm planning on getting a home security system put in. I just...I wanted to know how far away a deputy would normally be. Just in case."

"In case what, Vi? In case a fucking predator followed you here and breaks into the cabin? In case they escalate things further than creepy fucking messages and taunts? What if they hurt you? Hurt the baby?"

She held out her hand. "I'd like my papers back, please."

I'd messed up. Pushed too hard.

"Look, I'm sorry for being so...gruff. But I'd really like you to reconsider. If you move back in, you're on the ranch with my brothers, Jessie, and my parents. You'd have people around you. I'm almost your closest neighbor at your parents' place. That's too isolated."

I handed the folder back to her.

"I appreciate the advice, and the offer. I'm going to head back to Silver Springs and ask to speak with someone about home security. I'll try not to bother you with this again."

"Vi, no. This isn't a bother. Seeing you here still feels like a goddamn dream. But I'm wrapping my mind around it, okay? I'll get there. And no matter what, I want you to be safe."

"There's no reason to think anyone knows I'm here. The security system will be enough."

She stood, my hand grasping her elbow as she did. I didn't want to let her go. I couldn't.

"You should still come to the ranch one day. I know my family would love to see you. They'd love to celebrate the baby, too."

Her chin quivered, but only for a second. "I'd love that. I figured I might stop into the diner and see your mom. I'll ask about stopping in when I do."

VIOLET

I cried on the way back to Silver Springs. This pregnancy had turned me into a weeping willow, and I honestly didn't mind anymore. It felt good to let it out.

I passed the diner where I knew I'd find Colt's mom, but chickened out. The call of Dolly's key lime pie almost won out, but first, I really did need to get my security situation figured out.

"Hi there." A beautiful brunette woman stood from behind the receptionist desk of Montgomery Defense. "I'm Mae. How can I help you today?"

"Hi, Mae. I'm Violet. I just moved back to Silver Springs. Still not sure if it's a permanent thing, or just a 'for now' type of thing." My hand landed protectively over my belly, which I swear was bouncing from the baby's latest round of hiccups. "In any case, I'll be here until after this little guy comes, and I'd really love to have a home security system installed. I heard you offered that service here."

"Awesome. There are two guys here today, but I'll buzz back to my fiancé." I must have given her a strange look, because she smiled and laughed. "The other guy is nice enough, but can be a little rough around the edges. You can take a seat if you want, I'm sure it will only be a minute or two."

I nodded, but instead of sitting down which I'd done enough of in Colt's office, I walked a little deeper into the building. It very clearly wasn't just a home security business. There was a fully stocked gym with a boxing ring just beyond Mae's desk. *Interesting.*

"God, I just finished talking to Beau. Apparently Beckett is being a terror. I'm so thankful Hawk and I had the night away—" I recognized the frazzled voice the second she started talking.

Jessie Ford. Colt's youngest sibling, and his only sister. We stayed in touch sporadically over the years. Enough for me to send a gift when she had her baby boy two years ago. But I hadn't reached out about my own pregnancy...Had Colt told her?

"What are you doing here?! Oh my God, Violet! You're pregnant!!" Her eyes sparkled with tears as she made her way over towards me.

"I am. Can you believe it?" I let out a watery laugh, my emotions mirroring hers instantly as we hugged. "It feels so surreal."

"It feels surreal that you're here. I mean...When did you get in? How long are you staying? Oh my gosh, are you going to raise the baby here? *Does my brother know*? Shit...I need you to spill everything!"

I looked over at Mae, who was doing a very good job of studying her computer screen as if Jessie wasn't talking so loud that everyone in the building could hear her.

"Oh, God. I'm such a bad friend. Vi, did you meet Mae? I mean, of course you met her when you walked in, I just mean..." Jessie tugged on my hand and we walked back over to

Mae's desk. "Mae, this is my sister-in-law, Violet. She's Colt's wife."

"Ex-wife," I say at the same time.

"God, right. It's only been a freaking decade. You'd think I'd be used to saying it that way. His *ex*-wife."

Mae smiled and nodded. "You're the tattoo."

"Sorry?" I replied. I didn't have any tattoos.

Before she could respond, a man walked out from a separate hallway, smiling at Mae before nodding at Jessie and finally turning towards me.

"Hi, you must be Violet. I'm Stone Lawson, one of the founding members of Montgomery Defense. Mae mentioned you're looking for home security?"

"Vi?" Jessie squeezed my hand.

"I'm staying at my old house. My parents never sold it after they moved to Arizona, and my dad couldn't part with it after my mom died."

"I imagine it could use some added security."

"You could say that." I tried to laugh, but it sounded forced to my ears. I'm sure everyone else noticed as well.

"Okay, well I don't want to keep you from Stone, but please tell me you don't have plans later on?"

"The only plans I have these days involve soaking in the tub and going to bed early."

"So, you're free around, say...six tonight?"

"Free for what exactly?" I laughed.

"Dinner with me! I want you to meet Hawk and Beckett! Oh my God, our kiddos will grow up playing together! Please say you'll come to dinner!"

"I'd love to."

"Good. Six. The ranch."

"Did you and Hawk build?"

"No," Jessie smiled, "we're in the old homestead. Hawk

fixed it up for me while I was pregnant, and it's just so perfect! I'll have you over sometime to see it."

"Won't I see it tonight?" I asked, suddenly confused.

"No. Once a week Hawk and I take Beckett over to Colt's house for dinner. You can meet us there!"

My mouth popped open, and she just laughed.

"Jessica Ford. No."

"It's Jessica Morgan now, and you already promised! I'll see you there at six, Vi."

———

"Can I get you some water?" Stone's eyes dropped to my belly, but only for a second. I was still wrapping my mind around how I'd fallen for Jessie's trick, and trying to think of every way possible I could somehow alert Colt that I was, in fact, going to show up on his doorstep after I'd made such a big deal about not doing that exact thing an hour ago.

"No, I'm fine, thank you."

"Okay, well, why don't we start with your address and maybe what you're looking for in your security system."

I rattled off my parents' address, Stone smiling as I said the road I lived off.

"Are you familiar with that area?" I asked.

"A little. We drive out to see Hawk and Jessie a lot. The Silver Ridge Ranch almost feels like a second home at this point. Or, well, a third. Maybe a fourth."

"How many homes do you have?" I laughed.

Stone smiled. "It's complicated. We have an apartment here in this building. But we also have a house out past Silver Springs proper. And then we spend a lot of time on the ranch here, but also a lot of time in Montana with one of the guys who we founded the company with."

"Sounds lovely, to feel at home in so many different

places." I held back the shudder I felt bubbling up from my stomach. But I must not have hid it well enough, because Stone switched into serious mode.

"Where were you before you came to Silver Springs?"

"New York City."

His eyes went wide. "Wow. This is quite the change."

I nodded in agreement. "I prefer it here. There were just a lot of painful...memories I was running from. I wanted somewhere that wouldn't make me think of home."

Stone nodded. "Did it work?"

"Not at all," I laughed, but there was no humor behind the sound.

"But now you're back, and I imagine with a baby on the way, you want just another layer of protection."

"I really wasn't going to...even after my dad suggested it. But Colt mentioned there had been some teens breaking into places, and I had a bit of an issue with someone in New York before I left. I just feel like, yeah, maybe I do need something to put my mind at ease."

His fingers stopped typing. "What kind of an issue with someone in New York?"

"Oh, nothing that I think will spill over here. Everything in New York happened under my pen name. I..." I leaned back, the baby kicking my side letting me know he wasn't happy with the space I was giving him. "I'm an author. And I really did try as best I could to keep Violet Murphy separate from my author business."

"Okay, so this wasn't someone who knew you personally?"

"No, God no. I think it was just a reader. Someone who sent me some notes to my business manager. Got a little too comfortable with thinking they knew me personally."

"You responded to them?"

"No. Never. But maybe they came to a signing or something, you know?"

Stone's jaw clenched. "Okay. So, only ever mailed to a PO Box?"

"Mhm." Shit. No, shit. How had I not realized?

"Violet?"

"The last note...uh, why I decided to get out of New York for a while...it came to my apartment. I think I have it here..." I looked down to the folder in my lap, my hands shaking as I tried to rifle through the papers.

Stone stood from behind his desk, but I still hadn't found the paper I was looking for by the time he came to sit next to me.

"Here. Why don't you take this, and I'll look through those?" He held out a water bottle to me.

"Oh, no. I mean, it's not that big of a deal. I can find it."

Again, his eyes dropped to my belly. "I'd feel better if you took a drink of water. You're looking a little pale."

"I'm being ridiculous. It's just that...I didn't think about the apartment being in my name. My real name." I took a deep breath. "I'm so sorry."

"No need to apologize. You're scared. And that's okay. You're in the right place to make sure you're protected at home. I don't know if Mae mentioned this, but I'm also a paramedic. Of course, I'd really like to not have to use those skills today. So maybe you can take a sip of the water for me while I look these over?"

I nodded, unable to get my voice to work as I handed over my folder and accepted the water bottle.

"Can I call someone for you? I'm sure Jessie and Mae would be happy to sit in with us? Or maybe I could call Colt?"

"No!" I almost jumped out of my seat in my hurry to answer. "No, that's so kind of you, but I'm perfectly fine. I was getting thirsty, so thank you for the drink. You're more than welcome to look through the file. I already showed it to Colt before coming here."

That seemed to surprise Stone. "Alright. And he didn't say anything about the person knowing your address?"

"I only thought of it just now. I left New York because of what the note said. I was so worried about it, that the fact it came to my apartment instead of to my manager completely slipped past me. But I'll tell him. I really just want to be able to say there is someone coming out to install the system and my cabin is safe." God, I was second guessing my decision not to accept his help. "He tried to get me to move back home with him, and it's all just way too complicated for that."

Stone nodded, his eyes still focused on papers in front of him.

"Okay, well, I'm going to work up a package for you. We'll need to come out and survey the property. It would be helpful if Colt was there." I opened my mouth to argue, but Stone lifted his hand, effectively silencing me. "I know you probably think that's overstepping, but we normally work very closely with the Clarence County Sheriff's Department. And since Colt is a close friend of mine, who's already aware of your concerns and is wanting to make sure you're safe, I think it's for the best that we loop him in."

———

I swear the damn cursor was mocking me. While ghost writing during my marriage is what got my foot in the door, I'd been writing for myself since my divorce. Probably because there were so many things I couldn't figure out how to say out loud before leaving, that were then easier to pour into my stories once I had some distance. What was once a dream of publishing even a single novel has turned into an entire career for me. But since the day I heard back from the fertility clinic about my positive pregnancy test, I have had to *force* the words out.

In the last few weeks with my anxiety growing about giving birth on my own, and all the unwanted attention from my—God, it felt terrible to say stalker, but maybe that's exactly how I needed to start addressing the situation as—*safety issue*, the words would not come. I was questioning everything, and sitting in front of my laptop just made me want to pull my hair out.

The baby gave me a kick at the same time my phone rang. The picture I had saved in my phone for Ryan's number popped up. I smiled, loving the way we both were laughing in the picture.

"Hey, Ry."

"Wow, Callie. You remember who I am?" He knew my legal name, but always chose to use my pen name. "For a second there, I thought I was going to have to come all the way down to Arkansas to see for myself that you were still alive. I thought we agreed you would keep me in the loop?"

I cringed. "I'm in Texas, and yes, I'm alive."

"No sign of trouble?"

"No, thank God."

"And the words? How are they coming along?"

For all the ways I loved Ryan as my manager, sometimes he was a little too focused on the goal line and not enough on me as a human.

"They're..."

"Cal, we talked about this. I know you were wanting to get ahead of schedule before the baby comes, but—" A loud honk interrupted him. "Hey! I'm trying to walk here! Maybe don't almost run me over? Yeah, up yours, asshole. Shit, Callie, you still there?"

"Yeah," I laughed, "I'm still here."

"Well, as much as I'm sure living the small town life is excruciatingly boring, at least you don't have people trying to run you over all the goddamn time."

"That is true. The citizens around here are very good about not jaywalking."

"Oh, is that how we're going to play this?" he laughed. *"Fine, you caught me."*

"Look, I'm working my ass off. I know they want the draft done in a few weeks, but with everything going on, my mind is just…"

"Blank?"

"Yeah."

"We're already on extension. They're going to throw a fit if I try to get your agent to ask for another," he reminds me.

"I know. I know. I promise, I'm prioritizing it. I've unpacked. I've settled in. And now I'm going to get down to business."

"That's my girl. Love hearing that. Alright, don't forget to call me if you need my help, okay? That's what I'm here for."

"No help needed. I promise not to let you down."

"You never could, Callie."

"Bye, Ryan."

I stared at the cursor still taunting me before my eyes drifted towards the clock. I needed to get ready for my dinner with Jessie and her family. At my old house. Where Colt would be.

COLT

"Look, all I'm saying is that I almost got into an accident there today, and I really think you guys need to station someone there to slow down traffic and make sure people aren't crossing when they shouldn't be."

"Mrs. McNally, I appreciate that feedback, and I'll be sure to tell the Sheriff about your suggestion. Is there anything else I can do for you?"

I nodded at Jonesy as I walked out of the station. I'd read the report in the morning. Right now, all I could think about was how I was supposed to get through dinner with Jessie and Hawk without losing my mind, worrying about Violet.

Because I was worried. For someone who lived with a deputy for years, for someone who I fucking taught self-defense to when we were in high school, she was acting like leaving New York solved all her problems. And maybe it would. I fucking hoped whoever was bothering her stayed right where they were.

I pulled my phone out of my pocket, cursing when I saw it was set to silent. I had a message from my sister waiting for me.

Hey! I bumped into Violet at Montgomery Defense today! I can't believe you didn't tell me she was back.

I've only known a few days. I just haven't wrapped my mind around it.

God, took you long enough to reply! You're going to be late if you don't get your ass home now.

We can eat quick. I really just want some time with Beckett.

He's excited to see you, but I figured you'd want to get home before Vi gets here.

What?

I told her she had to come. To meet Beckett and Hawk.

I threw the phone down in the passenger seat and closed my eyes. *I could do this.* Hell, I wanted another chance to talk to her. To ask her to reconsider staying at the cabin on her own. Maybe I could rope Jessie into it, too.

———

"Supper smells good," I called out as I walked in the front door of my house. It always made me laugh that Jessie wanted to do dinner at my house. When Vi and I first got divorced, my sister spent nearly every night eating with me when we weren't having supper up at our parents' house. When she had Beckett and told me she wanted to start doing it again once a week, I couldn't really say no.

"Coco! Coco!" My nephew ran down the hallway right into my open arms.

"Hey, Beck! Were you a good boy today?"

"Res!"

I chuckled. Poor kid didn't have the best grasp of his words yet, but he was working hard on them.

"Okay, Uncle Coco has something for you then. Ready?" He nodded, his eyes going wide as I fished around in my shirt pocket. "Here you go! An honorary deputy badge sticker!"

"Ticker, Mama! Ticker!"

Jessie laughed as Beckett ran into the kitchen, waving the sticker around.

"Hey, Hawk." I held my hand out to shake my brother-in-law's as soon as I walked into the kitchen.

"Hey, Colt. Want a beer?"

"From my own fridge?" I joked. "Sure, I'd love one."

Hawk laughed. "Actually, I put a new six-pack in there. Nash brought down this IPA from a little brewery startup back in Montana. Figured you might want to try it out with me."

His buddy, who was actually my good buddy now, too, split time between Silver Springs and a small town in Montana where he was expanding a Montgomery Defense program. "Yeah, definitely. Thanks."

Hawk handed me a can from the fridge, and as I set it on the counter in front of me, I could feel Jessie's eyes on me.

"You need to go get changed," she scolded. "Vi will be here any minute."

"And?" I grabbed Beckett as he ran by, hoisting him upside down in front of me and tickling his belly, absolutely fucking thrilled with the string of giggles I got out of him. "She already saw me wearing this today. It's fine."

"Colt. Go. Get. Changed. I bet Vi is wearing something different from what she had on earlier."

"It's not a first date, Jess. She's my ex-wife."

Jessie set the knife down on the counter, holding out a small piece of cheese to her son who I had gently turned right side up before placing back on the floor.

"Your ex-wife, that you never got over, who is back in town all on her own…I'm just saying."

"Come on, Beckett." Hawk chuckled, scooping his son up. "Want to go check the steaks with Daddy?"

"Res. Les go, Daddy!" They were out the back door faster than I could blink.

Jessie pushed away from the counter, walked over to me, and wrapped her arms around my waist.

"What's the hug for?"

Jessie pulled back, and I knew what she was going to say the second she looked up at me. "She's pregnant."

"Yeah." My throat was so damn tight.

"Are you okay?"

I nodded. "I'm happy for her."

"And hopeful?" she asked.

"Hopeful for what?"

"She's not here with anyone, Colt. And I know you. I know you'd still want to step up and be there for her. Always."

"Of course I would."

"So, go get changed. It's your chance to *gently* remind her of that."

I nodded as I left the kitchen. Jessie was right. I wanted to show Violet she could open up to me. That I'd be a safe place for her and the baby, no matter what.

Christ. I felt almost as nervous as I was the day I asked Violet to have a milkshake with me at Ma's diner. I tossed my uniform on the chair in the corner of the bedroom and pulled out my favorite pair of jeans and a plain black Henley. Good enough. I started to head downstairs, but turned around and headed back to my dresser. I grabbed the bottle of cologne, and gave myself a single spray.

Pregnant women were sensitive about certain smells, and cologne could probably go either way. But this one was special for us, and I loved it still, after all these years.

I jogged down the stairs and smiled as I watched Vi's car pull into the driveway. *Good.* I'd have a chance to talk to her before she got bombarded with questions from Jess.

Opening the front door, I stood on the porch and watched Vi. She was sitting with her eyes closed, head tipped back, taking slow breaths. *Maybe I wasn't the only one feeling nervous?*

Her eyes popped open just as I knocked on her window.

And the scream she let out had my heart falling out through my ass.

VIOLET

This was a bad idea. A really bad idea. Even as I made my way up the long stretch of road on the main drive on the Silver Ridge Ranch property to the house my ex-husband and I used to share, I could feel the pinpricks of sweat popping up on the back of my neck. My own body knew this was a terrible idea, and was throwing symptoms at me left and right to try and get me to turn around between a churning stomach, shaking hands, and a baby boy who was wiggling so much I might actually pee myself before being able to ask to use the bathroom.

I just wanted to turn around and run—okay, waddle—my way back to bed. Even if the mattress my parents had in the house was a decade old and so hard I might as well be sleeping on the floor.

But seeing Jessie in town earlier, I just couldn't say no to the chance at finally meeting her husband and son.

I pulled up in front of the two story cabin, and a sharp pain began to throb behind my eyes. It was so silly to be emotional over seeing the place we'd built...but I'd spent my whole life thinking about bringing a baby home to this very house, and now I was pregnant, and Colt didn't know—

A knock on my window had a scream bubbling up in my throat before my brain could even place the hulking shadow at my door.

Speaking of Colt.

I shoved open the car door and swung my leg around, trying my hardest to kick him in the shin and make it look like an accident.

"Jesus Christ, Colt! Are you trying to scare me into labor?"

His eyes went wide as his hands landed on my arms, cautiously holding on as I grunted my way out of my seat. "Can that happen?"

"I'm sure it can! Any sort of stress can set off contractions!"

His hand flew to the back of his neck and he rubbed the skin there while giving me his biggest, most sincere apologetic eyes.

"Fuck, Vi. I'm sorry. I just wanted to open your door and make sure you got up the steps alright."

"The same steps I have at my parents' house and can navigate perfectly fine on my own?"

"Yeah, well, this is my house. My rules apply here. And I always get your door."

"Even if it used to be *our* house?"

I expected him to turn and run, but I should have known better. Instead of bolting like I would have, Colt reached down and took my hand. He helped me stand before leaning so close I could feel the heat radiating off his skin as he lowered his face towards mine.

"You should remember the punishment for not letting me get your door. Always did love the way you sounded panting my name when I bent you over my knee and turned that pretty peach ass of yours beet red."

I gasped, trying to remind myself I was in no shape to get worked up over a man I hadn't been near in almost a decade. A man who was so close I could smell him, the rich amber and smokey, charred maple washing over me in nostalgic waves. A man whose arms I desperately wanted wrapped around me, tattoos rippling as his hand tightened its hold. Our son rolled in my belly, as if he, too, wanted to punctuate our closeness.

No.

Not *our* son. *My* son.

My body flushed hot and then cold.

"You okay? I was only trying to tease. I didn't mean...I shouldn't have said that."

"No." I forced myself to smile as I shut the car door that had been left wide open during our exchange. "I'm fine. Just a lot of memories there I hadn't really thought about in a while."

Lies, Violet. You thought about Colt in the shower just before you came over here.

His eyes narrowed on my face, and for a second I thought that maybe Colt had gained the ability to read minds in the time since our divorce. But he just shook his head and gave a little chuckle as his hand landed on the small of my back, guiding me up towards the house.

"Jessie mentioned seeing you at Montgomery Defense. Did you talk to one of the guys about a security system?"

I nodded. "A very nice guy, actually. Stone?"

He smiled. "Good. I can come by when they're going to install it. Make sure they do it right."

I stopped, my hands resting on my hips. "You don't think they'll do a good job? Isn't Jessie's husband a part of that team? You trust him to keep her safe, don't you?"

"Of course I do. I trust all of them. It's just..."

"Just what? That you think you could do a better job?"

"That you're too precious," he whispered. The wind picked up, a strand of my hair flying free in front of my face. Colt reached out, tucking it back behind my ear. "I know you don't want me overstepping. But this situation is serious. I'm scared for you, and I really think you should reconsider—"

I held up my hand.

"I'm not here to discuss that tonight, Colt. I just wanted to meet my nephew." My eyes drifted over my ex-husband's shoulder to where my former sister-in-law was busy stirring something together in a big green bowl.

"He's not—"

My cheeks burned. "You really seem hellbent on pissing me off today. Your sister has been *my* sister since the minute she came into this world, even if the divorce strained things between us. Maybe you're forgetting the promises we whispered to her together when I came over to meet her after she was born?"

That we *both* would always watch over her. That we *both* would always love and protect her.

His features grew tight. "I haven't forgotten."

"Good. So please put this discussion on the back burner until I've had a chance to fawn over the two of them."

Colt stepped out of the way, his hand sweeping out in front of me like he was letting me into the most exclusive club in the world.

And to be fair, that's what it felt like for me, too. The divorce was devastating for so many reasons, but right at the top of the list was the loss of the brothers and sister I'd grown up with. In the blink of an eye, I was back to being an only child. Something I hadn't had to contend with since I was twelve-years-old.

"Vi!" Jessie's smile grew the closer she got to me. "Oh my God, I still can't get over how cute you look. This belly! I am so excited to be an aunt again! But on the Ford side of the family this time."

I wrapped my arms around the pipsqueak, grateful to get to soak in time with her twice in one day. She might be a wife and a mom, but she would always be the little girl who followed me around endlessly with hearts in her eyes. The one who made me want to be a mom myself.

"It's wild to me that you're not officially a Ford anymore."

Jessie scrunched up her nose. "It feels so weird. I mean, I love writing 'Mrs. Morgan', but I'm just not used to it yet."

"Speaking of Morgans..." A tall—okay, very tall and very handsome—man stepped into the house through the back door, bringing with him a wiggly little boy and a plate full of steaks that made my mouth water as he set them down on the table.

"Oh," Jessie laughed, "Vi, this is my husband, Hawk. Hawk, this is, well, for all purposes other than legally—which honestly is the least important—my sister, Violet."

I laughed at the description as I offered my hand to Hawk, who was balancing their son on his left arm. "It's so nice to meet you."

"Nice to meet you, too, Violet."

"And this," Jessie reached and scooped her son from Hawk's arm, "chunky boy is Beckett. Beck, say hi to Uncle Coco's friend, Violet."

"Hi Lielet!"

"Well, hello there, Beckett. It's so nice to finally meet you." My heart was about to burst out of my chest. "Jessie, he is the cutest! I'm just so overwhelmed thinking about our boys playing together one day soon."

Colt flinched next to me. I turned to look at him, wondering why the hell he was standing ramrod straight and staring at me. But then my words played over again in my mind.

He didn't know the baby was a boy. I'd just accidentally blurted out something I should have saved to tell him when it was just the two of us. When I was going to explain everything.

"I'm sorry," I whispered.

"Don't be." His fingers twitched, but he didn't move.

"Dinner's almost ready, everyone can find a spot to sit. Just don't sit next to Beckett unless you want to share your food with him." Jessie's joke broke the lingering tension.

———

"I talked to Stone today about the house. He's going to come and do a walk through so he knows he's ordering the right parts, I guess." I brought the glass of water that was sitting in front of me up to my mouth. Colt and I sat next to each other, him on my right and Jessie to my left. Beckett was currently pushing mashed potatoes all over his plate while Hawk and Jessie wrangled his hands to try and get them clean.

"Did he say when? I can be there," Colt offered.

I shook my head. "He didn't. But he did mention telling you, so you'd know."

"Good."

I pushed another bite of meat onto my fork. "This steak is delicious, Hawk. But I won't lie, I'm already eyeing those brownies."

Jessie laughed. "I've definitely upped my skills since you got me that toy oven for Christmas, and I made you two eat half-baked cookie dough."

"I don't know how I forgot about that," Colt chuckled. "I remember how many tears there were when you pulled the cookie tray out after thirty minutes and everything was still raw."

"Hey, you don't mess with a woman and her sweet treats."

I crossed my arms and winked at Jess. "I'm not sure why toy manufacturers think it's smart to try and have kids cook with light bulbs."

"It was special, but I just enjoyed getting to spend time with you both."

The conversation continued like that through the rest of dinner. Light. Fun. Reminiscing through the memories we shared together. No one brought up my pregnancy again, and I was grateful for that. Because even with as lovely as the night turned out to be, I was still standing under the giant shadow of a secret I needed to share sooner rather than later.

"I'm sorry I was so on edge when I got here," I said to Colt as I walked out the front door. "I know I need to face the fact that what happened in New York was scary and dangerous. I just...I'm trying to hold it all together on my own. Anyway, thank you for having me over."

"I want you to stay." Colt leaned against the doorway and reached for my hand.

"I don't have a change of clothes," I teased. "I wore this to look nice, not to sleep in."

His eyes traveled down my body, then back up to my face. "You do look nice, Vi. I haven't said it before now, but this pregnancy really suits you."

I could feel the heat hit my cheeks before my heartbeat thundered in my chest.

"Thank you." I looked over my shoulder at my car. Yeah, it was time to get out into the cool night air. Otherwise, I was going to cave.

"Look, I don't like what you told me this morning. I can't get those messages out of my mind."

I looked down at the place where our hands connected, truly surprised I couldn't find the energy to pull away. "They didn't follow me here. And worst case, you're just five minutes away if I need you."

"A lot can happen in five minutes, Violet. Please."

I pulled my hand away from his. "I need to go. Thank you for dinner."

"Wait." His command had me frozen in place. "Give me your phone."

"What?"

"Your phone. Let me see it so I can give you my number. In case you need to call me."

I grabbed my phone from my pocket, making sure to unlock the screen before I handed it over.

He held it out at arm's length. which made me smile. Until his eyes went wide and he handed the phone back.

"Everything okay?" I asked, confused by the shock I saw written on his face.

"You still have my number in there."

"Oh. I thought maybe you would have changed it."

He shook his head. "Nope. Still the same as it always was."

"Good. Mine's still the same, too." I had no idea why I offered that information to him.

"Is that an invitation to call you?" The smallest hint of a smile tipped the corner of his mouth. I needed to look somewhere else, but my eyes were glued right on his lips.

"If you ever need to, sure."

He took a step closer to me. I closed my eyes, waiting for what he'd say next.

"What if I want to...maybe just to check on you? To say good night, or good morning?"

I shook my head, the smile back in place. "We can say goodnight right now."

"Mm." He leaned back against the door frame and sighed. "Goodnight, Violet."

"Goodnight, Colt."

COLT

My hand slapped at the buzzing sound coming from the night stand. I loved my job—truly, I did—but if a deputy was calling to tell me there was some big after-hours issue when I'd just managed to finally fall asleep after that dinner, I might throw my badge out the window and set my uniform on fire.

I could still smell Violet's amber and honey perfume. It was like the second she walked into this house, it pulled the essence of her everywhere. She'd only been downstairs, but I would have given sworn testimony that she'd laid her head down on the pillow next to me with how I could still smell that damn intoxicating scent.

"Ford," I answered gruffly, clearing the sleep from my throat with a borderline indecent cough. Everything was silent, until a watery sniff came over the line.

"Colt?" Violet's whisper had the hair on the back of my neck standing straight up. Not only because she was calling me in the middle of the goddamn night, but because I could hear the worry in her voice. The room zoomed past me as I sat up in bed.

"What's wrong?"

"I-I need you. Can you come to the cabin?" The small hitch in her voice made my blood run cold. She was *crying*. Violet *never* cried. Not on our wedding day. Not from our divorce. She was always so steady. So stoic. Nothing except when we struggled to get pregnant. And...*oh fuck*. The last times I'd seen her cry were after the last miscarriage and when her mother died.

"I'm already on my way, sweetheart. Just take a deep breath." I was on my feet, sliding them through the legs of some jeans I'd thrown over the armchair in my room when I'd gone to bed after dinner. "Is it the baby?"

"No. He's okay. It's...I can't...please, just hurry. I'll explain when you get here."

"Fuck, Vi. I promise, I'm going as fast as I can. You want me to stay on the line with you until I get there?"

"Yes."

"Okay. I'm heading out the door right now. It'll take me five minutes to get in the truck and get to you. Just breathe. You don't have to say a goddamn word, but I better hear you breathing over this line the entire time."

———

I made it out my door, into my truck, across the ranch, and down the road to her place in three minutes. I should arrest myself for how fast I was driving.

"Violet? Hey, sweetheart, it's just me," I called out as the door knob twisted easily in my hand. Fuck. She better have just unlocked it, or I was going to lose my goddamn mind. The door swung open, and it only took a few seconds for my eyes to adjust to the dark, landing squarely on her.

Violet was hunched over, her elbows resting on the counter in the kitchen with her face illuminated by her laptop.

She was fully dressed...If it wasn't the baby, why was she still dressed in what she wore to dinner? Shouldn't she be in whatever she'd wear to bed?

Damn it. Now I was the one who needed to take a breath.

"Violet?" I called out again. But her body didn't move, her eyes just stayed glued to her cell phone.

"Vi," I whispered before I slid my hand to cup her cheek. She jumped at the contact, her hand coming up to slap me away.

"Christ, Colt. You nearly gave me a heart attack."

"Me? You stopped responding to me while I was driving over here, and then I came in and found you standing there like a goddamn mummy. What the fuck is going on?"

"I..." She winced, her hands moving to her lower back. My hand followed hers, pressing in right next to where her fingers were massaging. She groaned, her eyes closing, and the realization of how intimate the moment was slammed into me.

I wasn't the man who should be helping with her pregnancy aches and pains. She had someone—who knows where he was—that needed to step up and be by her side.

"You should be sitting down. Or do we...you're dressed? Do you need me to take you to the hospital after all?"

"What? No...no, I'm fine. I just..." Her head shook as her eyes dropped back to her phone.

"Come on." I wrapped my arm around her waist and slipped her phone off the counter before she could grab it. It took only a second to guide Violet over to the couch before I made my way back into the kitchen. Once I had a fresh glass of water, I marched it over to her.

"Drink."

"I'm not thirsty. I just want answers."

"Don't be stubborn. You've been crying, and you'll get a migraine."

Her eyes finally found mine for the first time since I'd gotten there. "You remember that?"

I nod my head. "Yeah, I remember. Drink. And then I want to hear about why you're wound so tight I'm afraid you're going to pop."

Violet's hand came up to rub her belly, the glass of water still sitting on the coffee table untouched. "I'm waiting for a phone call."

"At..." my eyes dropped down to my watch, "almost midnight? Who the fuck is calling you this late?"

"The Milton City Police Department."

Her dad lived in Milton City.

"Okay. Start from the beginning."

She sighed as I sat down next to her, my thigh pressing against hers on the small couch. "I drove into town after dinner, just to clear my head. I stopped into the diner to see if I could say hi to your mom, but she wasn't in. Her key lime pie is still just as good as I remember it, though. I had a terrible craving for it when I was sixteen weeks. The frozen pie my grocery delivery service got for me just wasn't the same, and I cried for three days over it."

"Ma would have shipped you up some if she'd known. But I don't think craving key lime pie is why you're so worked up right now."

She sighed. "I'm getting there. I got home later than I thought I would, but I know I turned on the porch lights and left the living room lamp on before I drove to your place."

Well, I officially didn't like where this was going.

"They weren't on when you got home?" I asked.

"No. It freaked me out, but I got out of the car thinking maybe the power was out... Why are you rumbling like that?"

I swallowed, stopping the deep growl that was running through my chest. "If you were freaked out, you could have called me. I was still awake."

"Because there weren't any lights on? Colt, come on. I've survived a lot of days on my own. Scary, dark nights included."

Fuck that. She wanted my help. "And yet you called me, sweetheart. So tell me why."

She nodded, her pupils dilating at the use of the pet name. And I liked that reaction far more than I should have. "I didn't see it at first. But the door was unlocked and—"

The floor above our heads creaked, and I jumped up, looking around the cabin...there were at least four rooms I'd need to sweep on this floor, then two bedrooms and a shared bathroom upstairs to get through before we could say the space was secure. And my wife—*dammit!* My very pregnant *ex*-wife who spent the morning telling me about how someone in New York made her feel unsafe—was just hanging around in here by herself until I showed up. I took a deep breath, trying to not fly off the handle. "Vi? The door was unlocked?"

Her eyes went wide, and she nodded. "I-I came inside and everything seemed fine. I grabbed a water bottle from the fridge and was getting ready to go upstairs, but I was still expecting an email from my business manager. I got on the computer to check real quick, only, the message I got wasn't from him. I-I read it and tried to call my dad, but he wasn't answering. Maybe I shouldn't be freaked out, but I called for a wellness check. That's why I'm waiting to hear back from the police."

"Is it still up on your laptop?"

She nodded.

"Good. I'll read it in a minute. Come on." I held out my hands, waiting for her to grab them so I could help her off the couch. She only blinked once before her hands were in mine. *Fuck.* I needed to get her out of the damn cabin, but the second she slid her hands into mine, I didn't want to let go.

"Where are we going?"

"I'm getting you out of this fucking house until I search it."

"Colt?"

There wasn't time for arguing. "Now."

I walked her, hand in hand until we were out the door, across the porch, down the stairs, and over to my truck.

"I forgot…"

"What?" I asked as I helped her up into my truck.

"The last note the person sent. It wasn't sent to my manager's address. It…it came to my apartment. I was so flustered by what it said, I didn't even realize it was delivered there. I remembered when I was talking to Stone earlier. If this guy knows my address, he knows my real name…" Her hand gripped my arm. I could feel the fear rolling off of her in waves. They ebbed when I first showed up, but they were crashing over her once again. "I'm sorry I didn't say something before. But now he's threatened my *dad*, Colt."

"It's okay. It's going to be okay now. Move your legs for me, just for a second." I reached under her seat, my fingers brushing against the lock box where my firearm was stored. Wrapping my hand around it, I slid the box back under her seat and discreetly placed the weapon in the holster on my hip.

"What in the world are you going to do with that?"

"Vi, someone could be in your house right now. I'm protecting myself. Now, take my keys. Don't you dare unlock this truck until you see me coming back out and I give you the all clear. Okay?"

"O-okay. Oh, my phone, Colt! I need to have it in case the police call."

My hand rested on her leg. "I'll answer it if they do. Just turn up the heat and get warm."

She nodded, and I gently closed the door. I waited until I heard the locks click into place before I turned around and marched back inside.

What the fuck had she been thinking, staying inside when she came home to an unlocked door? If she didn't want to move in with me, I needed to figure out how to make it clear I was moving in. God, I could just see it now, the way the tip of her ears would turn red like they always did when we argued.

As I walked through the kitchen, the floor above my head creaked again. I wasn't about to take any chances. My weapon came out of the holster. I walked through the kitchen to the small bathroom that held the washer and dryer. *Clear.* Once I was back out, I climbed the stairs to the second floor. The first bedroom was untouched. The bathroom in between was the same. But the second I opened the door to the room Violet was clearly sleeping in, my heart rate doubled.

I focused on the task at hand, walking down the room, checking for an intruder. When the space was clear, I pulled out my cell phone and dialed dispatch.

"Has anyone been in the cabin with you?" I grumbled as I sat my ass down in the driver's seat. The bag I packed with clothes from the laundry instantly went over my shoulder and into the back. I had my finger on the door lock a second later.

"What are you doing? Why are you putting my bag back there?"

"Vi." I set my hand on her arm, hoping the contact would make what I had to tell her somehow easier—it wouldn't. It's disgusting and vile, and for a second I think that maybe I can get away with giving as little detail as possible. "Has anyone else been at the cabin?"

"No. I've barely been here a week. Who the hell would be in the cabin with me?"

My fingers tighten around the steering wheel as I force the air from my lungs. "Someone *was* in the cabin. I've already called it in, gave them permission to come out here, and told them if they needed to speak with you they can come to the ranch tomorrow. Right now, I'm taking you home. And you're moving in with me. Tonight."

"Sorry," she gasped, "did you say someone had been inside? How do you know?"

"It was messy in your room. Things thrown around."

Her shoulders relaxed as her head hit the back of the seat. "I'm a messy person, Colt. That was just me unpacking!"

I grimaced, thinking back on the downright vile things that had been done to her clothes. "No. It wasn't."

Her head didn't move, but her eyes found mine. "What do you mean?"

"Your...uh..." I cleared my fucking throat, remembering how all her delicate undergarments were strewn about the bedroom. How they were placed on her bed. How they were violated... "Someone had been in your room. It looks like they sifted through your underwear drawer and they left some physical material behind. That's why I called in my guys. They'll get the evidence to the lab, and if there's a DNA match on file, we'll get this son of a bitch."

"I'm sorry...Did you just say *physical material*? As in what?"

"It looks like someone used your clothes for..." *Christ.* I didn't fucking want to say it out loud, much less to Vi. I knew she'd be horrified. "For an intimate sexual act, Vi."

A violent shudder rolled through her body.

"Oh my God. That's so...*ew*."

I reached out, my hand settling on her leg. "It's okay. I'm going to keep you safe while we get to the bottom of this. I'm going to take you home." It wasn't a promise I made lightly. Everything inside me was screaming to get Violet out of there and back to the ranch where I could make sure she was safe.

"No. I don't have to go to the ranch. You don't have to—"

"Your piece of shit baby daddy didn't stick around," I snapped, her eyes going wide at my outburst. *What was wrong with me?* "Look. You proved that you could do it on your own —I get that you wanted to do things your own way. But this threat is real, and the threat is here now. I'm not taking any chances. He didn't stick around to protect the two most precious people on Earth, but I sure as fuck will."

"It's not like that…"

"Then tell me what it's like," I begged.

Violet turned away from me, her head resting on the back of the seat.

"I'll go with you to the ranch," she whispered, closing her eyes and effectively ending our conversation.

COLT

Violet was silent as I helped her out of the truck and up the porch steps. With every passing second, I could feel the weight growing heavier on her shoulders. She'd physically shrunk into herself, and I just wanted to get her inside so I could wrap her up in my arms.

"I'll just head up to the guest room," she whispered, looking over at the bag in my hand. "I'll take that with me."

I cringed. "Uh, you can't."

"I can't go upstairs?"

"No, I mean you can definitely do that." My free hand came up to rub the back of my neck. "It's just...I turned the guest bedroom into a home office."

Her eyebrows lifted. "Okay. Well, I could manage something in the room we were going to use as a nursery. Do you still have that air mattress your parents gave us for Christmas that one year? The one that folds out onto its own frame?"

"No."

Her eyes closed for a second before she opened them again, looking towards the couch. Oh *hell no.*

"Okay. I'll just stay—"

I closed the distance between us in two strides, my hand pressing against the small of her back as I directed her towards the stairs.

"You're sleeping in my bed tonight."

"I don't think…"

Before she could continue arguing, I shook my head. "I'll take the couch; it's better this way. I'm by the door if someone is watching you and knows that you're here. If they try anything, the second story gives you better protection."

Her face blanched. *Fuck, I shouldn't have said that.*

"You think they could come here?"

"Well, if they know your real name, and they could find your parents' place, it's safe to say—"

The phone in my pocket vibrated.

"Oh my God." Vi gasped. "Is that my dad?"

I scooped the phone out, immediately smiling at the picture of Violet with her dad that popped up. Nodding, I passed it to her.

"Dad?" Her hand went first to her chest, then reached out for me. These moments of connection between us, they should feel cold and awkward. But one day spent sporadically together, and it just felt right again to hold her.

Jessie was right. My heart was already stitching back together.

I couldn't hear the other side of the conversation, but from the relief written all over Vi's face, I could tell Pete was okay.

"Yes. Okay. No, I'm safe. I'm fine." She sighed, her eyes finding mine. "Please don't worry. I'm…I'm going to stay with Colt for now."

Thank you, God.

I mouthed *good girl* to her and tried not to chuckle at the smile that pulled up the side of her mouth.

"Yes. I promise, Dad. I will. Please don't put your phone

on silent until we know more about what's going on. Okay? I love you, too. Bye."

Her hand dropped away from her face, and her eyes closed. I stepped closer, and held my breath as she dropped her head against my shoulder. My hands hovered awkwardly above her back for only a moment before I rested them against her. It took a couple of breaths for her, but eventually, she melted into my embrace.

"Vi?" I questioned.

"I'm good. He's okay." Her face nuzzled into my shirt. "He was sleeping, and his phone was on silent. Whoever this is...whoever sent that message, they didn't do anything to my dad."

She pulled back, and my jaw clenched, wishing more than anything that she would just let me hold her again.

"I'm glad he's okay. But what happened tonight at the cabin isn't. I know you just said you were staying with me—"

Vi shook her head. "I only said that so he wouldn't worry. He wanted me to call you the first time I told him about what was happening in New York." She huffed. "Like, you'd just ride up there on your white horse and keep me safe."

"I would have."

"I'm okay. I don't need to invade every part of your life."

"No."

"Sorry?"

"No. You *are* staying here. With me. There is no invading, Vi, because you never left. Besides, who the hell else is going to look out for you?"

Her mouth dropped open before it returned to a thin line.

I took two steps back, running my hands through my hair. I could feel the edges of my control fading. Violet stood tall, but her hands moved to her belly and rubbed small, slow circles on her side. I watched her eyes crinkle, but she was fighting whatever was going on inside her mind.

"What you told me in my office was scary. Really scary. It fucking killed me to let you go back on your own tonight. And then you call me, scared and crying. That email they sent you is beyond terrifying, Vi. Saying no one else has a right to you because you belong to them. That is a wild escalation from something that already made me want to vomit. We found out someone was in your place, for fuck's sake, and there's no doubt in my mind it's this bastard! No, Violet. Just no. I've tried my hardest to stay out of it, but wherever the fuck the father of your baby is, I hope he knows he's a piece of shit for leaving you vulnerable like this. For not protecting what's his. He's a fool for letting you go."

I watched the tears sparkle in her eyes, but she didn't say anything else to me. Violet simply turned and walked up the stairs, and I followed right after her.

Down the hallway I'd walked for years on my own. Past the closed door of my office. Past the closed door of the room I never went in anymore.

And then I was back in our bedroom, with *her*. For the first time in nine years, Violet was standing in our room with me. I forced my mind to focus on her, and not the thousands of memories pushing on the carefully constructed walls in my mind.

"Vi?"

She turned, sinking down onto the edge of the bed as one tear slipped past her lashes and ran down her face.

"It's still the same in here."

I ran my hand over my face. "Yeah. It didn't make much sense to change it around. I knew it was how you liked it."

Violet stared at me, unblinking. As if I had just stunned her with my admission that I was still living like she was coming back to me. Hadn't I made that clear when she left? Hadn't I told her I'd always be here for her, no matter what?

"I'm tired, Colt. I don't want to do this right now. I

just…" She shook her head. "I just want to take a warm bath, and let the water stop these painful Braxton Hicks contractions. I'm tired and I want to try to get some sleep."

My heart stumbled in my chest. It only took two steps for me to close the distance between us. In the next breath, I was on my knees in front of her, hand held out over her bump. "They aren't supposed to be painful." *Shit.* What was it that I read in that fucking baby book? Braxton Hicks could feel tight, like they were squeezing the baby, but they shouldn't be painful. Painful contractions were more likely to be real contractions.

"What?" she snapped.

"Braxton Hicks aren't supposed to be painful." My hand slid to the other side of her belly, trying to feel the tightening through her shirt. "At least that's what the book said. How long have you been feeling them? Is there a pattern to how fast they are coming? You've been having back pain. I don't even know how far along you are, and you could be in—"

Vi's hand rested on top of mine. "Slow down. I'm not having real contractions. My due date is still weeks away. I just need to take a bath. That always helps them calm down."

"How often does this happen?" I asked, storming towards the bathroom to start filling up the tub.

"All the damn time," Vi laughed from over my shoulder, and I felt the pressure in my chest loosen just a bit. "This one just likes to rile me up. Takes after his dad."

My eyes flew to hers, and all the color I could see in the darkness of the night drained right out of her beautiful face.

"We've fucking danced around it enough, Vi. Who is the baby's father? Is this shit that's going on…is it possible it's him? Is it possible he's the person stalking you?"

"No." Her tone was fierce. And final.

But that wasn't enough for me. "No, what? No, he's not

the person? No, you aren't telling me? Because you mentioned him, and now you look like you're about to pass out."

She was annoyingly silent as I moved around the bath-room, grabbing a new set of towels and placing them next to the tub. My jaw ticked as I watched her walk in from the bedroom, waiting for her to say something, *anything*, to make me feel better about this unknown asshole. But her lips were apparently sealed shut.

Just as I was ready to turn the water off, Violet groaned, bending forward against the sink as her hand circled her belly.

"Christ. What's wrong?"

"Nothing." Her hand swatted mine away as I reached for her elbow. "His butt is pressing weird on my side."

My eyes fell to her stomach, where, even in the pale moon light, I could see her belly was comically lopsided.

"That's wild."

"Yeah, he's a regular gymnast already."

I swallowed down my reply and stepped back, letting her stretch her back as she stood back up.

"I'll just...I'll grab your bag and bring it up for you." She nodded, but I couldn't quite bring myself to leave. "Vi? I'm going to stay in the room until you're done. Just... in case you need help, okay?"

"Okay. Thank you."

It only took me a minute to grab her bag and bring it up to her. She was sitting on the edge of the tub, waiting for it to fill up as I set everything on the closed toilet seat lid. I wasn't sure if I grabbed her something that would be really comfortable when I took what little laundry she had in the dryer, so I made sure to include a pair of my sweatpants and a worn-in shirt for her to use if she wanted.

And I was a fucking bastard for sitting on the edge of the bed with my heart beating like a racehorse, waiting to see if she came out wearing them.

VIOLET

He still had my favorite bubble bath under the sink.

Not used. Not open like I left it there while I was in a hurry and he just forgot about it in some back corner for all these years. Colt had a fresh—still sealed in plastic—bottle ready for me.

It smelled exactly the way I remembered it, too. I sank down deeper into the tub, letting the bubbles cover me up to my shoulders. The baby was clearly enjoying the warmth of the water. He was kicking and making the water ripple around my belly, which was so comically large it stuck up out of the water like an island.

There was a part of me that was panicking as the water cooled. Because I couldn't stay in the tub forever, and I already knew what I had to do.

Colt came for me. I called, panicked and disoriented about my dad, and he hadn't hesitated to get to me.

The second I'd realized he was there, I finally felt safe for the first time in months.

The pains in my belly had stopped almost as soon as my body touched the water, but the knot twisting in my stomach hadn't eased up. Because I knew I needed to tell him the truth. There was only one thing stopping me, and it was so sickeningly selfish it made me hate myself.

I didn't want him to look at me differently.

Colt's eyes had landed on me outside my parents' place a few days ago, and I could still see the love he had for me in his heart. He would have every right to be mad at me for keeping this from him. For not reaching out to say the transfer worked. For staying away as the pregnancy progressed. I couldn't stomach the idea that he'd be angry, or that the love in his eyes would change and shift into hatred.

It wasn't fair for me to sit in my selfish bubble. I couldn't keep it from him. Not for one minute more. The baby kicked again, pressing his foot out so it looked like a little mountain on the floating island. My pruned fingers pushed back, laughing as I got him to roll.

For just a second, as I worked out how to hoist myself out of the tub, I thought about calling out to Colt for help. But that would be awkward, and things already felt so out of sorts between us because of the secret I was keeping. But I wasn't going to keep it any more.

So I rolled like a manatee in a warm freshwater spring onto my hands and knees. What a ridiculous sight I had to be, but the safety of the baby was most important. I was tired, the last little bits of my energy hanging on solely from how nervous I was to talk to Colt. The last thing I wanted was to slip and fall.

I managed to get myself to my feet. Holding on to the edge of the tub, I stepped out, one foot and then the other. But as I found my footing, my head swam. *Jeepers.* The water hadn't been hot, but it still must have gotten to me. My eyes drifted shut for a second, my fingers still gripping the edge of the tub as the dizziness subsided.

First thing's first, I needed to get dressed. The most ridiculous giggle burst from my chest as I thought about walking into the bedroom naked. That would certainly be one way to distract him from the news I was about to deliver.

But that thought passed quickly as I eyed the pile of his clothes he'd brought in with my bag. In all the years we were married, I never wore my own clothes to bed. Maybe that wasn't a big deal to him, like the bubble bath under the sink. Maybe it was something he'd enjoyed on his own over the years, and he wasn't thinking of me. Maybe he'd just realized what a haphazard bunch of clothes he'd thrown together in my bag and didn't think about what wearing his clothes would mean to me.

I slipped the shirt he left for me over my head, groaning when I realized it didn't fit all the way over my belly. But I kept moving. I did retrieve a pair of my maternity panties from my bag, my face heating as I thought about Colt finding them in my laundry room and packing them away for me.

By the time I had his sweatpants on, I was out of breath. My butt hit the edge of the tub and I forced myself to work through every technique I'd ever learned to calm down. The decision was already made. I'd live with whatever feelings he had about me, because he deserved to be in his son's life. And our son deserved to grow up with a dad who was the best man I'd ever known.

COLT

"Are you feeling better?" I asked, trying to ignore the way my dick went instantly hard at seeing her wearing my clothes. Her belly was big enough that it poked out at the bottom between the waist of the sweats I gave her and the t-shirt she was wearing. It was fucking adorable, and took everything in me to not go to her and press my hand against the exposed skin.

"A little. My back is still bothering me, but I did a lot more today than I normally would. And it's late."

I stood, pulling back the comforter on the side of the bed that had always been hers. "Come on. You need to get some sleep."

Violet's hand wrapped around my arm.

"I need to tell you something." Her voice broke, fingers digging into my skin.

"Okay." Fuck, she was scared. I helped her sit then took two steps back, crossing my arms and hoping like hell I could stay calm.

"It's about the baby's dad." Her eyes dropped to the

ground, and I felt the heat rising in my chest. Because I knew where this was going.

"You *do* think he's the one stalking you, don't you?"

She shook her head, still not looking me in the eyes. "It's not him, Colt. He's the most annoyingly protective person I've ever met."

Fucking great. Now I'd be fucking pissed off about this *incredibly protective* baby daddy that in fact seems like the world's biggest douche-canoe for the rest of the night, because how the *fuck* is he so amazing if he left Vi and the baby all on their own this close to her goddamn due date?

"So why isn't he here? Why isn't he protecting you and the baby?"

"He is," she whispered.

I sank down on the mattress next to her hip. She was fucking talking in riddles, but the way her eyes didn't leave mine, the way it looked like she was willing me to understand what she wanted to tell me without saying the words, left me with a hope spreading through my chest like a wild fire. Her hand reached over, grabbed mine, and put it back over her belly.

I froze. "Are you saying...Are you telling me..."

"That you're the baby's father? Surprise..." A fat tear rolled down her face. "You're going to be a dad."

I jumped back, tripping over my own feet as her words slammed into me. I'd heard them before. Each time her voice sounded more tired, more afraid of what was to come. But this time...this time, the words were tinged with hope. Hope that I'd be happy? Hope that I'd be there for her? For him? My *son*.

I fell to my knees and cupped her swollen belly.

"Say something. Please," Violet begged.

"H-how?" I stuttered over the question.

But the truth smacked me right in the chest before I'd even gotten the question out. Tears burned in my eyes as I tried to swallow past the emotion sitting painfully in my throat. Deep in the divorce paperwork had been one single sheet of paper that I thought about every goddamn day for years. Our last chance at becoming parents. One tiny embryo, not graded that well and not expected to lead to a pregnancy, that I signed over complete ownership of as a part of finalizing the end of our marriage.

It felt like the final nail in the coffin. But now, all I could think about was how fucking happy I was. It wasn't the end. *It was just the beginning.*

Something in my chest cracked wide open. I pressed my hand against my heart, trying to catch the breath that had been knocked completely out of me. Beneath my other hand, my son rolled. His back pressed out hard against the pressure of my hand.

Fuck. I felt like my heart was going to give out. A pathetic groan left my body as I fell back on my ass.

"Colt?" Violet slid down, sitting on the floor with me. Her hand came up, pressing against mine. "Are you okay? You've gone really pale."

"I...I..." I couldn't get a clear thought out. "Jesus. I need to get my heart checked out."

Vi squeezed my thigh. "Are you having chest pains? Should I call an ambulance? Or one of your brothers? Jessie?"

"No. *Fuck.*" I cleared my throat. "No, Vi. Just...Come here."

I opened my arms, and she looked down at my chest for a moment before landing against me. My arms wrapped around her in an instant, just for a moment, before I remembered I desperately wanted to hold her belly, too.

"I'm going to be a dad."

"Yeah..."

"We're...the both of us...are having a baby."

She nodded. "I mean, I am. You don't have to be if you

don't want to. I made this decision on my own. It doesn't have to change things for you. I know it probably does, but don't feel bad if not."

Her fingers brushed on my face, and it was only then that I realized I was crying again. Just like I had the day she came home.

She's carrying my baby.

And she was worried. I could see it in her eyes, worried that I'd be upset. Worried that I'd turn her away.

"Why didn't you tell me you were thinking of using our last embryo?"

"We haven't spoken in years, Colt. You signed over your rights to me. And I just...I didn't know if I'd even get pregnant. And then there were all the worries about making it out of the first trimester. Getting this far...It was easier to think I'd come back once the baby was here. Once I knew I wouldn't break your heart with another loss. I didn't ever imagine you seeing me pregnant."

"I would have been there."

"I know. And it would have broken you all over again to have that hope taken away when it didn't work."

"But it did work. And you came back here. You came back to me."

She nodded. "I thought about you every single day. Not just during this pregnancy, but every single day after I left. I know it wasn't healthy. I know it wasn't right. I was the person who walked away, and I knew I had no right to ever just walk back in. A part of me feels horribly guilty that I had to come here. There just wasn't time for me to settle down anywhere else. It had to be here."

Our son decided to kick directly under my hand. God, it was the easiest thing in the world to accept, and yet somehow, I couldn't wrap my mind around it. Vi hissed at the pressure as soon as the baby moved. I could feel the rush of emotions pour over me in that second, and it was overwhelming. Our baby was there. I tightened my hold on her.

He was strong.

He was healthy.

He was going to be born in just a few weeks.

I was going to hold my child in my arms.

I was holding my wife and my child in my arms right now.

The room spun as the air left my lungs. "I think I'm going to pass out."

I'd missed so much of the pregnancy already. But Vi had done such an incredible job...I waited to feel the anger at being kept in the dark for so long, but there wasn't any to be found. Instead, the brightest, hottest pressure seared through my chest as I lowered my face to her belly.

"Hey, buddy. It's okay. I'm here now. Don't be mean to your mama. She's working hard to make sure you get here safe and sound."

Violet shook her head. "Colt, I...I'm so sorry. I should have told you the first day I was here."

The tears splashed over her lashes, and her beautiful lips trembled.

"When, Vi? I ran the fuck away as soon as I saw you."

"But I could have—"

"Why did you leave?" I asked instead.

"What?"

"Why did you leave? Why didn't you choose to stay? To fight for us? We were so much more than just our potential as parents. You were my best friend. The love of my life. Every dream I ever had come true. That's the only question I have. Why, Vi?"

She looked at me, not blinking. "Why are you asking me this now?"

"Because I was too much of a coward to ask you when you handed me the papers. I was so fucking furious at you for wanting to leave. But I knew you were slipping away from me for months by then, and I *let it* happen. Every negative test. Every time we lost..." The words stuck in my throat. "Every time we lost a baby. I'm going to tell you this right now, and I'm dead serious. This baby is a beautiful blessing, but this baby isn't the reason I want things to work out between us. You are enough for me. You've always been enough for me."

"You were always enough for me, too. I was just so lost in the grief. How could I do that to you, Colt? Tie you to someone who couldn't give you what you'd wanted your whole life. You deserved to be a dad, you talked about it all the time. I can remember you holding Jessie as a baby, telling me how excited you were to have kids one day. I wanted to give you that chance. I wanted you to find someone who could make that dream come true for you. Without the struggle. Without the loss." She sniffed, her hand coming up to bat away the tears streaking down her cheeks. "And I wanted to fall apart without worrying about upsetting you. Without you having to feel like you had to help me pick up the pieces. I needed time to know who I was now that I knew my body had betrayed us. You have every right to be mad at me. To never forgive me."

"I'm not mad at you." The way the words snapped out of my mouth probably made it seem like I was lying. But the truth should have been so clear to her. "I'm fucking thrilled. I was so happy for you, seeing you pregnant after everything we went through, that I went to my truck and cried on the drive back over here. I would have loved him no matter what, Vi. Just like I'll always love you."

"Colt."

"This changes everything, darlin'. Don't sit there for a single second and think it doesn't." I ran my hand over her belly, smiling at how perfectly round it was. "There isn't time to dance around it. I've prayed for this moment since the day you told me you needed to leave. That you would come back to me. There isn't time to be shy about what I want. So let me be clear. I want you."

"And the baby?" she asked.

I simply nodded. "*Our* son."

Violet was a whirlwind meant *only* for my heart, sweeping back into my life with an intensity that would blow everything else away. She brought the cold hard truth that I'd been afraid to admit out loud all this time...I would always be desperately in love with her. No amount of time, no amount of heartbreak or ache, would change that. We were being given a second chance, and there was no way I'd ever let her walk away again.

I lifted her shirt, dying to press my lips against the safe home my son was currently curled up in. But as soon as my eyes landed on a line of bruises, all in various stages of healing, I froze.

"What the fuck are these? Someone hurt you!"

"No," Violet laughed through her tears. Her hand dusted along the purple and green splotches. "I have to give myself an injection every day, it's a blood thinner. I'm at a higher risk of developing blood clots, so my OB prescribed it for the duration of the pregnancy."

"Christ. When do you do them? I didn't pack any medicine in your bag. What do we need to do?"

"I normally do the injection in the morning. We'll have time to go back to the cabin and get them before I have to do it tomorrow. Or, later today, now...wouldn't it be?" She yawned. I needed to get her to bed. It had been the most insane few hours.

"Right. Okay. Bed for you and the baby. I'll make sure your medicine is here in the morning, and I'll help you with the injection when it's time."

"You don't have to—"

"Stop right there. It's the *least* I can do. I know you've been doing it all on your own...fuck, I was furious when I thought there was another man walking through this with you, but I want to kick my own ass for not being there now."

Violet placed her hand on my chest. "How could you have been?"

"Tell my fucking heart that, darlin'."

She bit down on her bottom lip. "Okay. You can help with that in the morning."

"Good. Let's get you into bed."

Violet nodded, taking my outstretched hand as I helped her up off the floor.

"I think we need to go slow," she whispered as I pulled back the comforter for her to slide under. "I think tonight was a lot. And nothing good can come from making a decision one way or the other about things when there are a lot of emotions involved. We should...we should work towards being good parents. That's what is most important."

"Okay." I bent over, pressing a kiss to her hairline.

"Colt."

"I hear what you are saying, and although I think it's utter and complete bullshit, I know you are tired and need sleep. So, I won't remind you that while we work on being great parents together for our son, you and me? We've got a lot of great things we are going to be working on together for *us*. Got it?"

She smiled, her eyes closing as she let her head fall against the pillow.

"Got it."

I walked back to the side of the bed closest to the door, and slid under the blankets. Her body was stiff as I curled around her back, my hand sliding over her belly.

"I think that might be a dangerous thing to do," she whispered, wiggling until I realized she was waiting for me to slip my other arm under her head. As soon as I did, she sighed.

"I'm just holding onto my baby, Vi. Making sure you're both safe. Go to sleep."

Her body relaxed into mine, and after a few minutes, her breathing evened out. I was finally holding my whole world in my arms again. Except now, there were two of them to protect. Two of them to keep safe.

My wife was back, and I was going to be a dad.

Violet

"Vi?" Colt's hand was on my arm, but I couldn't comprehend why the hell he was waking me up in the middle of the night. Well, it felt like the middle of the night, at least. And once I cracked my right eye open and found that the room was still swallowed in darkness, I knew I was right.

"Hmm?" I managed to mumble back at him as my eyes tried to roll right back into my head.

"I have to go to work, I'm so sorry. I have your medication downstairs. Can I help you inject it before I go in?"

Well, I couldn't be mad at that. With my eyes still closed, but a smile creeping across my face, I sighed. "No. I do it at eleven. Don't worry."

"Okay. Shit. I'll try to come home for it, but there's some new evidence in a case and I need to be there for the briefing. There's a deputy..."

His voice faded as I yawned and drifted a bit. I wanted to hear what he was saying, but the gravel in his early morning voice had always been so soothing.

"Vi? Did you hear me?"

"Yep."

"You go back to sleep. Everything is locked up, you're safe here."

"I know I am."

Colt chuckled. "Good. I also asked my dad to keep an eye on things over here. He's up around now, anyway, and usually putters around the barn while Beau runs things out with the cattle."

My eyes flew open. "Did you tell him—"

"No. Figured we'd do that together. Sometime soon, seeing as how *our son* doesn't have much longer before he's in our arms instead of in your belly." His hand palmed my bump before he leaned in and pressed a kiss into the blanket. "Be good for your mama today." Colt looked back at me. "Call me if anything comes up."

I closed my eyes, waiting to hear his footsteps fade out of the room and down the hall. Instead, I felt him get closer to me. And as I fought to keep my breath steady, he leaned in, pressing his lips to my cheek.

"I'm not happy I have to go into work today, but I'm fucking thrilled I get to come home to the two of you," he whispered. "Best feeling ever."

I didn't open my eyes. I didn't dare move as his words wrapped themselves around my heart and squeezed. Ignoring the call of the bathroom—which happened every time I woke up now—I forced myself to breathe steadily as I listened to him quietly move around the house. A short time later, his truck started and he pulled away from our home, just as sleep pulled me back under.

———

Ugh. The bathroom was now an alarming need.

I groaned as I flung the blankets off myself, rolling a bit

more onto my arm so I could push my body up and off the edge of the bed at the same time. It was always a bit of a gamble at this point in my pregnancy, because my blood pressure liked to swoop if I moved too quickly. But it was either that or wet myself, and I didn't particularly feel like doing laundry first thing in the morning. I hadn't had a chance to even look around at our house with everything that happened, and I had plans on snooping...*No!* Not snooping. Just seeing what Colt changed in the time I'd been gone.

After using the bathroom, and taking the shortest amount of time possible to make me look somewhat presentable while still in my pajamas, I left the bedroom and padded down the hallway. My stomach growled, and my throat was suddenly so dry I almost gagged.

Weird. I held my belly as I made my way downstairs and to the kitchen. The sunshine immediately caught my eye. I always loved the way it danced through the side of the house in the morning, streaming in and making the kitchen the perfect place to soak in some early vitamin D. I looked out the window over the sink, my eyes first finding the spot where Colt's truck should be. A little pang of anxiety kicked in my chest.

I knew he loved being a deputy, but there would always be the danger of the unknown. And as tough as it had been to deal with when we were married, it was excruciating thinking about him not coming home now that he knew about the baby.

I shook my head, trying to silence the worry. Only a different vehicle parked outside the house caught my eye, and my heart sank. *Why the hell was there a deputy's vehicle out in the driveway?* It wasn't Colt's. I knew that immediately because it wasn't a truck, and he wasn't inside the house.

I slipped my shoes on, wrapped my jacket around myself so my belly wouldn't be sticking out, and marched out the front door. The brisk air greeted me, but only added to the urgency of finding out what was going on.

I raised my fist and knocked on the glass. The deputy inside smiled as he rolled down the window.

"Good morning, ma'am."

"Good morning. Is there a problem, Deputy?"

His brows pulled together. "A problem? No ma'am."

The feeling returned to my fingertips. "Why are you here then? I almost had a heart attack thinking something was wrong with Colt!"

He chuckled. "No, no, everything is fine. I promise. I'm just here to make sure you're safe. Per the acting sheriff's request."

My jaw fell open.

"He requested *what*?"

"Colt requested a deputy to stay here on the Silver Ridge Ranch to make sure you're protected. Which I will make sure you are, ma'am." The deputy's eyes dropped to my belly, and I shoved down the urge to groan. I knew I had to look absolutely ridiculous in Colt's old sweats and t-shirt, my bump no longer wrapped inside the jacket.

"Please stop calling me ma'am. I'm Violet." I held out my hand. He reached through the window and took my hand, giving it a firm shake.

"Deputy Johnathan Boone. But please, feel free to call me John."

"Well, John, it's very nice to meet you. Do you need anything? Coffee? Breakfast? You're more than welcome to come inside if you need to use the restroom..."

John smiled. "I'm all set here, ma—sorry, *Violet*. Thank you. If you need anything..."

"I'll get your attention. Promise."

He nodded, his smile never wavering, even if his eyes did look tired. "Alright. Have a good morning."

"Oh, I will."

And I would, because as soon as I was back in the house, I marched straight upstairs. Colt had filled my bag with the most ridiculous mismatch of random clothes possible, so it was going to be a black legging and sweatshirt kind of day. Lucky for me, my ex-husband still had his extensive collection of sweatshirts, so it was the dealer's choice. My eyes skimmed over the folded fabric until it landed on a gray sweatshirt that looked well loved.

Unfolding it, my breath caught in my throat. Embroidered across the chest was *Chesapeake Bay* and my mind was instantly back on the shore, eating so much seafood that Colt joked he was going to have to roll me back to the little bed and breakfast we were staying at for our honeymoon. I'd bought a canvas bag to carry my laptop in when we were shopping the day before we left, and I had insisted he get something to take home with him.

"I already have exactly what I want going home with me, Vi. My wife."

Smiling at the memory, I slipped the sweatshirt over my head and made my way back downstairs. Before I slipped my shoes back on, I grabbed my laptop and slid it into my bag. I marched over to the counter and removed my injection from the big box before slipping that into my bag, too.

Colt wanted me to be safe? He wanted to help with my medication? Perfect. I'd make it possible for all that to happen. But no way, no how, was a deputy wasting his time sitting outside this house all day long.

Slinging my bag over my shoulder, I opened the door, flipped the lock, and shut it behind me as I stepped onto the porch once more. I smiled as I walked in front of the vehicle. Of course, my car was still at my parents' place, so Deputy Boone was going to get the honors of driving me into town, all the way to the Sheriff's Department.

"Violet?" John's voice questioned me as I pulled open the passenger side door. "Are you okay?" His eyes dropped to my belly.

"Fine," I huffed, startlingly out of breath. "I just need you to drive me into town."

John nodded, his hand reaching to turn the key. The engine rumbled to life and I closed my door, slipping my hand around the seat belt and yanking it over my body towards the receiver.

"I would never normally ask this of you," I start, "but since Colt drove me here last night and left my car at my parents, this will have to do."

"I don't mind one bit. But could you let me know where you need to go so that I can let him know we've left, and I can get you there safely?"

I laughed. "Oh, you don't need to tell him where we're going. He'll see once we get there."

A smile pulled across John's face. "Ah. We're heading to the Sheriff's Department?"

"You would be one-hundred percent correct."

"To come home from our honeymoon and hear we were having twins a few weeks later was the shock of a lifetime," John laughed. I smiled as he finished telling me about his wife, Abby, their daughter Katy, and their twin boys.

"You certainly have your hands full."

"I do. But it's the best. You must be looking forward to the chaos."

"More than you could ever know."

John nodded as he flipped on the blinker and pulled into the station.

"Wait right there, I'll help you down," he instructed.

"I managed just fine on the way in."

"Yeah, I'm all for a woman standing in her independence and all, but I really would like to keep my job. Colt will suspend me with his temporary powers—no question asked—if he hears I didn't help you down."

I nodded. "Well, I can't be responsible for that."

Once I had two feet firmly on the pavement, I grabbed my bag, threw it over my shoulder and marched into the station with my head held high and the biggest scowl I could manage.

Of course, Colt wasn't milling about. I had figured with whatever investigation he was working on he wouldn't just be standing around, staring at the front door.

"Mrs. Ford, is everything okay?" Nate smiled from behind the glass partition.

I sighed, and for a moment let the title wash over me. It had been so long since someone had called me that.

"No sassy nickname for me today, Nate?"

"Didn't want to step on toes," he admitted.

"She's here to see Ford." John cleared his throat, a smile dancing across his face.

Deputy Jones nodded, pressing whatever magic button he had back behind the glass to open the door for us.

I fully planned to keep walking until I made it to Colt's office, but just as I stepped over the threshold, Colt came walking out of a different room. His eyes scanned over us, recognition flaring in an instant.

He stopped dead in his tracks, his eyes tracing over me. Searing heat lit up my body as he lingered on my torso. A smirk kicked up in the corner of his mouth, and I realized he recognized I was wearing his clothes.

I crossed my arms and stared back at him. *Holy hot sauce!* His sleeves were rolled up, exposing several of his intricate tattoos. His forearms had always been one of my favorite features of his. Strong from working on the ranch, but still soft enough that they felt so safe each time they wrapped around me.

And how had I not realized he was wearing glasses? I mean, yeah, he looked shocked to see me, and that shock morphed into worry as he walked closer to us, but my God. I could *not* stop looking at this man and his glasses. The salt and pepper edges of his temples were enough to make my knees weak, but pair them with an ocular accessory and I was downright almost panting!

They were hot. He was hot in them.

"Vi?"

Yeah, my hot and bothered self was too hot and bothered to reply. All sense of indignation went right out the window. I couldn't remember what I was doing there.

"Come on." His hand went to my elbow, and before I knew it, John's chuckles were just a distant sound as Colt shuffled me into his office and shut the door.

I set my bag on the chair, fully intent on sitting in the other, but as I turned, my head swam.

Shit. I hadn't had breakfast. A cold sweat hit the small of my back and I closed my eyes, willing away the flood of saliva and roll of nausea that hit me like a tsunami.

"Colt," I whispered as I reached out to steady myself.

"Whoa. What's wrong?"

I swallowed, breathing in his scent. I couldn't believe I'd been so wrapped up in my nerves that I hadn't recognized it last night. That scent took me right back to the first Christmas we lived together. The first year we were renovating the house. God, we barely had any money, but I'd gotten him the nicest smelling cologne at a fancy shop I'd found in Dallas. He wore it all the time. Even now. My heart galloped, the dizziness coming back in full force. Only this time, I didn't think it was because of my blood sugar.

"Vi? Hey, I'm going to help you sit down, okay?"

I nodded, letting him guide my body back into the chair that sat in front of his desk. The same one I'd sat in the day before, telling him about my stalker. So much had changed in so little time.

His thumbs traced steady circles over the back of my hands. "I don't like how pale you are right now. What's wrong?"

"I'm fine," I whispered. Hating how unsure that sounded, I cleared my throat. "I'm sorry. I was about to make breakfast when I saw Deputy Boone sitting in your driveway and made him drive me over here. The baby doesn't like when I forget to eat."

His thumbs stopped moving as he shook his head, his jaw ticking once before he swallowed. "I'll be right back. Do *not* move."

COLT

"Christ," I groaned, watching Violet sip on a glass of orange juice as the bagel I made her sat on the corner of my desk. I'd bitten the nail on my thumb right down to the raw, tender flesh, watching every move she made to see if she was still feeling dizzy.

"I'm fine. I told you I just didn't eat before I came down here. Stupid move on my part, but *nothing* to worry about. Especially now that you've fed me enough to put me into a coma."

"You're lucky I haven't cuffed us together and thrown away the key."

"Colton Ford." She leaned forward, pinning me with her eyes.

"I told you last night, Vi. I'm not playing around this time. I'm winning you back. I'm taking care of you. Both of you."

She rolled her eyes, but I didn't miss the way her lips turned up in the corner before she leaned back in her chair.

"Now," I continued, "why don't you tell me why you're down here."

"Well, I'm certainly not going to have you waste taxpayer dollars on stationing a deputy outside your house."

"*Our* house."

She bit her plump lower lip and shook her head. There was no way Violet wasn't aware of the effect she was having on me. Christ, I thought I might lose control of myself the second my eyes landed on her wearing my sweatshirt. Did she remember buying it on our honeymoon? Was that why she wore it down here?

"And I'm the acting sheriff. I get to delegate my force to wherever I feel the need is greatest. Besides chasing down a few teenage hooligans who were out tagging buildings on Ford Avenue last night, we've got the resources. And keeping you safe is my number one priority."

Her brows pulled together. "What about the big investigation you had to come into work for this morning? That's obviously bigger than what's going on with me."

I shook my head. "Let me be very clear here: you are my number one priority. Keeping you and our son safe comes before everything else. But we think there's a serial arsonist in Clarence County. Unfortunately, that's all I can say about that right now."

"Gosh, that's scary. But I understand."

I looked down at my watch. "There's only about an hour until you're due for your medication. Do you want me to drive you back home?"

She smirked. "Oh no. I told you, I'm not sitting at home with some deputy assigned to me. I'll be perfectly fine working right from here. And if you need to take a meeting in your office, I can use the break room. Besides, I have a few questions I want to ask Deputy Jones about procedural things for my manuscript."

"You can just ask me."

"You're too busy. I don't want to bog you down with my silly plot line questions."

"Vi," I grumbled. "You need help with a scene? You need help with dialogue? You need to test out a position or two that your characters find themselves in?" I winked. "I'm your guy. I'm the *only* guy. Not Deputy Jones. Okay?"

I watched her round cheeks flush a pretty shade of sunset pink as she bit down on that damn lip again, shifting in her seat. "Got it."

"Good."

————

The silence was driving me bonkers. There was so much I wanted to ask her. So much I was desperate to know. I hadn't wanted to push last night, but the glances I was not so sneakily stealing right now of the woman I'd loved my whole life, pregnant with my baby, wasn't enough.

"Are you craving anything?" I blurted out.

Vi's eyes left her laptop screen and found mine, a smile spreading across her face. "No, that juice and bagel were perfect. Thank you."

"I don't mean now. I meant...throughout the pregnancy. Did you have cravings at first? Are they the same now? Maybe we should go grocery shopping on the way home, that way I know I have stuff at the house you like to eat."

Her head tilted, and then laughter filled the office. "I promise, whatever you have at the house is fine. Your son is just hungry. All the time. Pickles? Great. Steak? Great. An egg salad sandwich and pasta with marinara sauce at two in the morning with a bowl of cinnamon pecan swirl ice cream to wash it down? Great."

"What about morning sickness? Heartburn?"

"I had some nausea in the beginning. Heartburn's been touch and go since the second trimester."

I nodded. "Will you tell me more? Please?"

Her eyes softened and she shut her laptop. Violet pushed off the chair, walking around my desk to me. She leaned against the edge of my desk, wrapping her hand around mine and bringing it to her belly.

My face fell. "Is he okay?" I asked. Her belly was bouncing slightly, but at a steady pace. It wasn't a kick.

"He has the hiccups," she explained.

The tension released from my shoulders and I brought my other hand up to cup the roundest part of her bump. I pressed my lips to the fabric of my sweatshirt, pulled tightly across her. "I can't wait—" The baby kicked out, Vi's hand covering mine as she laughed.

"I think you scared him!"

Her belly jumped up and down in my grasp as she continued to giggle. "Has that happened before?"

"No! No one has been close enough to my belly before for that to happen."

"I'm sorry, little one. Daddy didn't mean to scare you."

Violet stilled. *Shit! Did I push too hard?* All my fears seemed to be confirmed when I looked up and saw her eyes sparkling with tears.

"Vi, I—"

"No, I'm sorry. I'm really, truly, deeply sorry that you didn't get to experience this pregnancy with me. I convinced myself that I had to protect you from something going wrong. If I didn't tell you, until I knew he was here and he was safe and he was healthy, that if something bad did happen, I would be the only person heartbroken. There wasn't a part of me that considered how heartbroken you'd be over every good and happy thing that you missed. I thought the ends justified the means. And I was wrong."

I moved my hand off her belly to cup her cheek. My thumb caught the first tear that fell as she leaned into my touch. I traced my finger over a few of her freckles before shaking my head. "I know you were trying to do what was right. For you. And our son. And most of all to protect me. I'm not mad at you. You don't need to apologize any more. Do I wish I had been there from the moment you decided to try again? Of course. But not because I need those memories for fatherhood. But because I wish that we had that time together. For us."

Before she could respond, the phone on my desk rang.

"I'll let you get that," Vi responded, sounding a little out of breath as our connection broke. She walked back to her chair and opened her laptop while I took the call.

COLT

I opened the group chat I had with my siblings, typing silently behind my computer screen as Vi focused on her own work. I honestly couldn't remember the last time I'd felt so relaxed doing administrative tasks. It was like her proximity had reset my nervous system. Was that even possible?

HAYES:

BEAU:

Lachlan:

That doesn't sound ominous.

Jessie:

Lach, are you even going to be there?

Three dots next to my youngest brother's picture popped up, only to disappear a moment later. I knew what he was trying to type out. That no, he wouldn't be there. Because he didn't like to leave his house any more. And we didn't push him to.

My phone chimed into the silence of the office. Vi looked up from her laptop screen, smiling as I took off my reading glasses.

"It's time for your medicine," I said, watching her eyes drop down to check the time for herself on her screen.

"God, I was so lost in my manuscript it only felt like a few minutes had passed."

Well, that was good. Maybe she hadn't noticed the fact that I was constantly sneaking glances at her from across my desk.

"Must be a good story."

"I don't totally hate it at this point, which is odd, seeing as how last week I was certain I would have to delete the whole thing and start over."

I pushed up from my chair, walking towards her bag. "Is it okay if I get in here?"

She nodded. "There's just a pre-filled syringe in some packaging."

I nodded. "I took a look at the box when they were dropped off. And I looked at an article quick when I was waiting for the briefing to start this morning. Injecting it looks pretty straight forward."

Violet stood up from her chair and turned towards the door.

"Where are you going?" I asked.

"Oh, I...uh. I didn't notice the alcohol pads I use with the box, so I was just going to wash a spot on my belly in the bathroom before we did this."

I shook my head. "Hank has a first aid kit in his desk. We'll just grab one out of there. If we can't get back into your parents' place to grab the ones you have, I'll pick some up at the Shop and Save so we have our own supply for the next few days."

"You really think they won't have what they need by tomorrow?"

"It can take a few days to turn a crime scene around."

Shivers rolled through her body. "God. I hate how that sounds. *A crime scene.* I was standing there, not even knowing something had happened. If I hadn't seen that email, I would have gone upstairs...I can't imagine."

"I'm glad you didn't have to see it."

"I just want the baby's things. They were in one of my suitcases, but I hadn't unpacked anything yet. Did you see it up there? Maybe they won't need to enter it for evidence."

I winced as I walked around to my desk, not answering as I grabbed the first aid kit out and started looking through it. Just like I thought, alcohol pads were in there behind the bandages.

"Colt?"

"Come here." I guided her back, so her bottom was resting on the edge of my desk. Her hands went behind her, stabilizing herself on the desktop. It made her belly stick out further than I'd seen it before. There was no way I could stick a needle into her skin. *What if I hurt her? What if I poked through something important?*

No. I knew that was a dumb thought. The needles were short and c-sections had to cut through something like seven layers of skin, fat, and muscles to deliver a baby—yes, another thing I'd learned as I scrolled every possible new parent website for information about everything I'd missed, and everything that would be happening over the next few weeks.

I swallowed down my nerves. While I mentioned the article I'd read to Vi, I left out the fifteen videos I'd watched on properly injecting the medication, specifically in the belly during pregnancy. There was no way I was about to mess up something so important.

"Let me get through this, and we can talk about it."

She smiled. "This isn't surgery. I promise, it's no big deal."

"I'm about to push a needle into your body and inject you with medication. It's a very big deal." I knelt down between her legs, pushing my sweatshirt all the way up to the top of her belly. She was wearing some sort of maternity leggings, and my fingers reached out to pull them down over her bump, but I froze.

"Is it okay if I—"

She nodded, and I slipped my fingers under the band, pulling the fabric down so it rested across her hips. The line of bruises, all in different stages of fading, appeared.

I sucked in a harsh breath. "Christ, I don't know how you do this, Vi."

"The outcome is worth the cost."

I felt like I'd been kicked in the chest. Of course she felt like that. Before I ripped open the alcohol wipe, I pressed my lips quickly over the darkest looking bruise.

"Thank you for taking such good care of our son," I whispered, unable to clear the emotion from my throat.

I reached over her hip and slipped my glasses back on. The

antiseptic cloth came out of its packaging and I found a clear spot, an inch to the right of her belly button, just like the instructions online had said. Violet's muscles tightened as the cold cloth pressed to her skin.

"Sorry," I muttered as I cleaned an area larger than I needed to. Like I said, I wasn't about to take any chances that something could happen.

As soon as I lifted the cloth away, I blew my breath across her skin. Her breath hitched, but steadied as I took the syringe out, pulled the cap off, and in one smooth motion, pushed it into her skin.

"Go slow, it burns if you go too quickly," she instructed.

I nodded, pressing the small blue plunger as evenly as possible. Once I hit the stop, I pulled the needle out, capped it, and deposited it in the SHARPS container in the corner of Hank's office.

Striding back over to the desk, I removed the instantly ready ice pack from the first aid kit, snapping the mechanism inside and shaking it until it cooled. I tsked at Vi, who looked like she was getting ready to pull up the waistband of her pants.

"Wait one second. I read you could put a cold compress on it to help with the burning. Try this for a minute or two."

She laughed, taking the compress from my hands. "That's so sweet of you, but I don't think I should just stand here in your office with my belly exposed like this. What if someone walks in?"

"They'll knock first, and unless it's an emergency, it can wait five minutes while I make sure you're okay."

She didn't argue again. "You did a great job."

"I'm surprised you couldn't feel my fingers shaking. I don't know how you've done that to yourself this entire time."

"I wasn't very successful in the beginning. Something about the first trimester...trying to do the injections would always set off my gag reflex. So I'd be gagging the entire time I was trying to hold still while doing the injection. I'm sure I was quite the ridiculous sight." She placed the cold pack against her belly and pulled her pants up around it, tucking the sweatshirt back into place. "I actually almost passed out a few times. Had to lay on my bathroom floor for a good ten minutes before I could get up."

Her eyebrows shot up as a grumble bounced around my chest. "I should have been there."

"I'm sorry," she whispered.

"No. No. No more apologizing to me about it."

"I don't have to share—"

"Stop. Full stop, Vi. I want to hear every story. I want to know every detail. I told you already that I want you to tell me it all so I can write it into my memories like I was there when it all happened. But I don't think I can control the anger I feel towards myself for not being there to help. I know it's not rational, but I feel it."

She stood up from the desk, closing the distance between us. Her hair was pulled back into a messy bun, little strands poking out here and there. Her freckles were still out in full force, like she'd just come inside after sitting under the sun. God, I wanted to kiss each and every one.

Her hand reached up, cupping my cheek. This felt like a dream, but if it was one, I never want to wake up.

"How about this? I agree to stop apologizing, and you agree to absolve yourself of guilt that has no right to weigh you down."

"Deal," I agreed. "Should we seal it with a kiss?"

Violet tipped her head back and laughed. I hadn't noticed before, but she had the most beautiful lines in the corners of her eyes. Smile lines. Fuck, I could stare at them for hours.

"Keep wearing those glasses of yours around me, and I don't think I'll be able to say no to that offer."

VIOLET

Why had I agreed to this?

I was solely focused on the sound of our footsteps trekking across the gravel of Colt's parents' driveway, trying desperately to stop my mind from spiraling—it wasn't working. Of course, I was nervous when he told me we were having dinner with his family, but I forced it to the back of my mind until I remembered I had no nice clothes, and all of my makeup was still at my house.

I might have cried really hard in the truck as we left his work, and poor Colt looked so scared. As soon as I told him I was freaking out about looking absolutely disheveled wearing his clothes to a family dinner with people I hadn't seen in years, he took pity on me. We drove straight to the discount department store on the edge of Bell Ridge and I found a sweet little green sundress that actually fit over my belly. It almost touched the ground, too, so that was nice. I managed to grab a cute cream cardigan, a tube of mascara, and a round brush. Colt swore he had a hair dryer at the house I could use when we got back.

And then more tears came when I saw it was the hairdryer

I had left behind when I moved out. He'd kept it in the same bathroom drawer and everything.

My hand smoothed the fabric over my belly as we walked closer to the house. I didn't care if this was the only thing I had to wear for the rest of my pregnancy. It made me feel pretty, and that was a blessing.

"What's wrong?" Colt's hand squeezed mine as he stopped walking.

"Nothing's wrong? Why would you think anything is wrong?"

His eyebrows shot up to his hat, and he chuckled. "You haven't ever been this quiet before in your life."

I pressed the fingers Colt wasn't holding directly into the small of my back and sighed. "I'll have you know, I like being quiet these days. Quiet is my favorite."

"Not buying it, darlin'." *Christ.* Every time that cowboy drawl came out, it made my whole damn body flush. Who the hell was I kidding? Just because I was carrying his baby, just because we were about to tell his whole family about it, didn't mean Colt and I would find our way back to each other. We were two people with a past who would love our child no matter what, and I needed to hold onto that.

"Okay, I know you think I'm dramatic when it comes to checking in with you, but you are actually starting to worry me. Are you okay?" The gentle touch of his fingers on my elbow did absolutely nothing to chill the full hormonal flush that was creeping over my skin.

"I'm fine, I think I'm just having a hot flash. The baby makes it so damn hard to regulate my temperature." I pulled away from him and tried to shuck my jacket off my body.

"Vi?"

I wasn't fine. *Not at all.* Because Colt had been so wonderful about everything, but that didn't mean I wasn't walking into a situation where the rest of his family wouldn't be absolutely fuming that I hadn't come straight back to Silver Springs the second the pregnancy test was positive. And my damn hormones were swinging so fast these days I felt like sobbing, but I wasn't sure if it was because I was over-whelmed, or nervous, or scared, or so fucking horny for my husband that if he kept looking at me with concern in his eyes, I might just tackle him to the ground right here and rip his clothes off.

"I'm nervous, okay?!" The damn jacket fell into my hands and I waved it around like I'd lost my mind. Which clearly, I had. "I mean, I haven't seen most of your family for years, and I'm quite certain they're all on your side now, which of course it's not *about sides*. And they *should* be on yours. It's just that...I ran. I ran, and I left everything and everyone I loved here, and now I'm back and I'm having a baby, but not just *a* baby. I'm having *our* baby. The baby that would have meant we stayed together and had a happy life here like we always talked about, but instead we're living together in the house we worked so hard to turn into a home during our marriage, sleeping in the bed we made love to each other in, not touching the elephant in the room that is *what happens when the baby is born,* and we have to figure out how to split time. Because I know that's what you are going to ask me to do, Colt. I know you want to be in this baby's life, and I want that for you too. But you also can't take him from me. You signed away your rights and that means legally, he is mine and only mine. So if you think walking into that house is going to give you some sort of power over me, or if you think I'm going to let your family wrap their arms around me and hold me in place until I agree to give the baby over to you, then...then...I don't know." My voice hitched, and I swear my flushed skin sizzled as a tear rolled down my cheek. "I'm just scared."

Colt didn't say a word—he just moved. Before I could fall

apart even more, his strong arms were around me. Comforting me. Pouring in his own strength and silent promises to me.

"I would never take our son from you." His words vibrated through his chest as his hold on me tightened. "As for everything else you just blurted out in an adorable rant, don't give a second thought to my family. I'll always be on *your* team when it comes to facing anyone in the world, especially my knucklehead brothers and my sometimes overbearing parents. We already know Jessie and Hawk are Team Calliope."

I gasped and shoved my hand against his chest. "Don't say that name out loud! Someone could overhear you," I hissed.

He just laughed, his hands gathering my hair up off my neck. I felt a cool breeze dust over my heated skin, the effect instantaneous. My shoulders fell, the tension melting away.

"Better?" he asked.

"Better."

"Good. Now, if you feel like freaking out more, we can hang out here for another minute. Or, we can just tackle it head first and get it over with. Your choice."

"Run, and hide, and live with the hope that your family won't hate me forever and ever, please."

Colt laughed. "Sweetheart, my family would be so disappointed if we didn't give them a chance to love on the baby and support us."

———

The house was filled with conversation and laughter as we walked in, which would have been awesome if not for the fact that everyone literally stopped speaking and turned to look at us.

I swear, Hayes and Beau looked exactly the same as the last time I saw them, but I couldn't believe how much Beau's best friend, Birdie, had changed. Not in a bad way, either. She was always a cute girl, but she was absolutely stunning now.

"Hey, guys. Decided to go with a full on stare at Vi instead of a welcome wagon?" Colt joked, breaking some of the tension.

"Are they dating?" I whispered to Colt.

His brows pulled together. "Who?"

"Beau and Birdie?"

He shook his head at me, his face full of surprise.

"Violet! It's so great to see you again!" Birdie wrapped her arms around me.

"So great to see you, too. I wasn't expecting you to be here tonight, but I should have known better. You and Beau still attached at the hip?"

"Pretty much. Someone has to keep him from saying all the ridiculous things that his brain comes up with."

I laughed.

"Listen, this is probably so forward of me and you probably have things handled, but I know it can be tricky moving when you're close to your due date. Jess mentioned you might need someone...I'm a certified nurse midwife and work in Bell Ridge with Dr. Witten and the staff at St. Clare's hospital. I would be happy to make sure the office fits you into the rotation, or take you on myself as your midwife. Whatever you'd be comfortable with." Birdie's smile was so genuine it cracked open the wall I was quickly constructing around my heart.

"She delivered Beckett, actually, right here on the ranch. So, if you want a review of how she did, I can definitely give you one." Jessie smiled. "I'll tell you this, I absolutely wanted to throttle her when she said I wasn't going to make it to the hospital."

"But," Birdie laughed, "I was right. There was no way we were making it all the way to Bell Ridge. And you had an uncomplicated delivery, thank goodness."

"Except for a son arriving when we were expecting a daughter," Hawk laughed.

"Yeah, well, there's nothing I can do about that!" Birdie rolled her eyes.

"Alright, quit hoggin' her." Hayes stepped up next to Birdie, holding his arms out to me. I stepped into them, happy for the embrace.

"Missed you, Vee." The familiar nickname made my throat ache. "Jessie's been a real pain in my ass lately. Could have used that older-sister energy to put her in her place, you know."

"I can, with one-thousand percent certainty, say I'd be on Jess's side when it comes to dealing with you." I laughed as he stepped back, his hand coming over his heart as his face crumpled in fake pain.

"Ouch."

"Did I hear my daughter-in-law's voice? Or am I just losing my mind?" Colt's dad, Danny, stepped out from the hallway, a dish towel on his right shoulder and a *Kiss the Cowboy* apron tied over his chest. "Well, I'll be damned. Hey there, honey."

I waved my hand, unable to speak past the lump in my throat.

"Oh, bless us! Violet! Look at you!" Colt's mother had tears already welling in her eyes as she pulled me into a hug. Dolly had been a second mother to me, really like a true mom, from the very first time I walked into her diner. But once Colt and I became inseparable, she was someone I talked to about everything. Her advice and the wisdom she shared meant everything to me.

"Hi, Dolly. I've missed you."

She released me from the embrace, but her hands landed sternly on my arms. "None of that *Dolly* stuff. I haven't been Dolly to you in decades. Mama will still do just fine."

"How about Grammy?" Colt asked from over my shoulder. Dolly's face turned towards Beckett, who was busy riding back and forth on a rocking horse.

"Of course. You know I love that name. I hope you'll let the baby call me that too, Violet. You know you'll always be family. Even after...everything."

"I appreciate that so much." I knew what Colt was doing. He was trying to give me the chance to tell them, all of his family, that the baby was his. But I couldn't get the words out. I felt the heat of their stares all over my skin and I...just couldn't.

"Well, dinner's done. Why don't we all head into the dining room and eat. We have so much to catch up on!" Dolly's hands waved out in front of her, ushering her family towards the table.

"We do." Colt chuckled, and I fought the urge to send my elbow into his side. "Just give me and Vi one minute, okay?"

All those eyes were back on me again. *God, I couldn't do this...*

One by one, the voices faded into the next room. Colt's hand landed on my waist, turning me so I was facing him.

"What?" I asked.

"You need to breathe."

I blew all the air out of my lungs.

"You know," he chuckled, "I was trying to give you an in there. I basically set it up perfectly for you to give the news."

"I can't," I croaked, scared I might fall with how hard my legs were shaking. "I mean it, Colt. I...you've already done so much for me, been so understanding about this situation, but I can't be the one to tell your family."

He nodded, pressing a kiss onto the crown of my head. "Alright, sweetheart. I can do that."

My whole body went gooey at the term of endearment. This man had always been my undoing, and it was clear my body hadn't forgotten that.

He stepped back, slipping his hand around mine before pulling me into the dining room. I noticed three chairs were empty.

"Where's Lachlan?" I asked.

"He's at home. Like always." Colt shrugged his shoulders.

I expected him to elaborate on that, only he didn't. He took two more steps into the dining room, and froze.

"Violet and I have an announcement to make."

My eyes went wide as I watched his family turn, stunned at his booming proclamation.

"I know you all can very well see that Violet is pregnant. And I know that you've been walking around me gently since she came back into town and I had my little breakdown."

Breakdown? I squeezed his hand, and he dropped his gaze from his family to me. "I started to tell you...but after dinner, when we're back home in bed, I'll finish the story."

His whispered words were loud enough for Jessie to over-hear, and I watched as a smile spread across her face.

"Violet is pregnant with my baby. We're *both* going to be parents."

Beau stood up. His chair scraped loudly against the wood floor, and Colt's hand tightened around mine.

"What are you doing?" Birdie hissed. "Sit down."

"No." Beau wasn't answering her. I knew, because he was looking right into my eyes. He turned, storming through the kitchen. No one moved or made a sound as the back door slammed shut.

"Is there ever going to be a day in this family where everyone reacts normally to a pregnancy announcement?" Jessie mumbled, and I watched Danny's face fall. There had to be a story there I wasn't aware of.

"That's why you asked me about being called 'Grammy'?" Dolly asked. "I can't believe I didn't realize..."

"When were you back in town? You only saw Colt?" Jessie asked over her mother.

"No. I haven't been back in years," I admitted.

Colt cleared his throat. "Violet and I, when we went through IVF…There was an embryo left. Just one."

"And at the time," I continued, "after that last miscarriage, I was too heartbroken to keep trying. I was scared, and hurt, and I ran away from everyone and everything. I'm very sorry for that."

Colt turned, his hand squeezing mine again in reassurance. "You have nothing to be sorry for."

I nodded, feeling the painful sting of tears hit the back of my eyes. "In the divorce, Colt signed over custody of the embryo to me. And I kept paying for the clinic to store it, all these years."

My finger brushed at the tear tracking down my cheek. I didn't want any part of this beautiful miracle to feel embarrassing. But with nearly every member of the Ford family looking at me in disbelief, I couldn't help but feel that way.

"And this year, turning forty, I just knew I had to give it one more go."

"But Colt didn't know." It wasn't a question from Hayes.

"No. I didn't tell him. I didn't tell anyone. I couldn't." My voice got stuck in my throat. It took everything in me not to let the anxiety that was constantly humming through the back of my mind come out. A deep breath and a moment of staring down at the floor—or trying to, while really just weirdly eyeing my belly—seemed to help.

"Honey, you don't have to explain a single thing to us. We're welcoming a new member into our family, and we're getting an old one back. I'm thrilled." Dolly stood from her chair and wrapped me in her arms. "I know it must have been so scary to go through these last months by yourself. But you've got us now."

COLT

My boots crunched across the gravel as I walked to the barn, where I knew my brother would be stewing. The disappointed look on Violet's face had faded as my family wrapped us up in words of support and congratulations, but the sadness in her eyes never left. All because my brother was going to hold onto a grudge that wasn't even his to have.

I marched straight through the open door of the barn. Beau was busy mucking out a stall, his back turned to me.

"What the *fuck* is your problem?"

His back straightened, and the rake fell from his hand as he turned towards me.

"*My* problem? When the fuck are you going to stop letting your fucking broken heart lead you around by the balls, man? Violet left. She's been gone for almost ten fucking years. And you can pretend now that those ten years weren't hell. You can forget those years as fast as you fucking want. But I won't. I won't forget how scared we were that it wasn't just Vi we were losing. How we listened to Mom cry, and Dad try to reassure her that you would be okay. I won't forget how it was me, Lachlan, Jess, and Hayes who had to set up a rotation to check in on you when you were so depressed you stopped functioning."

"I never stopped—"

"You were a zombie for those first few years, Colt. We marched our asses to your house every fucking day to make sure you didn't do something stupid to take away the pain. She just left! She only cared about herself. And you're just going to let her lie like that? You're going to accept her back after she fucked someone else and left them behind, just like she left you? Did he realize she was a selfish bitch, and that's why he wants nothing to do with the kid?" Beau spit on the ground as my hands clenched. "Did she come crawling back to town to lick her wounds and then decide to hook you back in to play daddy? You're a fucking idiot."

My fist connected with his jaw in one smooth motion.

Fuck. The bones in my hand cracked and electric pain— hot and sharp—radiated up my arm. But the blood my brother spit onto the barn floor filled me with such fucking relief that I almost fell over.

"I see how it is," Beau laughed, his hand coming up to wipe away the blood dripping down his face.

"No, you fucking don't. Because Vi is pregnant with *my baby.* Mine. Not some other man's. She was never with anyone else."

Beau scoffed, his hand rubbing along his jaw. "So she says."

"And so I believe."

"If you believe that, please, tell me how the hell a baby is conceived when two people haven't spoken to or seen each other since their divorce? I mean, I'm not living in an alternate reality where her pregnancy is going one hundred times slower than a normal one, am I? Christ. Jessie told me about some weird alien romance she was reading a few weeks ago, but those pregnancies only lasted half the time. Is that it? Are you here to tell me Violet is actually some weird intergalactic being with a decade-long gestation period?"

His mocking made me want to punch him all over again. "Shut the fuck up, and listen to me. There was an embryo left over from the IVF we did."

Beau shrugged his shoulders. "And?"

"And..." My non-throbbing hand rubbed against the stubble on my chin. "I signed over my rights to it in the divorce. It was hers to decide what to do with."

His eyes went wide, and the color drained from his face.

"She got to decide..."

I nodded. "And earlier this year, she made the decision to try one more time for a baby. It took. Now she's here—"

"Now she's here. Holy fuck." Beau took a step towards me. "Please tell me you aren't stupid enough to believe this. Please tell me you called the fucking clinic. That you asked for the records. That you're getting a paternity test done!"

"I'm going to fucking punch you in the mouth again," I warned. "I don't need any of that."

"Yes, the fuck you do! You're so blinded by your love for her and this golden carrot she's dangling in front of your face, that you can't even see it! You think we haven't noticed the sadness creeping back in after Jess had Beckett? That we didn't see the way you pulled back into yourself because you were thinking of every time you lost your chance at fatherhood?"

"I haven't—"

"Save it. The others might want to tiptoe around you, but I don't have the fucking temperament for it. Jesus, I want to shake you, Colt. Be fucking smart for one goddamn minute. Demand a test. Make sure you're stepping up for the right reasons."

"If you want a paternity test, I'll be happy to do it." I spun on my heel. Violet stood in the doorway, her jacket wrapped tightly around her body.

"Did you walk out here alone?" I growled.

"I'm perfectly capable of walking on my own."

"I told you to wait inside for me."

"The ranch is safe, Colt. And I'm glad I didn't wait. If you feel like what Beau is saying has any possibility of being true, then I want to clear the air. I'll have the test done."

My jaw clenched. "I don't. I know that baby is mine, and I don't want to do anything that could hurt him, or you."

She took a step closer to me, her eyes flicking to my brother before settling back on my face. "But he's right. You shouldn't just take me at my word. If it makes it easier, I'll show you the paperwork from the transfer. It has all the dates on it, and our information. And the paternity test wouldn't hurt me or the baby. It's just a quick blood draw."

I moved to her. "How would you know what a paternity test entailed?" I asked, cupping her cheek.

"I just thought you might ask. You have a right to, you know? And I'll do it. No questions asked."

"I don't need it," I sighed.

"You can think about it. Before things are complicated."

Behind me, my brother chuckled, no humor in the sound.

"You got something to say?" I asked, whipping around to stare him down.

"Just feels like things are already complicated."

"I swear, Beau—"

"Could I have a minute with your brother?" Violet's request hit me like a ton of bricks.

"Vi?"

"Hawk and Jessie wanted to talk to you about something, anyway. Head back up to the house. I'll be there in a minute." She stood on her tiptoes, pressing a kiss to my cheek.

My brother faded away as I stared into her eyes, fighting

every urge I had to slip my hands around her waist and pull her in for a real kiss. One that I could pour my heart and soul into. One that would show her she was right where she belonged. One that made her feel the love I was ready to share with her all over again.

"What was that for?" I asked, the warmth of her lips lingering on my skin. Fuck, I loved that feeling. I'd *missed* that feeling.

"For trusting me. For standing up for me. For not hating me." Her voice caught on those last words.

"Never. I could never, ever hate you." But I knew my brother could. I dropped her hand, turning towards him. "You stay the fuck over there and listen to whatever she has to say. Don't take a step towards her. Don't be an asshole. If she walks back up to the house with a single fucking tear in her eye, your sore jaw will be the least of your worries."

Violet nodded, her hand coming out to squeeze my arm as I walked out the door. But I couldn't leave her. I had to hear what Beau was going to say—what she was going to say—so I stopped walking as soon as my shadow made it out of the doorway.

"I'm sorry, Beau," Violet said softly. *Shit.* I took a step back towards the barn, my ass hitting the wood of the building as I tried to press my body flat against it.

"It's not me you need to apologize to." My brother sounded irritated.

"Yes. It is. I owe every single person in this family an apology. I was so wrapped up in my own grief, in my own pain and failure, that I couldn't see beyond that. To any of you. To Colt. And you were here when I couldn't be. You kept him going. You helped him through. The very least I owe you is an apology."

Beau sniffed. "You don't know how bad it got, Vi. He's loved you every day of his life since he was twelve goddamn years old. He's never stopped, not for one single breath. And he would never admit how bad it got, because on all the days when one of us had to go drag him out of bed and force him to eat something, force him to get fresh air, to move his body, he still talked about *you*. He talked about protecting you from the pain he caused you by not being able to give you a child. So I don't need your apology. *I don't fucking want it.* I'm happy that you're getting what you want now, but I have to protect him. He won't survive when he finds out the truth—that you've come back for protection, or support, or whatever the fuck it is you need, and the only way you knew to get that from him was to tell him this kid in your belly is his."

"This is his baby, Beau. I know it's wild and it's weird, but this is his child. When I walked away, it wasn't because I didn't love Colt any more. He's been *the only one for me since I was twelve, too.* I have never stopped loving him. Do you know what it's like to know in your soul that you've walked away from the greatest gift life ever gave you? To have to leave so that maybe, just maybe, that person who is everything to you will be able to go on and have their own happiness?"

"You want me to pat you on the back for breaking his heart because you thought maybe one day he'd find someone else? You're not a martyr, Violet! And you're not family. Not anymore."

She didn't respond right away. The hair on the back of my neck stood as I heard her clear her throat. "I know that you want to make me into a villain, Beau. That you want to have someone to hate for the heartache he went through, and that's fine. I deserve to carry that. But this baby is his family. His son is your family, too. I just wanted to say that I'll stay out of your way now, and after the baby's born. When he's with Colt, you're more than welcome to have whatever relationship with your nephew that you'd like to have. And because it's painful for you that I'm back, I'll stand off to the side. I know how important it is to Colt to have his family by his side. I want that for him. I want that for you, too. And for my son."

I heard her walking towards me, but never in a million years did I expect her to walk out of the barn with her head held high. She closed her eyes for a second before turning towards the house. And that's when I saw her realize I was still standing there, waiting for her.

There was no doubt in my mind an argument was coming, which is why I was so shocked when she walked over and wrapped her arms around me.

"Vi?"

"You stayed." Violet's words were muffled against my chest. "You weren't supposed to hear all that."

I saw how flushed her cheeks were as she walked out of the barn, so I didn't hesitate to put my fingers back through her hair, lifting it off her neck so the night breeze could cool her down. "I'm so proud of you. You never would have said any of that to my family before."

"It didn't feel good."

"But it needed to happen."

"Yeah." She shrugged her shoulders. "I'm really tired. Do you think we could head back home now?"

Home. Not my house. But *home.*

My finger slipped under her chin, tilting her face towards mine. "Of course. Want me to carry you?" I teased.

Her smile returned as she rolled her eyes at me. "Don't even try. I'm perfectly fine on my own two feet."

VIOLET

Colt and I had settled into a comfortable routine over the last few days. He didn't even try to get me to stay at home, just smiled as I got up every morning when his alarm went off—which was always at an ungodly hour—and I always felt his eyes lingering on me as I went into the bathroom to get ready.

The Sheriff's Department has actually been the perfect place for me to work. I wasn't alone with my thoughts any more. Colt was there, forcing me to take breaks, still giving me my injections, and distracting me occasionally with a question about the pregnancy or the baby.

And at the end of the day, he'd slip his hand over mine, and we'd stay like that until we got back to the ranch. The little touches—his hand on mine, a grasp of my elbow to steady me, his fingers brushing over where the baby last kicked —felt more intimate than sharing a bed together.

Which had become the norm. I couldn't deny him the time with his hands on my belly, enjoying our son's midnight shenanigans. And selfishly, I couldn't deny myself the relief that washed over me every time his arms wrapped around me.

I knew I was safe, and that was something I hadn't felt in a very long time.

"You know I'm going to get my ass handed to me for this —taking the interim sheriff's pregnant wife away from the office for some fried chicken." Nate shook his head as he pulled the SUV into the parking lot of Dolly's.

"Colt shouldn't have left his pregnant *ex*-wife on her own at dinner time then, should he?" I laughed. It wasn't his fault. Something was happening in Lark Lake that he had to support. I told him to go, but I also didn't expect it to run into dinner. The baby wanted fried chicken, and it was one of those things where I was about to sit on the floor and cry if I didn't get some. "I'll totally fall on my sword for you. He knows I've been dying for this all day. Besides, I'm getting some for everyone back at the station. We'll be back before he even notices."

"You are nothing but trouble. I just got off of desk duty," he mumbled under his breath. I laughed as I unlatched my seat belt.

By the time Nate came around the front of the vehicle, I was quietly shutting my door.

"My God, it's like you want me to get fired! You should have waited for me," he scolded me.

"You're awfully jumpy. You know Colt is just a big teddy bear, don't you?"

He looked at me like I was growing a second head. "Yeah, sure. The man definitely gives off teddy bear vibes. Come on, let's go get your chicken before you decide to run into traffic *just for fun*."

I laughed, grabbing my belly so it wouldn't shake. Out of all the sensations and feelings in pregnancy, under-standing what the stories meant when they said "Santa's belly shook like a bowl full of jelly" was something I truly did not enjoy.

"Are you going to let me get the door for you, or would you like to just run through the glass?" Nate groaned.

"I would love for you to get the door for me."

He nodded, stepping up to grab the door for a family coming out before ushering me in with an enthusiastic sweep of his hand. He really had been such a hoot to rile up.

"Vi!" Much to my surprise, Jessie and Hawk sat at a booth right off the entrance of the diner.

"Go say hi," Nate encouraged. "I'll put the order in at the counter."

"Are you sure?"

"I can keep an eye on you from there."

I smiled as I turned to walk towards the booth.

"Hey, you two. Where's Beckett?" I asked.

Hawk laughed. "Mae and Stone scooped him up right out of Jessie's arms when she brought him in to say hi at the end of work, and they refused to give him back to us until after dinner."

Jessie reached over and picked a french fry off of Hawk's plate, popping it into her mouth. "I won't say no to a few hours of kid-free time, especially now that he's not attached to my boobs for hours at a time!"

"Ouch. I don't know if I'm looking forward to that."

Jessie shrugged. "You get used to it. But there's nothing wrong with bottle feeding if you want to do that instead. Oh, I just got so excited that next year, both our sons will be running around here like wild little things."

I placed my hand on my belly. "You think he'll be walking before he's one?"

Hawk laughed. "We're still debating if it's the Ford genes or the Morgan genes that made Beckett so rambunctious, but every time I see one of Jessie's brothers up on a horse, I'm certain it was her genetics that programmed him to be so wild and carefree. No doubt Colt's DNA will instill that in your little one, too."

"Got it." I sighed. "Start panicking now."

"There's no way Colt is the less protective parent out of the two of you." Jessie pointed the end of another french fry at me. "Remember when you took me to swim in the creek and Colt flipped out on us?"

I laughed. "God, yes! He was always such a worrywart. You know what...good. I'll happily let him take on that anxiety. I've had so much just trying to get through this pregnancy."

"Speaking of my brother...Where is he? I'm surprised he let you out of his sight."

"He's still in Bell Ridge, got called out of the office for something. Not sure what's going on, but I sent him a text and told him Deputy Jones was coming with me to secure dinner. I'm dying for your mom's fried chicken and coleslaw. We're going to order some for everyone at the station tonight."

Jessie's eyes went wide. "He's going to be mad when he realizes you left."

"He can't get too mad. I could have Deputy Jones take me home. He made your poor husband spend hours the other day installing a security system in the house. What good is it if I can't rely on it?"

"True." Jessie picked up another french fry off her plate, dipping it into her vanilla milkshake before biting into it. That combo sounded divine, and the baby rolled, clearly in agreement.

"We're almost done. Why don't you sit with us while you wait for Duke to package it all up for you?"

"No, no, I don't want to interrupt kid-free time. You two enjoy the end of your meal and I'll just drool over the dessert display."

"Actually, I was going to come over to talk to you and Colt

tonight about the security system stuff at your dad's cabin, but if you're here now, we might as well go over it." Hawk waved to the opposite side of the booth.

I looked at Jessie, who was smiling and nodding.

"Okay."

I sat down on the seat, barely fitting between it and the table. Jessie laughed, clearly aware of my awkward struggle.

"God, I don't miss those days."

"I feel like I don't fit anywhere anymore," I admitted as I turned to Hawk.

"Were you able to get the system installed at my parents' place?"

"We were. I wanted to let you know that we used the same codes as the one we put in at Colt's. The only people who have them are you, Colt, Stone, and myself. I'm sure Colt will tell the family, too, but that's up to you guys."

I nodded. "That's great. Thank you. I feel awful about what happened there. I haven't even been able to wrap my mind around telling my dad about it."

Jessie's hand slid across the table and covered mine. "It was a complete violation of your personal space."

I bit the inside of my cheek. "I know it's gross that someone went through my things and did...that...to them, but I don't understand why they had to ruin the baby's things, too."

"What do you mean?" Jessie asked.

"I haven't really let myself buy anything. I...Well it seems silly, but I'm scared of tempting fate. Like if I allow myself to be too excited, he won't make it."

"Vi..."

I waved my hand in front of my face. "Like I said, it's silly. Honestly. I did allow myself to buy things. A pack of diapers. A sleep suit. Practical things, you know?"

Jessie nodded.

"I did get one little thing that wasn't just for the sake of being practical. A soft blanket with little horses on it." Colts. I bought it because the horses had reminded me of my husband.

"That's lovely."

"It was. Whoever was there that night found it on the rocking chair in my room, and they cut it up. I don't think Colt wanted to tell me, but I'd asked about it specifically, and he couldn't lie. The thing was destroyed."

"Can you order another one?" Hawk asked.

I shook my head. "I wish. It was vintage, from the year Colt and I were born. I might be able to save some of it, make it into a new quilt one day."

"I think that's a great idea."

I looked over at Nate, who was accepting large brown paper bags from the cook.

"Oh, I have to scoot. I'm supposed to be paying for that." I excused myself from the table and walked over to help Nate with the bags.

"Violet, absolutely not."

"I can carry something."

"No. I don't want to get fired."

"Colt wouldn't—"

Nate pinned me with a stare so ridiculous all I could do was smile and sigh. "Fine. Give me a second to pay and we can head back to the station."

"All taken care of, doll." The server at the register smiled as she handed me the receipt.

I glared at Nate, who had the audacity to laugh.

"Come on, everyone knows you don't let the pregnant person pay for food. That's one of the perks. Let's get this food back to the station before it gets cold. You can scowl at me all the way back if you want."

I'd grown up with Colt's little brothers driving me up a wall like they were my own—Nate reminded me a lot of them.

Jessie and Hawk stood up just as I turned, taking the smallest bag off the counter with a huff.

I smiled as Jessie walked over to me, waving at the woman behind the counter before looping her arm through mine.

"Oh, we parked right by each other! That's fun!" Jessie stopped walking as soon as we got to the parking lot, wrapping her arms around me and squeezing tightly. My head was suddenly stuffy and my eyes burned. *Damn hormones.* "Send me a text when you make it home later, okay?"

"What a good mama bear you are," I joked as I tried to cover the sniffle that escaped.

She laughed, shaking her head at me. "It's just payback for all the times you forced me to stay home with you and Colt so I wouldn't be out drunk in a field somewhere with my friends."

That made me snort. "God. You'll be exactly the same way when Beckett gets to be that age. Make sure you give him a cuddle for me tonight."

"Of course."

"Bye, guys." I waved as I turned to Nate's patrol vehicle. I heard the locks release before I walked to the door he had opened. But a piece of paper on his windshield caught my attention.

Wasn't it illegal for people to solicit that way? I thought I'd read something in the news. Certainly not a great idea to leave it on a Deputy's patrol—

I dropped the bag of food, and the ground spun as I tried to comprehend what I was looking at. If my hands would stop shaking, I might be able to convince myself it wasn't what I was seeing. Dark dots danced at the edge of my vision, and I heard someone in the distance gasp.

Or was that me? It was hard to tell with the panic swelling in my body. Cold sweat dotted my skin as my stomach flipped. Oh, *I was going to be sick.*

I turned, my eyes locking on Jessie and Hawk as they walked back towards me with a million questions written on their faces. Nate was asking me something, but the ringing in my ears was too loud.

I held out the paper to him, and then everything went black.

VIOLET

I shifted my hips, trying to get comfortable while the monitor wrapped around my belly continued to track the baby's heartbeat. It was loud, and steady, and filled the silence that fell into place as Jessie held my hand.

"Jess, honestly, I really appreciate you being here, but you can have Hawk take you home."

"We're not leaving," Hawk grumbled, lifting his eyes from his phone. "I have to make a call. I'll be right back. Don't leave them alone in here."

That last part was directed at Nate, who was so pale I thought *he* was going to be the one that needed a hospital bed in a minute.

As soon as Hawk was in the hallway, I appealed to Jess. "You can't stay. Aren't you supposed to pick up Beckett? He'll be missing you."

"That boy would leave me in an instant to get time with any of his aunts or uncles. Besides, Mae won't mind watching him for a little longer. Honestly, I wouldn't feel right leaving until we know you're not going to pass out again, and that nothing's wrong."

"I didn't *pass out*. I simply wilted a little from the shock. And being hungry. I should have shoved a piece of that chicken in my mouth before Nate insisted on rushing me here."

"*Wilted a little*, my ass," Nate grumbled.

"I'll make sure you get that chicken. Can't deprive my sweet nephew of that." Jessie crossed her arms and sat back in the chair next to my bed. God, I missed it when Jessie was thirteen and thought I hung the moon. She was already too far into her maternal instincts. "Vi, what's going on? Who the hell would have been at the ranch taking a picture of you like that?"

Before I could answer, I heard boots stomping in the hallway, urgent steps walking up to the nurses' station. My room was just across from it, so the four of us had already been privy to two frantic dads bringing their laboring wives in while we waited for the doctor to come back in and check me.

"Where is she?"

No. My eyes flew to my sister-in-law's. *What a little skunk she was!*

"Where is *my wife*?!"

"Jessie," I groaned, my eyes closing as the heart rate monitor attached to my finger picked up.

"I didn't tell him anything, Vi. I'm not sure—"

The partially closed door flew open, and a frantic looking Colt filled the door frame. He pointed at Nate.

"You're fired! Get out."

"Colt!" I yelled.

Nate nodded. "I'm really sorry, Ford. I—"

"I don't want to hear it. Get. Out."

"You are absolutely not firing him over this!" I barked, the monitors beeping a little faster as my heart rate skyrocketed with my rage.

Colt shook his head. He closed his eyes, his shoulders

rising as he sucked in a harsh breath. "Vi's right. I'm not...I'm not going to fire you. Just...give me two seconds to get my head on straight here, and we'll talk."

"I'll be in the waiting room down the hall." Nate looked at me. "I hope you feel better, Violet."

"You did absolutely nothing wrong." Tears stung my eyes. "Thank you for making sure I was okay."

Nate nodded, closing the door behind him. The rage on Colt's face melted the instant Nate left.

"Jesus Christ, are you okay?"

"You were so mean to Nate! And for what? I'm fine," I croaked. Colt was moving towards me before the words even finished coming out of my mouth. His body was stiff with tension, but his eyes held a well of emotion I didn't know how to react to.

And then he shocked the hell out of me. Colt leaned in, his arms wrapping around me in a tight hug. I felt him relax against me, his breath pulling in deep as if he hadn't allowed himself a single inhale in the time it took him to get to me.

I didn't want to move, because through that hug, I could feel the same dread, the same anxiety I'd been living with for the entire pregnancy in the soft, cautious way he was holding me. Like I might fall apart. Like I'd need him to be the strong pillar he once was for me.

His arms finally released me, except I wasn't ready for the emotions the loss of his hold would bring to the surface. Jesus. These hormones were a nightmare.

"Tell me what happened. When the hospital called...Jesus, Vi. A decade shaved right off my life. At least." One of Colt's hands pressed down on my head, caressing my hair, while the other rested on my belly between the monitors tracking our son's heartbeat and movement. "I thought you were safe at the station."

"I got hungry, and I wanted food from Dolly's. I had a silly vasovagal reaction when I was getting in the car. Everyone made sure I was okay, and I only agreed to come here out of an abundance of caution."

"It wasn't a silly reaction," Jessie muttered from the chair. She reached into her purse and pulled out the white—now crinkled—piece of paper that I'd found on my windshield. "Someone left *this* on Deputy Jones's car. She was looking at it when I heard her gasp, and then she turned around, white as a damn ghost. Nate caught her before she hit the ground, thank God."

His gaze slammed into mine. "Vi?"

"I…"

Colt opened the piece of paper, and I swear his entire body froze. No words came out. He was locked on to the picture, the same as I had been.

It showed us walking hand in hand outside his parents' house. Except there was a large circle around me. And a note.

Still looking so beautiful. Can't wait to take that dress off you one day soon. You're mine, baby. All mine.

The door opened, and Hawk slipped back in behind Colt.

"I just got off the phone with Gage. He's going to come out to the ranch tomorrow and work on figuring out where this dickhead could have been on the property to take that picture. If you're not able to take the time off because of Hank being out, I'll stay home from work and can figure out something with your brothers."

"I can be home for that. No one else needs to be there," I offered. "Remember, state of the art security system? Newly installed? Ring any bells?"

The room felt so heavy, I tried my best to lighten the mood. It fell flat.

"I'm calling Hank the second the doctor comes in here

and clears you, and then we are going home where I'm not leaving your side."

"Colt, I think you're being—"

"Do not finish that sentence. My *wife* is being fucking stalked and tormented by some freak, and I'm not taking that lightly. The most important thing to me is that you and the baby are safe and healthy. That's it, Vi. That's why I could throttle Deputy Jones for being so careless with you."

"I'm not your wife anymore." I meant for my words to lighten the mood, but the way his eyes widened and his jaw ticked told me I only succeeded in doing the opposite.

"I'll change that soon enough," he growled.

Hawk chuckled, and both Colt and I looked over at him. But he was staring right at Jessie. "Is this what I was like when you were pregnant with Beckett?"

She stood, walking over to place her hand on his chest. "Worse, if I'm being completely honest. But I loved it. Come on, Chief. It looks like these two have everything covered here. Let's go pick up our boy."

———

"Colt." I sighed, trying to pull the blankets up over my belly. Something was caught near my feet and I was struggling to move my body enough to fix it. God, I was beyond ready to close my eyes and forget this day.

My ex-husband had just walked past the bedroom door for the fifteenth time since we'd gotten home and I'd come up to bed.

"Colt's downstairs." His voice trickled through the closed door.

"Right. Then who am I talking to?"

The door opened, his face popping into the opening.

"Sorry. I wanted to come to bed, but I didn't want to come in here while I was still feeling so…"

"Upset with me?"

"What? No. No, Vi. I'm pissed at myself."

"I'm fine. But I'm not going to be if your clomping feet keep running back and forth in front of the door all night."

"Got it. I'll walk quieter."

I groaned. "No. You need to come to bed. I'm *fine.*"

Colt shook his head as he walked fully into the room now, his hand running over his face before he crossed his arms over his chest. "Okay. I'll stop pacing in front of the door."

"Thank you—"

"If…"

"If what?" I forced myself not to sound pissy, even if I was starting to feel outlandish rage at the man standing before me.

"If you promise me you won't take off like that again." Before I could open my mouth, he continued. "I know you sent me a text and you just went to the diner. I know that you felt safe doing that, but it's clearly not. Someone is following you, Vi. I don't want to let you out of my sight."

The damn man had tears in his eyes, and I fought so hard to stop myself from holding out my arms and pulling him into bed beside me.

"I'm sorry I let my craving for fried chicken tempt me into leaving the station without you."

He chuckled. "Mom's fried chicken is just about the only temptation I'd say is worth breaking the rules for."

"No silly stuff," I joked, trying to lighten the mood. "Just… two adults sharing a bed after something scary happened. Agree?"

I was certain it came out huskier, and more sensual than I meant. But looking at the glimmer in his eyes, and the way one of his eyebrows flashed up quickly before returning to its normal place on his face had me second guessing that.

"I've been a gentleman since we started sharing the bed... haven't I?"

I nodded, my greedy little heart wishing that maybe there would be a day when the chivalry slipped...

Colt

"Go to sleep, Violet." I sighed as I watched her eyes pop up to my face. She'd been caught red handed staring at me, and I had to shove it to the back of my mind because that heat in her eyes was sending signals to my body that I didn't want to press her on.

Grabbing the bottom edge of my shirt, I yanked it up over my head. Violet gasped, and my head whipped around to see what was wrong.

Her mouth dropped open, and she pointed at my chest. "What is that?"

Shit. There was a reason I'd been changing in the bathroom all this time. Aside from it being a little weird to get naked in front of each other when we hadn't been that intimate in years, I wasn't sure how she would react to the newest tattoo on my body.

"It's a tattoo," I answered, trying to keep my voice even and unaffected by how wide her eyes were.

"Obviously it's a tattoo," she whispered, pointing to my chest. "I'm asking why the hell you have a *violet* tattooed on you."

"Are you mad?"

I'd told her seven years ago, I would never give up on us. I'd already had the tattoo for two years at that point. She was always with me.

"I'm confused. Why would you do that?"

Come on, Vi. I told you the truth. You know it. You know you'll always be the only person I want.

"You can't think of any reason?"

"Why a violet, Colt?" She wasn't going to back down.

"It's my favorite flower." I winked at her, but she just crossed her arms and sighed.

"No it's not. Tulips are."

There was no way I could hold back my laughter. "You *know* I only said that because it riled you up, Vi. I like it when you're flustered with me."

"Colt."

"It's not a big deal." I shrugged my shoulders, turning to the dresser.

"It's a very, very big deal."

I could feel her gaze roaming across my body again. My tattoos were all special to me. In fact, Violet was there, sitting next to me for each one I put on my body. In a weird way, it felt fitting that the one I would carry with me through the void of our divorce to feel close to her, was the singular tattoo she had no idea about. My tattoos covered my arms, my thighs —but my chest was clear, except for two dates. The first was when we met, all those years ago in middle school. And the second was the day we were married. They were faded now, both more than a decade old. The flowers were faded, too. They'd been on my skin, a part of my body, for years.

It made my heart ache. All that time, gone.

"When did you get it?" she asked.

"The day our divorce was finalized." There was no use lying.

She nodded, but her eyes went unfocused and drifted toward the ceiling. "Why?"

"Because I wanted to have you with me. Always. I knew I needed to let you go, but I couldn't. Not completely. This was my way of giving you what you needed, and still holding on to you."

I finally pulled a fresh shirt over my head. My hand slid along the wall until it hit the light switch and drenched the room in darkness. I marched over to the bed and got in beside her, wrapping my arms around Vi so that she was pressed against my chest and I could hold her belly. And then I did something frivolous. Silly. Wonderfully reminiscent of a time I'd wanted for so long to go back to. I kissed her temple.

"You're the only woman I've ever wanted, Vi. I let you go knowing that. There isn't another person out in the world that I want to lay down next to at night and wake up with my arms wrapped around in the morning. It's always been you."

And it always will be.

VIOLET

My eyes drifted to the corner of the laptop. Three hours. I'd been writing like a woman who was running out of time. And all that time had passed by in what felt like five minutes. I'd grabbed a snack and run—okay, waddled, excruciatingly slow—to the bathroom, but other than that, I was glued to my computer screen.

My entire body flinched at the sound of my phone ringing.

"I promise I'm working on my writing," I answered, smiling as Ryan's laughter filled the line.

"That's my girl. How are things looking?"

"Uh..." I bit down on my lip. "I think I'm in a good spot."

"And the deadline?"

"We might just make it..."

"Cal."

"I know. I know. I promise I'm doing my best to not have this be a disaster for us all."

"It won't be a disaster. And even if it is, that's what you pay me to handle. We'll get to the other side, together."

"Thank you," I sniffed, trying to hide the wave of emotion that crashed over me.

"Please tell me you aren't crying."

"No, of course I'm not. It's just the hormones. Pregnancy is wild."

"I'm sure it is." His words were clipped, harsh almost. But that was Ryan. Supportive and yet, still direct. "And being in Texas? Has it been all you were hoping for?"

I smiled, my hand rubbing circles over my belly where the baby was pressing his butt out. "Yeah. It's been better than I hoped it would be. I mean, the bar was set low because I really had no hopes other than getting away from..."

"Right. Have you heard from him again?"

"Yes."

"Shit, Callie, I'm sorry. You're being safe, right?"

"As safe as I can be."

"Good. Look, I have that trip to Canada coming up, but if you need me to cancel—"

"Ryan, no! No. I promise. I'm fine. Go be with your family. You've earned that time off."

"But you'll still keep me in the loop, right?"

"Always."

"Good. Alright, I've got to run. And you've got words to write."

It was my turn to laugh. "Yes, sir."

We exchanged our goodbyes and I sighed, leaning against the back of the chair to help stretch out my lungs. My eyes drifted back to my manuscript before my fingers started moving across the keyboard.

Finally, my writer's block seemed to have lifted, and the words were flowing out of me. I was feeling inspired again. Hopeful again. I might be eons behind and nowhere near close to done, but it was all a step in the right direction.

An hour more of working, and I'd managed to write *the steamiest scene* of my career. It certainly had nothing to do with the fact that I was hugely pregnant, hadn't had any spicy action in years, and was now living in *very* close proximity to the one and only man I'd ever loved, the only man I'd ever been with. Oh, and that I'd seen him with that towel slung low across his hips this morning, still dewy with droplets of water from the shower before he went into work. His chest was more defined than I remembered.

Mercy! I was glad I opted to stay home today. It meant some poor deputy was parked out front again, but I couldn't focus on that. I needed to get words written. And I needed to figure out what the hell I was going to do about my body feeling so damn... frisky!

My core ached with need. My pussy was a *thirsty, traitorous bitch*. Because what the hell was I going to do about my horny heart? Every time I closed my eyes, Colt's bare chest was there, and I just wanted to reach out and touch him. To feel his hands brush down my arms. We'd gone to bed with my belly cradled in his hands, and I prayed for his fingers to slide down my body—

"Damn, girl. Pull yourself together," I mumbled as I pushed back from the table. It was only two in the afternoon, and after sitting in front of a screen for hours, I should get some fresh air...

Instead, I walked up the stairs. My maternity leggings were down by my ankles and flung off into oblivion the second I walked through the bedroom door. I waddled over to the bed, plunked down on the mattress, and sighed as I flopped back against the pillows.

A very undignified grunt escaped as I grabbed Colt's pillow and wedged it on my left side, turning until my belly was resting against it. God, I moved like a beached whale, and

I knew that no one would ever find me sexy in my current state. Thank God I knew how to take the edge off.

I slipped my fingers under the blanket, down my body until they rested against my clit. It was almost a miracle I didn't have to contort my body to reach past my belly. No. Nope. I wasn't thinking about that. I was going to give myself one respectable orgasm and get back to work. Just something to take a little bit of the tension away.

My finger moved in slow circles. Jesus, my hips were already twitching to move. My body begged for more friction, and I wished I could give it to her. But this was going to have to be enough.

I closed my eyes, lifting my leg just a little so I could get a better angle. Yes. Oh, shit. Yes. My breathing picked up, and I let my mind wander...

What if it wasn't my hand making me feel this way? What if my husband—

My hips bucked at that thought, and suddenly, I could feel him there between my legs. The echo of his five o'clock shadow scratching my thighs as he licked, and sucked, and sent me over the edge. My fingers slowed and their movements became more deliberate as I found the perfect pace.

Yes. The memory of that night in the cabin was one of my favorites. The way he'd looked at me, the love I felt pouring out of him...

"Oh, God! Colt!!" *Fuck me.* My orgasm slammed into me, the sound fading out as blood rushed away from my head down to my throbbing core. Everything became hazy as I let my body melt into the afterglow of my orgasm.

My heartbeat was thumping so loudly in my ears it sounded like someone was running up the stairs. I laughed, silently thanking my body for remembering to take care of this instead of leaving me in misery for another night.

Until I felt frantic hands land on my arms, shaking me.

I screamed. Louder than I had ever fucking screamed before in my life.

"Violet! What the fuck is going on? What's wrong? Is it the baby?" Colt's frantic eyes searched my face.

"What…What are you doing home?! You scared me half to death!"

"Me? You screamed my name out just a minute ago! I thought you were having the baby!"

"Go. You have to get out. You're not supposed to be home. I can't…I'm not…"

Colt's eyes dropped to my chest, his own breathing picking up. "Oh. I…fuck, Vi. I'm sorry. I didn't realize." He cleared his throat and stood up. "I'll just…uh…Fuck. I should leave, right?"

I was on the verge of either hysterical laughter or sobs, and honestly it could have gone either way. His big brown eyes looked up from the floor the moment the first fit of laughter broke through.

"I can't believe I didn't remember that's what you sound like when you fall apart," he said, his voice filled with gravel.

"Why would you remember?"

That was clearly the wrong thing to say—because Colt came back to the bed, sitting with his hip resting against my belly. His hand came up to rest against my cheek, and suddenly that laughter felt so much closer to a sob than I wanted it to.

"Violet. That sound was always the most beautiful thing I'd ever heard in my life. From the very first time I got to hear it to just now. I think about it every time I fuck my goddamn hand in the shower. It's etched in every last cell of my brain. It's my *favorite* sound. I should have fucking known."

My breath caught in my throat. "Oh."

"Can I hear it again?"

His question made my body flush red hot, like cinnamon had been sprinkled across me. And Colt was standing there, looking like he wanted to lick me clean. "You want to..."

"Hear it again. But this time, can I be the one responsible for you screaming out my name again? Can I make you feel good?"

God. Yes. Yes!! Please!! No. I needed to breathe, because every inch of my body was pulling towards him. I was practically panting over the idea of him touching me again. His strong, tattooed arms holding me, the corded muscles tense as he worked my body.

I closed my eyes and swallowed.

"We shouldn't." The words felt forced and metallic as they came out of my mouth. "The lines are feeling..."

"Blurred?"

"So blurred!" I bit my lip to stop the nervous laughter that was bubbling up again.

"Mm. But just once wouldn't hurt? Just to get it out of our systems, now that I know I'm not the only one consumed day and night by these fucking thoughts."

"What if I don't want it to just be a one-time thing, though? What if I know that the second you touch me, I'll want it to be a forever kind of thing?" I whispered, laying all my cards right at his feet. We were too old for anything else. No more games. No more talking in riddles. "Can you forgive me?"

His head reared back like I'd slapped him.

"Forgive you? For what?"

"For leaving. I shouldn't have pushed you away. I should have stayed, and fought through my depression. I should have known that I wasn't protecting you from me...from all the heartache my body caused. I was hurting you by leaving."

"Vi. How many times do I have to say it before you'll believe me? There is nothing to forgive. I'm the one that should be showing you I'm sorry. That I am trying to fix things—"

"No. Absolutely not. I walked away. I gave up on us when you never, ever did. If anything, I should be bending over backwards to prove myself to you."

His eyes bounced between mine for a moment before he leaned in and kissed me. Every anxious thought, every second of trying to piece together how the hell I was going to make it up to him, left in the desperate whimper that erupted from me.

"I should have fucking been there for you. I should have taken time off of work. I should have brought you to therapy... fuck, I should have fucking went to therapy with you. Violet... you walked away to save yourself. I have never, and I will never, hold that against you. I thought the only way to give you peace was to let you go. I'm the one who needs to apologize. I'm the one who needs to beg for forgiveness. Please, Vi. Please forgive me. Please say there's a chance that you'll let me back into your heart."

"You never left," I whispered. "You've always been there."

His lips pressed down my neck. Over my collarbone. Onto my shoulder. The hair from his unshaven face tickled, bringing heat to the surface of my skin.

"This is it, Violet. Tell me to walk away," he whispered. Colt's voice broke, and his eyes grew misty. My hand reached out to rest against his face, but before I knew it, his hand was wrapped around my wrist, bringing my hand up to his lips. One single kiss, pressed directly into the palm of my hand, and I was melting. "Tell me you don't want me to do this. That we're still divorced, and you don't have those feelings for me anymore. Because if I kiss you right now, Vi, I'm never letting you go again. You and the baby are mine. *Mine.* So, if you have any doubts, you need to say them now. Because I can feel my heart stitching back together every time I'm close to you."

He placed my hand over his heart, the rhythm picking up and banging erratically. If he hadn't just seen his doctor, I might actually be concerned for his health.

"I'm scared," I confessed.

"I am too," he replied. "I don't ever want to lose you again."

COLT

I sat on the edge of the bed, taking her hand and pressing a kiss against her wrist. "Tell me no one else has touched you, Vi. Tell me no one has had these beautiful lips pressed up against their own. No man has touched you where only my touch should have ever been."

Her breath caught as my thumb brushed against her pebbled nipple. "No one."

"Say it again," I begged, my dick jumping at the sight of her bottom lip being pulled between her teeth.

"I haven't been with anyone else. I didn't want to date, but there was this one time my agent set me up to have coffee with her brother, and I felt like I couldn't say no. It was the worst. He didn't even open the door for me."

A growl ripped from my chest as I pressed a kiss against her neck. "I want his name, Vi. I'll teach him how to treat a woman. Not you, *because you're mine to take care of.* But for the rest of the world full of women, I'll teach him a lesson."

"I don't remember it," she whispered as my hand slipped under the blanket and my fingers ran over her hip. Violet gasped, and I could feel her skin pebble beneath my touch.

"I love hearing that, darlin'. The only name I ever want in your mind is mine." My hands pulled back the blanket, exposing her needy pussy. My God. I was going to fucking come in my pants before I even touched her.

The sight of Violet, so round with my baby, writhing with need killed me. I palmed my erection, groaning as I tried to find some sort of fucking relief from how goddamn hard I was.

"Is this position okay? On your side like this, for you and the baby?"

"Yes. God. We're fine. Please...please don't make me wait... I need you."

My fingers slipped between her legs. She was already so wet, so ready for me that I wanted to just bury myself deep inside her. But that would come. After she did.

My thumb found her clit, remembering the pressure and speed she loved like the last time we'd been in this position was just hours ago, instead of years.

"Colt," she panted, her head flung back, eyes closed. I pressed my other hand against her thigh, opening her up to me.

I couldn't take it any longer. I had to taste her.

I climbed onto the bed. My face lowered and the second my tongue licked along her entrance, Violet's hands were in my hair. Pulling me. Guiding me. Telling me exactly what she wanted me to do. I chuckled, my mouth taking over for my finger, giving attention to that sensitive bundle of nerves that I knew was about to throw her over the edge.

"M-more..." Her voice shook, fingers tightening their grasp. I licked and flicked my tongue, sucking against the bud as my finger slid inside her.

Violet's hips bucked in timing with my own. I ground my hips harder into the mattress, my body begging for friction, but not wanting to come yet. Not until I was inside her. My tongue and fingers were moving in perfect harmony. I could feel her body growing more tense. I knew that she was going to—

My finger grazed over the velvet-like spot inside her, and Violet screamed my name so loudly I was sure the windows rattled.

I sat back, watching her come down from her orgasm. Her face was flushed, her eyelashes fluttering even though her eyes were closed. Her mouth was open and she had one hand over her heart, the other was over her belly. I leaned over and pressed a kiss to the hand resting on her bump.

"You okay?"

She shook her head, and for a split second, panic swelled. "I'm going to need you to do that about a hundred more times."

I laughed. "I don't know if I can manage a hundred, Vi. But we can give it a go."

Her eyes popped open, dropping to the very noticeable erection I was still sporting.

"Are we going to do something about that? It looks uncomfortable." Her bottom lip raked through her teeth as her eyes found mine.

I made quick work of getting undressed, and when I looked back at Vi, I nearly came undone. She'd taken her own shirt off. Her breasts were exposed, dark nipples pulled into taut peaks. I licked my lips, acutely aware of what part of my wife's body I planned to tease next.

"I forgot," she whispered, her eyes wide as she stared right at my cock. "I mean, I didn't forget what it was like. I thought about it all the time. But I just forgot how big..."

"Don't worry, Vi. This has always been yours." I walked around the bed, climbing up behind her. She shifted her shoulders, so they were flat against the pillows, but her belly stayed on her left side. I took her hand and wrapped it around my aching shaft, my hand on top of hers gently pumping up and down, groaning as her eyes became hooded. "I was made for you. Only you. And you were made for me. It'll fit. And it will feel so fucking good. You're going to take it all, aren't you, Vi? Like a good girl."

I grinned like a cat about to lick its way though a pint of cream, still stroking myself with our hands. "You remember how good it felt. All those times I made love to you." My eyes dropped to her chest where her nipples were waiting for my attention. Her breath shortened to desperate pants and her legs dropped open; my head tipped so I had the perfect view of her pussy.

Fuck me.

I let her hand go as I positioned myself behind her. It had been too long. I couldn't risk exploding all over my fucking hand like I had when I was eighteen and about to taste her for the very first time.

"Are you going to be comfortable like this?" I asked, kissing her shoulder.

"God, yes. On my side is great. Just hurry. I feel like I'm going to die while I wait for you to get inside me."

"Bossy thing, aren't you?"

She laughed, her ass wiggling back against me. "And you're the man who said you could never forget something about me."

I wrapped my hand over her calf, pushing her leg into a more bent position. Fuck. Her ass was still incredible.

"*Colt.*" The way my name slipped off her tongue like a desperate prayer only fueled my own frenzy. I dragged my cock along her entrance, teasing for just a moment before I pushed inside her.

My hand slid up her belly to her breast, my fingers circling her nipple at the same time I entered her. The world was silent except for the way her breath hitched as she wrapped around me.

God. This was everything. My head dipped, teeth raking across her shoulder as my hips rocked us gently.

"More. I won't break," she whispered. "You feel so good."

"I don't know how..." I groaned. "It's better than I remember."

I moved gently in and out of Vi, not wanting the moment to be over. But I knew I was close to losing control. An all too familiar tingle had started at the base of my spine. It was spreading fast...I needed to get her there, too.

The motion of my hips became erratic as I lost myself in the sensations of having her wrapped around me.

My fingers slid down to find her clit, swollen and needy. I rolled my thumb across it, my eyes roaming over her body. She moaned, and I watched as her own hands began teasing her nipples. The sight was going to be my undoing.

"I'm too close...nine years of waiting. For this. For you. I need you to let go," I panted, my balls aching for release. I felt her walls start to flutter around my cock, and that was it. Our orgasms seemed to happen simultaneously, her perfect pussy clamping down on me as my balls drew up and I spilled myself inside of her.

"My God," she whispered as I slid out of her, rolling to my back for a second. I needed to get up and take care of her. But that orgasm was so intense, I was worried about standing up too quickly.

"Not God, darlin'. Your *husband*," I teased, reaching over to brush her hair off her face.

"My *ex*-husband." She winked at me and smiled.

"Shouldn't take me long to fix that." I meant for it to come out teasing, but the second I heard her sniff, dread shot through me. Because I did want to be married to her again. Hell, I'd been fiddling with finding the right time to bring out her wedding band that I still had safe and sound in my dresser.

But maybe that wasn't part of her plans.

"Hey, what's wrong?" I asked, feeling sick to my stomach at the tears gathering in her eyes.

"Nothing. It's not anything—"

"Violet. Don't bullshit me."

"It's just..." She breathed in so deeply her shoulders pressed into the pillows. "That was so intense, and wonderful, and I feel like I've been thinking about it every day for the last nine years, and especially in this pregnancy. The hormones are making me crazy frisky, so I thought maybe we both would scratch an itch and then you'd see that you didn't really..."

"Want you? Violet. Get that nonsense out of your head right now. You're all I want. You're everything I've ever wanted." My voice held steady even as the truth forced my own emotions to the surface. I rested my arm against her, my palm stretching over her belly. Just like before, when we were married, her fingers landed on my forearm, tracing the lines of my tattoos.

"It's overwhelming for me. You know?" she whispered. "Being back close to you. Feeling that peace of being so connected with a part of my own soul that lives in another body. I just can't..." Her breath caught on a shaky exhale, and her chin quivered as the tears poured out. "You're this perfect man, who loves me so completely, and is so sure that everything is going to work out. And I'm this ball of anxiety, not trusting that the goodness of these last few days is here to stay."

"Vi, I—"

"No, Colt. It's in the way you move around me. Always centering me. Always at my back to protect me. Or at my side to make me feel safe. I thought...maybe this would be different. Maybe it would just be sex for you. But of course it wasn't. And I'm scared. Because I didn't want it to just be sex. It meant something to me. Everything. You mean everything to me, and I'm terrified to keep fighting what I know is right in my heart."

"You don't have to fight anything, darlin'. Let yourself be happy. Give in. I'm here. This is safe, and good, and we'll work together to never fall apart again. I'm not going anywhere. You're right where you belong." That was a fucking promise I had every intention of keeping.

Violet

It felt good to finally get out of the house again. Aside from Colt taking me to a doctor's appointment earlier in the week, I'd been staying home, trapped in my own mind. As much as I tried to focus on how amazing our afternoon of unexpected delights was, I couldn't get past the fear simmering underneath my skin.

He was here. Watching me. Waiting.

I couldn't figure out how he knew to come to Silver Springs. There wasn't a logical explanation for it. But every time I started to think about it, I could feel my anxiety wrapping its sticky tentacles around my heart.

I blew out a sharp breath as Hayes turned the corner onto Cherry Street.

"You okay?" he asked, his eyes darting over to me before they made their way back to the road.

"Yeah, of course. Just thinking about how nice it is to get out of the house. Sorry you're stuck carting me around, though."

"It's no problem." He flipped on the turn signal and we pulled into the parking lot.

"Wasn't that Mr. Hennigan's barber shop?" I asked.

"Yeah. He died maybe five years ago? I think it sat empty until last year when this bookshop opened."

Part of me expected to come back and still see the town I grew up in completely unchanged. But that seemed like a silly notion, especially when I was coming back as a different person.

The bookshop was absolutely adorable. A smaller store, brick front and a super cute sign out front. Reminded me of my neighborhood bookstore back in New York. Hayes held open the door for me, and we walked inside.

"How long does something like this normally take?" Hayes asked, his eyes roaming over the rows of books in front of us.

"Jessie said they'd stocked a few different books of mine. It shouldn't be too long. I just want to make sure I can sign them all. I never imagined Silver Springs would have a bookstore that wanted to stock my stories, you know?"

"Hi there, welcome to Romantically Yours," a woman, probably in her late twenties or early thirties, greeted us. "I'm Maggie. Can I help you find something specific today?"

"Actually, yes," I answered. "My name is Callie Ford, and my friend Jessie mentioned that some of my books were stocked here. I was hoping you wouldn't mind if I signed them?"

Her whole face lit up. "Of course! Oh, that would be amazing. Let me see..." She walked out from behind the counter. "We've got your books right here, on our local authors display."

Maggie was kind enough to direct us to a table next to the display which had two plush seats flanking it. *Perfect.* As much as I was happy to get out of the house for something other than a doctor's appointment, my back was in knots and I was exhausted just from the walk into the shop.

Hayes picked up a book from the first stack on the table and turned to me, a big goofy grin plastered on his face.

"I think this one was my favorite of what you've written so far, but I'm excited for Daphne and Jack's story. You think you'll be finishing it up soon? Or...probably next year, right? With the baby and all..."

I stared at Hayes. And then I blinked, trying to focus on the book in his hand. *Over the Sunlit Hills.* I'd definitely written that. My pen name was in big, bold letters across the front of it.

"Sorry. Did you just say the book you're holding right now in your hands was your favorite of the ones *I've* written? As in, you've not only read that book, but you've also read the others?"

He chuckled. "Of course I have. Colt made us. There's a separate group chat that resurrects every time a new Callie Ford book comes out."

"Who's in the group chat?" I squeaked. My throat was suddenly very dry. *A whole ass group chat about my books? Between members of the Ford family?* I officially wanted to melt into the floor.

"All of us. I mean, not Dad. But Ma, Jessie, Colt, Me, Beau, and Lachlan."

I groaned. "No."

"Oh yeah. Colt told us all we weren't allowed to read the spicy scenes because it was 'like seeing Violet naked' and he was the only one allowed to do that, but—"

"Do NOT finish that sentence."

"Fine, fine." He held up his hands next to his face and smiled. "I'll just say, thank you for writing that one scene where Amelia and Grant are out in the field and she—"

"Hayes!"

"What? It's a great scene. I'm thinking of using it when I find my girl one day."

"Just take a picnic blanket with you. Those two didn't end up with friction burns from what they were doing, because I didn't want to write that into the story. But in real life, that could have been very painful."

He lifted his hand and mimed writing in a note book. "Got it. No. Friction. Burns." He closed the imaginary notebook and slid it into an imaginary pocket on his chest.

"I now need to forget that everyone in the family has probably read that scene. Oh God," I groaned. "Hand me that pile of books and change the subject, quick."

Hayes passed a stack of five or six books my way.

"What do you want to talk about?" he asked.

"Anything except me. How's everything at the fire house?" My marker glided smoothly across the title page of my book as I asked.

"Good. We eat a lot. Shoot the shit. Occasionally have a call to pull a cat out of a tree or walk an old lady across the road."

I laughed. "Sounds like a good time."

"It is. I know Ma wishes I had chosen a different career, but I just couldn't resist the adrenaline. It's addictive."

I raised my eyebrow. "And it's nice to help your community."

"Oh, yeah. That too."

"Alright, hotshot. So you save kittens and help old ladies. Have you had to deliver a baby?"

Hayes' eyes went wide. "Why? Are you having contractions? I can get us to the hospital, just don't push!"

I laughed so hard tears pricked the corner of my eyes, and I had to hold the side of my belly. "No, my God. But your instant panic was hilarious to watch. I was just trying to see if you'd be any help if I went into labor on the ranch. My due date is only two weeks away, and my new doctor mentioned I might not make it there. But I'm guessing you won't be any help."

Hayes shook his head as he pressed the heel of his hand into his chest. "Christ, Vee. No. I mean, I could help. I'm a great driver. But that's *all* Colt. He's in the backseat with you."

Now I was really surprised. "He's delivered a baby before?"

Hayes nodded. "A few years back. Stranded motorist. I don't think he would have said anything, but I was at the station and heard him make the call for the ambulance."

He'd delivered a baby. I couldn't wrap my mind around the emotional toll that must have taken on him. Guilt washed over me. I should have been there. For him to come home to. For him to have someone to talk to about it.

I had thought, for all these years, I was saving him from needless pain. But instead I'd caused so much of it. He didn't move on like I thought he would. Colt lived a life absent of the love and support a partner should offer him. All because he was waiting for me to come back.

Hayes took his phone out, but I didn't pay attention to what he was doing at first. I just figured he was letting Colt know everything was still fine and we'd be heading home soon. But when I looked up to swap books, I saw the phone directed at me.

"What are you doing?" I asked.

"Colt would want to see this! You signing your books...it's bad ass." I smiled and he nodded, tucking the phone back in his pocket. I turned back to the last three books I wanted to sign. "I'm proud of you."

His whispered words hit me right in the heart.

"I'm proud of you, too. Silver Springs is lucky to have you to run to the rescue. Can't say I love the idea of my brother running into a burning building. That definitely hasn't changed since I left."

"Your brother, huh?"

"You guys, and Jessie, will always be my brothers and sister. You know…" I looked back at the page in front of me. What I was about to admit was too emotional. Too vulnerable. "I tried to push this all away. I did push all of you away. But I never stopped caring, or loving you guys. I read every edition of the *Silver Springs Times*. I would search your names to make sure everyone was still okay. When Lach…" My voice hitched. When Lachlan had been hurt, it nearly killed me to stay away. The only thing that stopped me from running right back was Jessie keeping me in the loop with his prognosis and recovery.

"Vee."

"I know it's not the same. Beau told me what happened to Colt after I left. That he wasn't okay."

A tear slipped down my cheek before I could swipe it away. Hayes' eyes went wide. "Don't cry."

"I thought I was doing the right thing. But I messed it all up, didn't I?"

"I'm sure what I'm about to say is exactly what Colt has probably told you a hundred times since you came back. You did what you had to so that you could survive. You gave Colt the chance to move on and be happy with someone else. But the thing is, Vi…if you'd stopped to ask anyone in his life, if you'd stopped to really think about it, Colt was never going to fall in love with anyone else."

"I just didn't want to hold him back."

Hayes' hand landed on my arm. "You both could have handled things differently. And if you're feeling regret now for the decisions you made, it seems like you've been given the perfect chance to handle things differently this time. To trust Colt when he tells you how he feels, or what he wants."

I nodded, my eyes dropping back to the last few books sitting in front of me unsigned. I went back to work, numb as I signed them, thinking over what Hayes had just said. A minute later, when I'd finished and stood up from the chair ready to go, I noticed Hayes hadn't moved.

"What's the matter?" I asked.

"I don't like this sign. It feels like it's asking for trouble." His eyes were locked on the sign announcing the books featured on that table were by local authors.

The breeze from the shop's door opening only fueled the chill that was settling in my bones.

"He already knows where I am, Hayes. He could decide to escalate things at any point. A little sign in a bookshop saying I'm local being removed isn't going to protect me."

"Apple-anche?" I turned to see Nate strolling towards us. "Long time no see."

I smiled, wondering what the hell he was doing in a book store in the middle of the day. "God. I owe you the biggest apology."

Hayes held out his hand. "Nate."

"Hey, Hayes. Heard you guys think we might have a firebug on our hands?"

"Yep." Hayes slid his hands back into his pockets. "That old warehouse on Wickham Road went up last week. And three weeks ago the same thing happened to an abandoned place near Lark Lake we got called to assist with. Seems like someone is setting them on purpose."

"Well, you know we'll help out however we can."

"Appreciate it. Violet, I'm going to talk to Maggie about that sign. At the very least they can move your books out of the display window."

"Oh sure, Hayes. I don't want to be in the best spot in the store, or have my books noticed right as customers come in." I rolled my eyes. "It's fine."

"I'm talking to her. Don't try to slip out of the shop without me."

Nate laughed. "So I'm not the only one you give a hard time to?"

"No. Of course not. But I do really want to say I'm sorry for everything that happened. I told Colt under no circumstances are you to be punished for my choices as a grown, independent woman."

"How did he take that?"

"He growled something about me being his wife and needing to keep me safe, but I reminded him you did *just that.*"

"Colt's been absolutely fine, you have nothing to worry about. I'm not in trouble."

"So you just *happen* to have the day off today?" I looked him up and down. He very clearly was not on official duty in jeans and a hoodie.

"Yep. Scheduled weeks ago and everything. I promise it's all good. My girlfriend put an order in and asked if I could swing by to pick it up after I got done working out. So, here I am."

"That's nice of you."

He shrugged. "Seems like pretty basic boyfriend duty stuff to me." His eyes went to the table behind me. "Are those your books?"

I felt the heat immediately in my cheeks. "Oh, yeah. They just got some copies in. I was signing them."

"Signed copies! Count me in." He strolled past me and picked up one of each book.

"No! You don't have to buy them. I'd give a set to you...or your girlfriend. I mean, she's probably the one reading romance, right?"

"Actually, I read all the same books she does. It's like a road map to how she loves and wants to be loved."

Alright. I was actually going to swoon from how precious that was. "You're a real catch, Nate. She's lucky to have found you."

"Nah. I'm the lucky one."

"Don't let Colt catch you calling him a catch, Vi. He'll exile the poor guy to patrol the quarries."

Nate shivered. "Those places always give me the creeps."

"You ready to go?" Hayes asked, turning towards me.

"Yeah. Thanks for supporting a local artist," I joked.

"Are you kidding me? I'm excited to read these. Come visit the station again soon so I can share my thoughts."

I waved over my shoulder as Hayes and I left the store.

Colt

S hit, this day was dragging. I just wanted to be home with Violet.

I miss you.

Miss you, too. Hayes is being a pain in my ass. Won't even let me stand up without hovering because I told him I needed a nap after our trip to the bookstore.

I laughed, knowing damn well my brother was just listening to my orders.

Good. I told him if you broke a nail today, I'd bury him out back.

What! You're being ridiculous. I'm fine. Just trying to busy myself with work now until you're back.

Worried about me?

Of course I am.

There's nothing to worry about. I just got back to Bell Ridge, and I'm bringing home half a dozen cupcakes. Figure we can enjoy them in bed later.

Omg! Please tell me they had chocolate and chocolate! I'll swoon right now.

Like I'd pick up anything else. No swooning though. Are you feeling light headed?

Stop it. I'm literally fine! But we'll have to eat those over the sink before we go to bed. I've been dropping all my food on my belly lately and I don't want to make a mess.

Suddenly, my mind was filled with the image of licking frosting off of Vi's belly. Yeah. That was *definitely* happening.

We're taking them to bed, Vi. I'll lick you clean myself.

Three dots appeared...and disappeared. Then they popped up again, only to vanish a second later.

Flustered, baby?

Colt! Hayes just asked me if I was okay because "your face is really red and you're breathing weird". So yeah. And now I need you to hurry up and come home.

> Just wrapping things up. I'll see you at supper time.

> Can't wait.

> And just so we're clear, I want to lick you clean, too.

I had never once in my life thought about shoving my dick into a cupcake, but I wasn't about to disappoint my wife.

The radio spiked, my mind immediately leaving Vi to focus on the call coming in.

"Unit 20 be advised, there's an unknown trouble at 2216 West Lake Lane, Bell Ridge, at The Broken Spoke Bar, for reports of a physical fight in progress. Two males fighting in front of the bar. Weapons unknown. Time out is 16:18."

It wasn't my unit, but I was close enough to respond and provide backup if necessary. I picked up the radio and followed Unit 20's call back with my own.

It took two minutes, sirens and lights on, to make it down the road from Sprinkles to The Broken Spoke.

I slammed my SUV into park and jumped out onto the gravel parking lot. The door to the Broken Spoke swung open like some old time western movie, and as I stormed towards what I already heard was a large disturbance, I clocked several people rushing out of the place. Two deputy vehicles were already there. Once I stepped inside, I clocked Johnathan Boone and Mikey Dixon doing their best to get the situation under control.

John had one guy pinned to the ground, while Mikey held back another guy who looked like he's ready to kill someone. Probably the guy under John.

"What's going on here?"

"That fucking animal put something in my girl's drink!" The guy lunged, but Mikey still had a good hold on him.

"Calm the fuck down," I instructed. "John, take him outside. Cuff him."

Deputy Boone nodded as he locked his cuffs around the guy's hands who was on the floor, and jerked him up off the floor.

"Paramedics?" I asked, looking at the woman who was holding her head in her hands, her body swaying a bit in her seat. "Shit. How much did she drink?" I asked the guy.

"Let me go!" he yelled at Mikey.

"You gotta calm down like a hundred notches, man."

"I'm calm. I'm fucking calm. Just let me be with my girl! She's fucking sick."

I turned to the guy standing behind the bar. My eyes drifted to the camera mounted on the wall behind him.

"Gonna need to see the footage that system captured."

"Yeah. One sec." He looked down the bar at the other server. "Sydney, I gotta show this deputy to the office. You good to cover for a minute?"

The tall brunette nodded as she filled a glass with an amber liquid that was on tap. "I'm fine. You remember how to make a copy if they need it for evidence?"

"I think so. I'll holler if I don't."

She nodded, and the guy started walking out from behind the bar. I followed him down a hallway and into what was clearly a very disheveled office.

"Sorry. Our boss is like the most unorganized person in the world. Sydney tries to pick up the slack where she can, but it's...a lot."

"No worries," I answered. "Sorry, I didn't catch your name?"

"Anderson. But my friends call me Andy."

"Okay, Andy. Did you pour the drinks for that woman?"

"Nope. I was restocking when I heard Syd shout for help. I saw what was happening, called for you guys, and it felt like maybe a minute later the first deputy was here. I didn't see anything except the aftermath."

"Right."

"Anyway, here's where you can see the security footage." Andy pointed to a secondary laptop on a small table in the corner of the office. "I'll just click into the folder for today. They are broken down into hours, and there will only be a file up until ten minutes ago. The system rights new files—"

"Every ten minutes."

"You got it. I'm just going to head back out to help Syd. We're short staffed today. Let me know if you need anything else."

"Thanks," I replied, sitting in the small fold out chair next to the table.

Fifteen minutes later, I'd called back the bartender to email me a copy of the file and headed out to find Deputy Boone standing by his SUV.

"Hey, Johnathan!" I called, raising my hand in a wave as he turned to face me.

"Colt. Thanks for stepping in to help."

"Didn't think my day in Bell Ridge was going to be quite so exciting."

"What'd you find?"

"Video evidence of our friend there placing his hand over the woman's drink, stirring it with his finger, then sliding it back over to her before getting her attention that it was ready to drink."

"Okay. I'll take him over to the jail and start booking him in. The ambulance just took the woman to St. Clare's. I don't think anyone managed to get a statement out of her yet."

I looked down at my watch. Damn. Two in the afternoon...It was a gamble on how long it would take for her to be coherent enough that we could get a statement from her that would hold up. I guess it really boiled down to what the hell the guy slipped in her drink, and if the hospital could flush it out of her system.

"I'll head over to the hospital, see if I can't get a statement from the boyfriend first, then her."

"Thanks, man. Owe you one."

"Yeah, I'll put it on your tab."

John laughed. "You do that."

I nodded as I turned, walking across the lot to my vehicle. I hoped the DA brought every charge possible against his sorry ass. He deserved to get the max sentence for the shit he pulled and the harm he inflicted. My patrol vehicle sat parked on the edge of the lot, right where I left it. I'd hopefully be able to grab the victim's statement and head home to Vi without too much of a delay.

Leaves from the tree next to my cruiser had landed all over the windshield, and I took a second to clear them. The crunching of the leaves had to have masked the sound of someone walking up behind me, because one second I was thinking of Vi and our cupcakes, and the next, I was falling to the ground.

VIOLET

The smell of the supper I was cooking filled the entire house and felt like a warm hug in my chest. I was working hard to distract myself from Colt's words playing over and over in my head. The last thing I needed was Hayes asking me why I was so damn flushed again. I was pretty sure he wouldn't keep accepting my excuse that the extra weight from the baby was making me hot.

Thankfully, the girls were also helping keep my mind occupied.

Jessie:

> It doesn't have to be anything big. Think of it more like a coming home party than a baby shower!

Birdie:

> I mean, there will be baby presents. Lots of baby presents. I got some really cute fabric at Thread and Needle this week, and I've got the cutest pattern for baby overalls!!

We just want to celebrate you and Colt and the baby.

I bit the inside of my cheek. It wasn't that I didn't want to celebrate the baby. Or the fact that I was back in Silver Springs. Or the fact that Colt and I seemed to have found our way back to each other. I just…

Sizzling interrupted my thoughts as I pushed away from the counter I was resting my hip against, grabbing the wooden spoon to stir the potatoes. The girls had kept me giggling all damn afternoon with their texts, mostly about trying to get me to cave about a baby shower. It would be wonderful to celebrate the baby, but part of my heart still felt like I was tempting fate.

Right as I plunged the spoon down into the pot for another frivolous stir, the timer for the oven went off. My eyes lifted to look at the clock on the stove. Thirty minutes later than the last few days. Colt must be having a rough shift turnover meeting.

"I don't know what I did to get Violet babysitting duty on meatloaf night, but I'm just going to quietly count my blessings." Hayes got down off the stool at the breakfast bar and walked over to the stove. "I'll grab it out of the oven."

"You don't have to—"

He just looked at me, slowly shaking his head back and forth as he slipped on the oven mitt.

"Fine, fine. Have at it."

I laughed as I walked to the fridge and grabbed everything I would need to make the mashed potatoes. On the counter, I heard one of our phones buzzing.

"Is that—"

"It's mine," Hayes replied. He grabbed the phone, answering it with a smile on his face. "Hey, Beau. What's up?"

I brought the ingredients over to the counter and started opening Colt's cabinets. I'd seen the electric beaters a few days ago, but for some reason they were hiding on me now.

"Yeah, one sec." Hayes pulled the phone away from his ear and looked over at me. "I'm gonna step outside for one minute. You need anything, holler."

"The alarm is set. Just reset it before you go."

"Right. Thanks."

I flipped the switch for the hot burner to off, drained the water from the potatoes, and went to work adding the milk, butter, and chives to the pan. Just as I snapped the second beater into place, Hayes knocked on the door.

My eyes dropped to the handle. *Of course he locked it on his way out.* I opened the door, the alarm chirping until he was back inside. The cold air that had come in with him hit me, and my body shivered.

"God, it's really getting cold out."

"Vi."

I hadn't thought to look at his face when he came in—but I should have. One look at him, and I didn't need to ask what the phone call was about.

"No." Pain lanced through my chest as concern filled Hayes' face. Colt had told me years ago if anything ever happened, it would be one of his brothers who told me. That's what was happening. Hayes was standing in front of me, reaching out like he was going to catch me if I fell. Because what he had to tell me was going to rip me apart. "No. Don't you dare!"

"Maybe you should sit down." He took a step towards me as his eyes dropped to my belly. I hadn't even realized I was wincing as I clutched at the place where my baby was sleeping.

Colt's baby.

"Don't you come in here, and hold on to me, only to tell

me he's gone, Hayes. Don't you dare. He's coming home with cupcakes. We're supposed to have cupcakes in bed."

Hayes didn't listen, his hand locking on my elbow as he walked us back towards the table.

"Christ, Violet. That's not what...He's okay. But he'll literally kill me if you go into labor over this, so please...*please* just take a breath. Colt's had a shitty day, and I think missing the birth of his son would send him over the edge."

My hand covered my heart, and I leaned back until my head clunked against the wall. "You scared me." I waited a second until I felt my heartbeat slow, then popped open one of my eyes to scowl at him. "What happened?"

"In the grand scheme of things, it could have been so much worse."

"*Oh, God.* That's what you came up with to *calm me down?*"

He shrugged, grabbing my tea from the counter and setting it in front of me. "Don't get upset, okay?"

The baby chose that moment to start wiggling, his bum pressing out against my side. I watched as the bump that had grown to a size I didn't even know was possible stretched and morphed into a pyramid.

"Holy shit." Hayes stood next to me, white as a sheet. "It's like there's an alien in there."

"It feels like it, too," I grunted as I pushed against his little body. "You better sit and tell me what the hell happened. Fast."

Hayes nodded, pulling a chair away from the table. "Beau didn't have a lot of details to share, but I guess another deputy found Colt down behind his patrol car in some bushes with a laceration on his head. They're finishing up at the hospital now, and he's going to be okay."

I pushed up off the seat, trying to remember where I'd put

my keys. *Were they in my purse? Or were they in my laptop bag?* "Let's go."

"Vi." Hayes jumped up, his hand resting on my shoulder. "Beau was bringing the truck up to the hospital doors to get him when he called. They should be here soon, okay. So, you're just going to relax. I'll finish up supper."

"I'm not hungry." Honestly, the thought of eating made my stomach flip. Even the smell of the meatloaf, now resting on the counter, was making me nauseous.

"I bet my nephew is, though," he pushed. "Got to fatten him up still. Beckett will bowl right over him if you don't."

"Probably should wait until after he's exited my body to fatten him up."

Hayes cringed. "Damn. Yeah. Fair enough. But you still have to eat."

I nodded, not really meaning to agree with him as my mind wandered to Colt. I wasn't his emergency contact. Of course I wasn't. He was a first responder. He needed someone who was here to be it. But that realization hit me like a ton of bricks. He had rushed right down to the hospital to be by my side, but he had Beau call Hayes to tell me. He didn't want me there when he was hurt? I know that it was a practical thing. He wouldn't want me trying to drive myself anywhere right now. But he was *hurt. And I wouldn't have known if—*

Lights flashed into the house, and I was out of my chair before Hayes could stop me. I moved through the house with a speed I didn't know I was capable of, but I still wasn't quite at the door before them. I could hear Beau or Colt knock for a second before giving up.

Wrenching the door open, I expected to see Colt, but the doorway was empty.

"Jesus, Vi." Hayes wrapped his hand around my arm and pulled me back. I watch a delivery guy get back in his car and back down the driveway. My eyes dropped to the porch where a thin envelope sat. I should have known it would be too soon for them to get here all the way from Bell Ridge.

"It was just a delivery guy."

"That's weird. Usually all our stuff gets delivered up to Mom and Dad's house."

The alarm panel started beeping more rapidly.

"Crap. Would you grab it for me? I'm afraid we're about to set off the alarm." I gestured to the panel behind me.

"Oh shit. Yeah."

Hayes brought the envelope inside, setting it on the table Colt tossed his keys on every night. My eyes dropped to the address line.

It was for me.

"You want to wait for Colt?" Hayes asked, clearly picking up on my apprehension.

"No, of course not. I was expecting something from my business manager. He said I'd probably be getting some legal documents to look over in the next day or two. That has to be what it is."

I grabbed the envelope, tearing the sealed paper open. Reaching inside, I felt one single sheet of thick card stock material between my fingers. *That was weird.* If it was my contract coming through from Ryan, it would have been an entire document.

"Violet?" Hayes sounded like he was a mile away, under water, as I pulled what I could see was a picture out. The envelope fell to the floor almost as quickly as my knees gave out.

Because there, printed on the paper in front of me, was Colt's body. Sprawled out in the grass with blood surrounding his head. He looked...God, he looked dead.

I hadn't stopped staring at the paper, but somehow I was moving. Not falling. Not anymore. Cushions hit the back of my legs as I could still hear Hayes trying to talk to me, but none of the words he's saying were getting through to me.

I inhaled sharply as dark dots started closing in on my vision.

"Vi? Let me have that. Please. I need to take it. Colt will need to see it."

I swallowed, trying to force the ache from my throat. My fingers didn't want to move, even as I was screaming at them to let go. The picture was burned into my mind. I didn't need to look at it to know it would haunt me forever.

"This is my fault."

Lights flashed in front of the house again, and I yelped. My nerves were officially fried.

Hayes walked over to the window, and I watched his whole body relax as he turned back to me.

"It's Beau and Colt."

I nodded, pulling my bottom lip between my teeth and biting down, trying desperately to stop myself from losing it before I even had the chance to see with my own eyes that he was okay.

Hayes opened the door, Colt walking in before Beau. I pushed up off the sofa with a groan.

"Are you okay?" I asked, hesitating to reach out and touch him. His head was bandaged, and I could see where blood had matted his hair down.

His arms opened and I slid against his chest. "I'm fine. You know I have a hard head. Just a couple of stitches and I'm good as new."

"A couple of stitches and instructions for how to care for a concussion," Beau mumbled. He held out a packet of papers to me. "That's his discharge paperwork. It's just a mild one, but he was out for a few minutes they guess. Better to be safe than sorry. Wouldn't let the nurses fuss over him too much, kept saying he had a wife at home who was going to nurse him back to health."

"Well." I smiled as I lifted my head off his heart. The

steady rhythm had calmed me down more than I should probably admit. "That's very true. You just sit right over there on the sofa and I'll fix you all a plate for supper. Are you feeling hungry? Or do you just want some ice for your head? Is your stomach feeling off? I'm figuring they gave you pain medicine, and I know it can make some people nauseous."

The three brothers just stared at me.

"I'll get everyone a plate for supper, including you," Hayes volunteered.

"No, that's not necessary. I don't mind."

"Violet. I just caught you when you nearly passed out—"

Colt's face snapped from his brother to me.

"What is he talking about? Are you okay?"

"Of course, I'm fine. I was worried about you, and then this package came."

His eyes narrowed, and he winced. *I needed to get his stubborn ass over to the couch.* "What package?'

"Can I get you something to eat first? At least let me get your brothers something."

"Violet."

"Vi."

"Goddamn it."

All three brothers growled some version of opposition at the same time. Beau's was a little more unbecoming than the other two. But he still wasn't my biggest fan.

Colt's hand grasped my elbow as he walked me over to the couch.

"Let me see it." He held his hand out to Hayes.

"I'm so sorry, Colt. This is all my fault. You were hurt because this person is trying to hurt me," I blurted out as Hayes brought the picture to Colt.

"Fuck."

VIOLET

"Thank you for bringing him home." I reached out and took the bag from Beau's hand, turning for the kitchen. "I don't want to keep you guys. I'm going to put some supper for you on a plate, okay?"

"You don't have to—"

"Stop. You brought Colt home. You made sure he was okay. This is the smallest way possible for me to say thanks, but it's all I have right now."

Beau nodded. I shuffled around the kitchen, serving two portions of the meatloaf and mashed potatoes I'd made. Securing them with plastic wrap, I handed them both to Beau.

"Make sure Hayes gets one for me, will you?"

"Of course." Beau cleared his throat. "Call either one of us if you need anything, okay?"

I knew how much that offer must have cost him. He didn't want to hear from me, and I knew he only made it to help out his brother, but it still meant a lot to me.

"Sure." Crap. I was starting to lose to the panic threatening to pull me under. I could hear Colt's voice becoming more animated in the living room, and I knew the discussion was around me and my safety.

I turned away from Beau, grabbing the bag with Colt's shirt. I opened it, not surprised to find blood on the collar. In the laundry room, I stood on my tiptoes, belly pressed against the washing machine, trying to reach the detergent he kept on a shelf.

The noise of his brothers saying goodbye filtered into the room. I turned the tap on, trying to make sure the water wasn't too hot, but also not wanting to freeze my hands while I scrubbed the stain out.

I noticed the flap on his chest pocket was open, the button no longer through the loop holding it closed. Not wanting to put loose change or a battery through the wash, I slipped my hand inside the pocket.

A folded piece of paper slipped between my fingers. Probably notes he was taking during the shift, good thing I checked.

I pulled the piece of paper out and set it on the dryer. But my husband's handwriting wasn't on it. No. In fact, I didn't know whose handwriting it was, but the message they were sending to Colt was clear.

SHE'S MINE.

"Hey, what are you doing in here?" Colt stood in the doorway, his arms folded across his chest.

"Did your brothers leave?" I asked, working overtime to keep my voice steady.

"Yeah, after reminding me to check in with them tomorrow about how I was feeling forty-five times. They said thanks again for sending dinner along."

I ran the collar of his shirt under the water, adding detergent and scrubbing the fabric between my hands. Streams of pink water swirled down the drain and made my stomach churn.

"Vi?"

I sniffed, not turning around to face him. "You should go up to bed. I'm just going to get this in the wash and pick up from supper. Are you hungry? Take a plate up with you, and I'll be up when I'm done."

His arms slid under mine, resting in a hug with his hands on my belly. The scratchy stubble from his beard scraped against my cheek as he pressed a kiss there.

"I have more of those shirts. Let's just throw it out. And then we can both have some dinner and go to bed."

I shook my head. "I'm not hungry."

The pressure of his hands left, and he turned off the water, taking the shirt from my grasp and draping it over the edge of the sink.

"Turn around, baby."

"I can't," I whimpered. "I don't want you to see me fall apart."

"Breathe, darlin'. It's okay. Everything is going to be okay."

Anger surged, burning red hot across my skin. "It's *not*. I brought him here. He threatened my dad, and now he's actually hurt you! It's because of me."

Colt slipped his hand around mine and turned me around so my back was resting against the sink.

"We don't know that what happened today was connected to you. And no matter what, you don't take that on. Someone is stalking *you*. Someone is threatening *you*. We're going to figure it out, and I'm going to keep you safe."

I grabbed the paper off the dryer. "We *do*. This was in your shirt pocket."

Colt unfolded the note, his eyes wide as his body vibrated with anger. "This doesn't make it *your* fault, and you will not take that on, you hear me?"

I nodded. "I need to put the food away."

"Go upstairs, get ready for bed, and relax. I'll take care of things down here and be up in a minute."

What else could I say? How much more could I argue? I slipped past Colt and the messy kitchen, wishing more than anything the night had ended with cupcakes and kisses.

———

Colt shuffled into the bedroom just as I reached over to turn off the lamp on my nightstand. "I bagged the photo up and the note you found. A deputy is coming out in the morning to get it."

I was sitting in bed with my back against the headboard, trying to not let my mind wander with all the possibilities about how far this could all escalate.

"How bad is your head hurting right now?" I asked.

"I'm fine."

"I know you are. Now, how bad is the pain?"

"Barely there. I promise."

"Good. Come lay in bed."

He pulled his shirt over his head, and then stepped out of his pants before sliding under the sheets.

"You don't have to ask me twice."

I grabbed his pillow just as he was sitting down and laid it over my lap. Colt didn't ask a single question. He just laid down, resting his head on the pillow over my legs.

My fingers went to work, combing through his hair, careful not to come close to the spot where he was stitched up. I massaged his temples. My fingers gently moved to his eyebrows, and down his jaw. They traced over the violets on his chest. He melted further into the mattress as his body went lax under my touch.

"I forgot about this," he muttered at one point.

"It always made you feel better after a stressful day." Colt turned his head towards me, moving just enough so he could kiss my belly.

"How long are you out of work for?"

"Seven to ten days for my head, but Hank agrees it's best if I start my paternity leave now. John Boone will fill in until Hank comes back in a few days."

We hadn't even talked about him taking a leave once the baby came, but I should have known he was already planning on it. "Paternity leave? Don't you want that for after the baby comes? You won't get as much time with him..."

"It's fine. This doesn't count towards my time after. Hank is a family first guy. He'd make it work for anyone."

"That's really nice of him. So, no more deputies in the driveway?"

"Nope. Just a deputy in your bed."

"Jackpot." I giggled. "As long as it's only this one deputy I've had my eye on for a while now."

"Ma'am, if you describe him to me, I might be able to put in a special request for you."

"Well, you see, he's older."

"Ouch."

"Excuse you? I'm older, too. Older is wise. Older is understanding. Older is hot."

"Well, when you put it that way...continue please."

He smiled as my fingers made their way back to his jaw. He was carrying so much tension in his body. I pressed firmly into the joint, loving the groan that resonated in his chest.

"And he's got these two incredibly sexy salt and pepper patches of hair starting at his temple."

"Oh yeah?"

"Yeah."

"What else?" Colt egged me on.

"Well, he wears the hottest reading glasses known to mankind. Seriously, the government should look into labeling him a weapon of mass destruction when he puts those things on."

"Mm."

"And he has a lot of tattoos, but you'll know it's the right guy because of one very special tattoo."

"Right over his heart?"

"Right over his heart."

"Sounds like the kind of man you'd want to keep."

I knew he was joking, but when one eye popped open, I couldn't help but answer truthfully.

"He's the kind of man I never wanted to let go of. The kind of man who is so good, so safe. He makes everything scary and bad fade away. He makes me believe that no matter what, good things are coming for us." I dropped my voice to a whisper, scared out of my mind to keep speaking. But I did. "I've loved him my whole life."

Colt's hand came up off the mattress and captured mine. I melted as he pressed his lips to the center of my palm. "He's loved you his whole life too, darlin'. I promise."

Violet

I jerked awake, my face wet with tears as I blinked into the darkness. It felt like I'd been stuck in that dream for days, but it was still the middle of the night.

Groaning, I lifted Colt's arm off my belly, only to replace his touch with my own.

I waited for one kick. One roll. Anything.

Please, baby.

That dream had felt so real my heart was still pounding in my chest. I could feel the emotions burning in my throat.

The baby was in my arms and then he was just...gone.

And I knew he wasn't missing. I knew he'd been born. But he never cried.

He never took a breath.

I never got to see his eyes.

My chin quivered as a shiver rolled through my body. I pressed my hand over my mouth, trying to cover the sob that tore through me, but I wasn't quick enough. Because at my back, Colt moved.

"Vi?" His deep, sleep-filled voice filled the space between us. I couldn't answer though. The phantom weight of our son was still pressing down on my arms as more tears poured down my face.

"Fuck," I heard him mumble as his weight left the bed. In a heartbeat, he was kneeling in front of me. Colt clicked on the small lamp next to my side of the bed, wincing before his worried eyes focused on me. "What's wrong? Why are you crying?"

His hands rested on me. One on my thigh, the other on my belly. I covered my face with my own hands and lost it.

"Violet? Jesus, this is scaring me, baby. Tell me what happened. Are you in pain? Is something wrong? What can I do? What should I be doing?"

I'd fully lost it. All this time, all this anxiety building up inside, there was always going to be a point when it came crashing down. Because it wasn't just the relentlessness of this faceless threat that was getting to me. It was the silent monster of battling infertility that had been scaring me from the very beginning. Of getting pregnant, but not being able *to stay* pregnant. When it finally happens, everyone expects that the worry will go away. Once you make it to the *safe zone*. Once you're in the second trimester. Once you feel the baby kick. But it *never goes away*. It's constantly there, the worry that once again, I'll wake up and my baby will be gone. That he'll be born, but he'll never—

"Breathe, sweetheart. Christ. Just breathe. It's all going to be okay. Whatever this is, it's going to be okay."

"He...he d-didn't...he couldn't...open his eyes. I held...h-him." God. The words were just getting stuck in my throat. Falling out all jumbled and indecipherable as snot and tears poured down my face. "I h-held him..." My breathing stuttered. "He was b-beautiful. But he...our b-baby w-wasn't...a-alive."

"Oh, darlin'." His deep voice rumbled in his chest. "No. That's not going to happen. No. Come here." I closed my eyes, the bed dipping down as Colt sat next to me and wrapped his arms around my shoulders. I turned into him, into his chest, and lost it all over again.

"Just breathe, Violet. Try and breathe. You're okay. The baby is okay. You're doing a perfect job of keeping him safe. He's going to be born soon. We'll hold him in our arms. He'll be here. He'll be safe, and warm, and so squishy. He's ours, and he's going to be just fine. You've done it. You've done such a good job. You're so fucking strong and I'm in awe of you. Just breathe, baby. Just breathe."

I couldn't say how many minutes passed with us just sitting like that. Colt slowly rocked me back and forth as I cried until there were no more tears left inside me.

"Was that the first time?" he asked, his thumb gently wiping away what I hoped were the last of my tears.

"No. It was torture in the beginning. I'd have a nightmare that I was in bed and there would be blood. So much blood. I'd wake up screaming for you."

He looked so heartbroken at my admission. "Vi."

"It's fine. It should have gotten better. It *has* gotten better. Everything escalating just feels...wrong. You, getting hurt...It just set me on edge." I brushed my hand over my bump. "I wish he would move."

"Do you want to go to the hospital? To just check that everything's okay?"

"No, no. I'm being hysterical."

Colt stood, pressing a kiss to my head. Then he walked back to his side of the bed and grabbed his phone, motioning for me to meet him back in the middle of the mattress.

"Give me one second. I just need to go to the bathroom. Splash some water on my face."

"I'll go with you." He set his hands against the mattress, but a simple shake of my head had him stopping.

I smiled. "I'm okay."

"Leave it unlocked."

"As if those muscles couldn't bust down that door if you needed to," I teased.

"Oh, I'm sure they could. But I don't want to waste any time if you need me to get to you. Leave it unlocked, please."

I nodded, padding into the small room. I heard Colt speaking quietly, but couldn't make out what he was saying. By the time I washed my hands and was back in the bedroom, he was sitting silently, waiting for me.

The baby rolled, delivering a kick to my ribs that had me both wincing and sighing in relief. My fingers pressed against his foot, another little wiggle from him calming my nerves. I moved as best I could, settling back on the thick pillows that felt like heaven to my aching back.

"Were you talking to yourself while I was in the bathroom?"

He shook his head, looking up from the illuminated screen of his phone. "No. I called Birdie."

"Oh?"

"She said vivid dreams like that can be common in pregnancy, but if you feel like something is wrong, not to ignore it. She's working tonight and said she'd have no problem with you going in to see her, just for reassurance if you need it."

I climbed back into bed, more on his side than my own. I didn't want to admit it, but I needed his arms around me. "That's really kind of her, but it was just a dream. He's moving around now that he has more room since I emptied my bladder."

Colt nodded, his hand settling over the largest part of my bump. "Are you sure you don't want to go in?"

"I'm sure. Nothing feels off. It was just that dream…just my mind…"

He wrapped his arm around my shoulder and pulled me

into his side, pressing a kiss to the top of my head as it rested on his shoulder.

"Think you can go back to sleep?"

"No. I might just get up and try to write for a bit. But you should go back to sleep. Your head—"

"I have a better idea."

———

"Colt, honestly, you need to be resting. Is your head bothering you?"

He smiled over his shoulder as we walked down the stairs. "Not one bit."

"Liar."

"Fine. Maybe a little. But nothing a cup of coffee and holding my girl won't fix."

My eyes rolled to the ceiling, even though I knew he couldn't see my sass. "Smooth."

"Always have been. Always will be."

We stopped for a minute by the front door, where Colt draped one of his Carhartts over my shoulders. I slipped my arms into the sleeves and laughed, knowing there was no way I was going to be able to zip it up over my belly, but grateful for the extra warmth. I was only wearing an old shirt of Colt's because I got really hot at night. And my cotton undies really weren't thermal at all.

"I fear I've grown too large to share your clothes." There was a tinge of self-doubt in there, but the way Colt's gaze lingered on the extra curvy parts of my body washed it away in an instant.

"No need to zip it. I'll keep you warm if you start to get cold."

We stopped in the kitchen, where I opened the cupboard

and pulled down the bottle of over the counter headache meds I knew he kept in there.

"Here. Take two of these." I passed over the pills and watched as he swallowed them down dry. My whole body shuddered. "That's still as horrific as the first time I saw you do it."

He just chuckled as he tapped the code into the security system and opened the door to the back porch.

The air was crisp. Chilly, but not terribly cold. And the sky...my heart skipped a beat as I looked up at the sky, full of bright, shining stars.

"What are we doing out here?" I whispered, sinking back into his chest as he moved in close behind me. Our hands found each other and we gently swayed back and forth.

"We're going to watch the sunrise. It's not too far off now. Maybe another five, ten minutes and we'll start to see the sky light up."

I tipped my face up. "There are so many stars. I missed this."

"Too much light pollution in the city?"

"Yeah. And I never had a reason to look at them, you know? Life just gets busy, and these really slow and purposeful moments just sort of start slipping by."

Colt's grip tightened on my hand. "Are you warm enough?"

"Yes. Your son usually makes me feel like I have a furnace attached to me. The air feels nice."

We stood there, silent for another moment. The very first colors of sunrise caught on the horizon.

"See that little clearing over there?" Colt pointed off to the left, where a small cove had been carved out of the trees that led to the forested part of the property.

"Did you pick up lumber-jacking as a hobby after I left?"

"No." He chuckled, pulling me into his side and wrapping his arm around my shoulders. "Lachlan and Hayes helped me clear it out about a year after our divorce. It was hard; an old oak tree kicked my ass. But I won in the end."

"Why did you clear it out?"

"You can't see it yet, but when the sun comes up, you will."

And he was right. The sun kept rising, not yet quite over the edge of the land, when I could finally see beyond the porch and into the trees.

"You put a swing out there?" I didn't know how I'd missed seeing it in the time I'd been back at our house. It was tucked out of the way, so anyone who wasn't really looking for it could easily never find it. But still...

"I did. Planted an entire patch of violets around it, too. I spend a lot of time out there. Reading your books. Feeling close to you."

I looked over our shoulders to the second floor of the house. The nursery window faced that spot.

"Colt."

"I've been thinking about how sweet it will be to let the baby play over there when he's a little older." His head lowered, pressing his lips to my head.

"I missed this," I admitted softly.

"This?" he asked.

"Living life with you."

"I missed it, too."

He leaned down, his face so close I could feel the warmth radiating off of him. "Can I kiss you, Violet?"

"Yes," I panted. "You don't have to ask. I'm yours."

"You are. Mine. Only mine. And I'm yours."

His lips crashed into mine. It was passionate and explosive, and yet it felt like that kiss narrowed the world down infinitely small to a space where just he and I existed.

Colt's hand moved from cupping my chin, ever so gently lifting my face to reach his, his other hand going down my body. He stopped at my breasts, groaning at the way he could feel how ready and willing I was to receive his touch. My nipples were hard, the shirt doing nothing to hide the way they strained against the fabric. I was desperate to feel his touch there. Desperate for him to kiss all over my body.

As if he read my mind, Colt broke away from our kiss. His hand slid up under my shirt, palming my belly as his mouth wrapped around my nipple. One second I was standing with both feet firmly on the ground, the next I was floating, as every nerve ending in my body lit up with excitement.

"God," I hissed.

"Quiet, Vi," he whispered after he pulled away. "My dad is up and likely walking the ranch somewhere right now. We don't want to get caught."

The thought of that should have made me want to run inside and hide, but it only added to the throbbing between my legs.

"Naughty girl. You like the idea of us sneaking off to do something, don't you?"

"Reminds me of the first time you made a move, and we ended up in the hay loft."

"Hayes was a real cock block that day. Couldn't stop yelling out for me."

I laughed. "We made up for it at the springs that night."

Colt groaned. He walked us over to my favorite spot on the porch. Sitting down in my chair, he guided my body closer until I climbed on top of him.

"This can't be comfortable for you."

"Everything about this is excruciating, Vi." His hips moved, pressing his erection to my core. *Oh shit.*

"You're so fucking beautiful, Mama. So fucking sexy. So full with *my baby.*"

I gasped as I rocked my hips. My hands went to work, finding the waistband of his pants and pushing them down below his hips. I reached into his briefs, wrapping my hand around his shaft and giving it a little pump as I pulled it out.

"You're in control, darlin'. Take what you need."

That was all the instruction I needed. I sank down on top of him in one swift motion until he was seated fully inside me, the stretch delicious and all consuming. Each rock of my hips changed the pressure inside, the sensations climbing and warming my body. His lips were on my neck as I dropped my head back, arching my body so my belly pressed against him. With my eyes still closed, I felt the heat of his breath moving down my body, until he pulled one of my nipples into his mouth. The wet fabric of the shirt sent me spiraling into what felt like another dimension.

"Shh, baby." Colt's mouth popped off my breast. "I love those sounds, but any louder and I won't be the only person hearing them. I'd hate to have to shoot one of my brothers for hearing what's only meant for me."

"I. Can't...It feels too good. *You* feel too..."

"I know. You focus on what feels good. I'll take care of your mouth."

I rode him harder, chasing that feeling that I knew was just a moment away from slamming into me. I could feel my walls fluttering around him, milking him. Begging for his release in time with mine.

Just as my vision started to darken, Colt's mouth was back at my breast. His teeth raked over my sensitive nipple, and that was it. I tipped my head back towards the sky as my orgasm slammed into me. I opened my mouth to scream, but his mouth was somehow there, lips on my lips, swallowing down every last moan.

When he released me from his kiss, I smiled, tucking my head down against his chest.

"Good morning, world," I laughed, trying to catch my breath.

"Good morning, indeed."

Colt

The eggs popped in the pan as I flipped them over. *Shit*. If I wasn't careful, I was going to burn them.

My mind was all over the place. There was something about the photo being dropped off on my porch that I couldn't quite wrap my mind around. It felt familiar. Maybe a case I'd worked on sometime in the past? Maybe something I'd seen in a movie? I didn't understand why I couldn't pinpoint exactly where that feeling was coming from.

Two arms wrapped around my waist, and I smiled as I felt Vi's belly press into my back.

"Morning, again," she greeted me. "Something smells great."

"Figured we needed to get some good fuel into you. We never did eat dinner last night, and we burned a bunch of calories out under the stars."

Violet laughed as she snagged a piece of bacon off the paper towel-lined plate. "Oh God, this is delicious."

I bent down, kissing her, letting my tongue lick the salt from her lips.

"Mm, you're right."

Her eyes were wide, pupils blown out. Her mouth had popped open and the cutest silent *oh* sat unspoken on her soft and still kiss-swollen lips.

"Too bad we didn't have those cupcakes," she joked. "Bacon and cupcakes in bed would have been a real treat."

"I think we can find other ways for spending the day in bed to be a treat, don't you?"

"Actually," she laughed, patting her hand against my arm, "I need to spend some time writing this morning. Ryan is going to kill me if I fall any further behind schedule. I'm almost thinking he's going to need to ask the publisher for another extension, but I doubt they'd give it to us at this point. I'm *that* far behind."

"It's not like those things have been in your control though."

"No, and it's not the end of the world. We'll figure it out." She smiled at me, sneaking another piece of bacon when she thought I wasn't paying attention.

I turned, crossing my arms. "Can I read what you're writing?"

"Oh, absolutely not." She waved the piece of bacon out in front of her like a baton. "It's a mess, and meant only for my eyes."

"Are you writing a second chance romance?" My bottom lip slipped between my teeth as I winked.

She laughed. "I think we're writing one of those together, don't you?"

I nodded, placing my hand on her belly. "I think it's your best work yet."

She sighed, but the flush that bloomed across the bridge of her nose told me she felt the same way. "After I'm done writing words that you are forbidden to see, I'd like to see the storage room, if you're up for it. We don't have to move things out, I just want to see what we're working with."

Fuck. I knew I couldn't keep her away from that room forever. I just didn't know if she was ready...

"Yeah, that all sounds great."

Vi sat at the table, her laptop open while she typed like she was running out of time. I brought her over a glass of orange juice and got a smile as she gulped it down.

The eggs finished cooking just as I pulled our plates down from the cupboard. Vi gasped, and I whipped around, our plates clattering on the counter as I dropped them to get to her.

Her eyes were wide and watery, and I swear I watched as her normally flushed face drained of all its color.

"What is it?"

"He...he emailed me again. I don't understand. No one should have this address."

I turned the laptop away from her, my eyes running over every word. Trying to commit them to memory.

But I couldn't, because they were already there.

"Violet. Holy shit. I can't believe I didn't think of this before." Every nerve in my body buzzed as adrenaline dumped into my veins. *How had I not seen it? How hadn't Violet?*

"What are you talking about?" she asked.

I pulled my phone out as I turned to walk through the house.

"Hey, Colt. Everything good?" Gage Walker, the cyber-security expert at Montgomery Defense, answered on the second ring.

"I need you to hack into my wife's laptop and trace an email for me."

"That...uh...I can do it, but I just need to know...is this my friend Colt, the Clarence County Sheriff's Deputy asking, or is this Colt, the worried husband who is going to look the other way so I can get him some results?"

"The second one. You need to come over to do it?"

"Nope. I'll access it from here. Just leave it connected to the internet. I'll send you a text in a minute with the info I need from you, then just leave it to me, okay?"

"Thanks, buddy."

"Anytime, man."

Violet huffed up the stairs behind me as I hauled my ass down to my office.

"Colt?" She stumbled over my name as her eyes scrutinized every book on the shelf. Violet melted into me as my hands settled against her hips. The baby rolled as I pressed my hand against their little bum—or their head. I tried to remember how the doctor had said they were positioned when we were at the hospital.

"You have them. You have all of them?" Her books, every one that she'd published after our marriage fell apart, sat on display in my office. Even the special edition books, with commissioned artwork and painted edges, sat displayed on a shelf with their own lights to highlight them.

Stealing Hope.

Vanishing Dreams.

Finding Home.

Book after book with her name and mine on the spine. *Callie Ford.* A play on the name I always loved and cherished, that I kissed across her body so many times it was branded on my heart, too. And the one she never let a single one of our friends or family call her.

"I thought you hated that name." I smiled as I pulled the first book off the shelf. Fuck. I'd had these words memorized from the first time I read them. My eyes dropped to the pages as I flipped through all the annotations and highlights. Where the hell was that scene...

"I hate Calliope. You know I couldn't get rid of it fast enough. The only person who ever called me that name and made me want to love it was you. Hayes told me you read them, but you even have my special editions?" She gasped. "You have a copy of my book box collab?"

I nodded. "Why did you use that name, Vi?"

She stared at me for a moment before shrugging her shoulders.

"Out in the publishing world, being Callie Ford, it's always been my armor. It was a way I could still be protected by you." Her whispered words warmed my tight chest. "What does this have to do with him, though?"

I smiled. "I thought something about all of this was familiar. Just chalked it up to another case I was maybe involved with in the past. But that email he sent today, I think that's going to be his undoing."

"What do you mean?"

"You didn't recognize the words?"

"No. Not at all."

"You wrote them," I said.

"No, I didn't..."

"The proclamation of love? He's taken that from *A Love to End Them All*, and put your name in there. And the way he's only ever written that you're his? What if that is supposed to reflect the way your heroes are always so protective and possessive?"

"Ew. I wrote the words he's been torturing me with?"

I shrugged my shoulders. "I think he's using your stories as a blueprint to get you to want to be with him."

A shiver rolled through her body. "I'm never writing again."

"No, Vi. This is good. We can cross reference everything he's sent so far. If things line up, we might be able to see where the hell this is going. We might be able to catch him before his next move." I pressed a kiss to her forehead. "I think we finally have the upper hand."

I had clearly gotten ahead of myself. My theory was proving right, but the time it was taking Violet and myself to try and decipher a pattern to this lunatic's madness was taking its toll.

Violet had been shifting more and more in her chair the last hour. I watched several times where her hand slid to her belly for a moment and she held her breath, only to groan slightly or close her eyes before returning to whichever book she was looking through.

I didn't know if they were just Braxton Hicks or real contractions, but I was timing the hell out of them.

"I think I need a break," she said as she pushed off the chair.

"Everything okay?"

"Yeah. I just...this is a lot. Maybe we could go decide what we're doing with the storage room. I'd like to focus on something happy for a bit."

"Okay." I grabbed her hand and brought her down the hallway, past our bedroom, and to the room at the end of the hall. I took a big breath, and opened the door.

Violet was silent as she walked in, her head scanning the clean and cleared out space. The crib she'd picked out almost a decade ago, but never watched me assemble, was sitting in the corner, a precious horse and cowboy hat mobile gently swaying. I asked my mom years ago for my grandmother's rocking chair. She never asked me why I wanted it, just simply patted my shoulder and told me I could have it. It sat in another corner with a table and lamp, perfect for midnight feedings.

"Colt?" *Shit.* Her voice cracked. I moved quickly, walking until I could see her face. Silent tears tracked down past her jaw. I'd messed up.

"I'm so sorry, Vi. I should have told you..."

"When did you do all this? Did I sleep through you putting this room together?"

"No. It's been like this for years."

"Years?"

I nodded. "After your mother's funeral. I just...I needed to feel close to you again. And it was still on the list of things for us to tackle on your honey-do list. So, I started with the crib, and I just sort of didn't stop." My fingers brushed away her tears. "If you hate it, we can change whatever you want."

"I love it," she whimpered. "It's perfect. Everything I used to imagine before I gave up on this dream. I'm sorry you had to do it alone."

"No." I tucked a strand of her hair behind her ear as her hand landed on my chest. "Don't be. I got to do something that gave me hope. And look where it led."

"A true manifesting king," she joked.

"Something like that."

"Can I look closer at things?"

I nodded, stepping out of her way. My heart was still thumping like crazy. She groaned, her hand rubbing her belly again as she sat in the rocking chair. Her eyes drifted close, and I looked at my watch.

Still irregular. But I didn't like how much pain she seemed to be in.

By the time I looked up from my watch, her eyes were open, locked on the changing table.

"Is that..."

I smiled, walking over to grab the blanket she'd finally seen.

"I asked for it to be released from the evidence since it had already been swabbed and photographed. I washed it in some baby detergent Jessie recommended. It's not perfect because I could only remember how to do a running stitch, but I hope that's okay."

I placed the baby blanket in her arms.

"It's perfect, Colt. Thank you. For all of this, for—" Her gasp filled the nursery. My knees hit the floor in front of her.

"What's going on?" Could I hear the fear in my own voice? Yes. Did I give a single fuck about it? Absolutely not.

"I think..." We waited as she breathed in and out slowly until the pain seemed to pass. "I think this is probably just prodromal labor."

"Labor? I think you need to let me call an ambulance." My poor heart was going to give out. I was forty-fucking-years-old, and it was the second time in only a handful of weeks that I thought I was about to have a heart attack. Violet just sat there, holding onto the arms of the rocking chair, panting through a contraction like the baby was about to exit her body in the next five minutes.

And then she laughed. "I will never understand how you can be so calm in a million different situations, but fall to pieces when it comes to me."

"You can't figure out why?" The rumble that tore through my chest was a perfect reflection of the tornado ripping through my soul at the sight of her in pain. In a blink, I was holding her face in my hands. Her cheeks were flushed, painted with the prettiest shade of pink I realized had been missing from my life since she walked out the door all those years ago. A shade of pink I never want to go another day without seeing.

"Why?" she whispers, her eyes as wide as saucers.

"Because I love you, Vi. I love you more than anything else in this world. I have since the day we met in seventh grade, and I haven't stopped fucking loving you for one goddamn minute since."

I expected to see the corner of her mouth twitch, a smile she'd work to conceal, to keep away from me even though I'd just spilled my heart out at her feet. She'd always been the more reserved one. The one who said "I love you" only when she'd thought I was asleep, or too far away to hear it.

Instead, her face crumpled and one hand went to her belly as she sucked in a harsh breath, the other grabbing onto my arm like I was her only lifeline.

"I'm calling that fucking ambulance." There. No room for argument from her. Except there was—of course she was sitting there, shaking her head at me.

"Stop it. This could just be nothing. It's normal to have weird contractions in the last few weeks, and it's probably not going to progress into full blown labor. It happened the other night too, I just didn't wake you. And they never get closer together. They never get stronger."

Stronger?! Christ, she looked like she was about to pass out every time a contraction rolled through her. How the hell was she going to be okay if they got stronger?

"Never again, Vi. You wake me up. You let me help you, okay?"

———

"Hey, are the contractions back?" I asked, my voice thick with a bone-deep tiredness I hadn't felt in a long time. My head was aching, but I couldn't stop looking through her books for a clue I'd missed. Even after Vi went to bed, I just needed to find something that would point us in a direction for what was coming next. Anything to give us the upper hand.

I'd heard her feet pad down the hall, past my office, but when she didn't come back upstairs after a few minutes, I decided to see if she needed me. But the second I rounded the corner into the kitchen, I knew it wasn't me she was searching for.

Her hand was wrapped around a fork, and it took me a

minute to realize the jar in front of her used to be filled with pickled beets.

"Oh God," she groaned as a smile formed on her lips. "Well, this is embarrassing."

"Embarrassing?"

"I'm fine. The contractions haven't come back. But I woke up and I couldn't get comfortable because you weren't there, and then I remembered I saw the jar of pickled beets in here earlier, and I had to have them."

I laughed, taking a few steps to close the distance between us. "I remember how much you liked them."

"They're better than I remember. And our son really seems to be enjoying them, too."

My eyes dropped to her belly. "May I?"

"You don't need to ask." Her hands slipped to her back and she turned so she was facing me. "He's yours, too."

"But it's your body, Vi." I reached my hand out, settling it on the top of her belly. "I'd never want to touch you if you didn't want it."

"I want it," she whispered, the double meaning flashing in her eyes. I pressed my lips to her forehead.

"Good to know. But for now," my hand slid over her bump, palming her belly, "I think we need to get you both back to bed."

She nodded in agreement. "Did you find anything?" She yawned as we reached the stairs. "In the books?"

"No. Not yet." But I knew I was close.

VIOLET

"It's going to be great." Colt lifted my fingers to his lips and kissed my hand as we drove across the ranch to his parents' house.

God, my stomach was in knots. I blew out my breath, hoping the slow release of pressure in my lungs would somehow relieve the pressure behind my heart. Since he was attacked, I couldn't stop these sticky, all-consuming thoughts about how I was responsible for what happened. And that made me want to run.

My free hand drifted to my belly. Our son was quiet this morning, probably saving his energy for all the kicks his aunts and granny would request. I had been so stubborn about not celebrating him because there was still a small voice in the back of my mind telling me we weren't going to cross the finish line. That we weren't going to get the happy ending we'd prayed all these years for.

"Hey." Colt let go of my hand, moving his to my bump. "Is he giving you trouble this morning?"

"No," I laughed. "He's actually been pretty quiet. Why?"

His brows pulled together. "You look upset."

"Not upset. Just…"

"Thinking about too many things?"

"Yeah. My brain is not a quiet place these days."

He nodded, parking the truck next to his brother's.

"Lach's not here."

I'd noticed while all the other Ford brothers, including Colt, had black trucks, Lachlan had a white one sitting in his driveway when I went to visit.

"I didn't figure he would be," Colt said, worry thick in his words.

"But you hoped." It wasn't a question. I knew Colt was concerned about his brother. I knew everyone was.

"Yep."

"Alright, Deputy. Don't use up your daily allotment of words all in one go here."

He clicked his seat belt receiver, and then reached over to do the same for mine.

"Come on, Vi. There's no room for worry right now. Today is about celebrating you and the baby."

"And you," I added. His eyes went wide. "You're the reason he and I have a family. You're the reason this place, this life, this love that we share, has always felt like home. I love you. *We love you.*"

Colt turned and slipped out of the truck. The soft clatter of the door shutting had my heart tumbling. He'd been so clear about wanting the baby and me, but was I expecting too much to have him say those words back to me?

My door opened, and Colt's strong and steady hands were there, all but lifting me out of the seat before closing the door. He pressed into me, sliding us to the passenger door. The fire in his eyes, the way his leg pressed between mine, had my breath rushing in and out of my lungs.

"I thought you were mad at me," I whispered as his lips

slid against my neck, sucking first before letting his teeth rake over my flushed skin.

"No, baby. I just couldn't say it back without kissing you. Without my arms wrapped around you. Not without our baby between us. I love you so fucking much, Violet Ford. You've always been mine. You'll always be mine."

His breath was hot on my ear, and yet, the rest of my body shivered as my skin pebbled under his touch.

"Say it again," he growled. "I want to hear you say it as I taste you."

"I love you."

His lips crashed against mine. It was more than a kiss to close the decade we'd been apart from each other. It was all the love that spanned from the first part of our lives, over the void, into now. It was the forgiveness we held in our hearts for each other. The love that waited quietly in those darkest, loneliest moments. The tears that fell to the Earth when it felt like everything had shattered, helping to grow stronger roots in our foundation.

"I love you," Colt whispered as he pulled away, not trying to hide the way his eyes shimmered full of tears. He stepped back, his hands bracketing my belly before he gave our son a kiss. "I love you both so much."

My fingers ran through his hair as he came back and kissed me again. I giggled, the realization that this was happening where his family could see making my body flush red hot with embarrassment.

"Alright, lovebirds," Beau called from the porch. I jumped, hiding my face in Colt's shoulder. "As much as the girls are swooning in here at your little display, it's time to get the show on the road."

Colt flipped his brother off, Beau laughing loudly as he walked back inside.

"I'm never going to hear the end of that." He smiled, slipping his hand behind my back and helping me get my footing as we walked away from the truck.

"I think it was worth it."

He stopped, his eyes dropping to my lips and then back up to my eyes. "One thousand percent. Top five memory for us, Vi. Top five."

I laughed. "What other memories are in there for you?"

"Number five? Definitely the first time we went skinny dipping together at the springs."

"That was a fun night. I remember thinking you had a really cute butt."

"Hey," he grumbled. "I told you not to look."

"Sometimes a girl just can't help herself. Number four?" I egged him on as we climbed the stairs.

"Our wedding day."

I nodded. "Number three?"

Colt sighed, running his hand along the back of his neck before shrugging his shoulders. "The rest are all tied. Because I can't possibly rank the first time I saw you back and realized you were pregnant against the moment you told me I was going to be a dad. And you can absolutely forget about asking me to rank those two against the moment the love of my life, when the woman I've been obsessed with for almost thirty years, uttered the words in my truck on the way to our baby shower that I prayed to hear again every damn day while watching the sun rise alone in the house we turned into a home together."

"Oh." My chin quivered, and I bit down on the inside of my lip to help push down my emotions.

"Say it one more time before we go inside? Give me something to brag to my boneheaded brothers about while I'm stuck showing them how a real man uses a grill."

"I love you, Colton Daniel Ford. I've always loved you. And for as long as I live, for every minute there is air in my lungs, there will be love that is only meant for you in my heart.”

"I absolutely cannot wait to have you over for book club!" Lily, Jessie's friend who was married to one of the guys who ran Montgomery Defense, smiled as she held out a pretty blue drink in a glass to me. My baby shower was in full swing, and although it was small, with Jessie, Dolly, Birdie, Mae, Lily, and their other friend, Sloane, in attendance, it made me feel so cherished and special. Especially for these other women to attend just because they loved Jessie and she loved me.

"We're a small group, but it's lots of fun! Jessie and our other friend Lacy usually lead up the shenanigans, but Lacy and her husband Nash are up in Montana for the next two months," Mae shared.

Lily smiled as she sat next to me. "Lacy wanted to be here, and she made me promise to bring along her gift for you and the baby, which of course, I did."

"That's so sweet of her. But you didn't have to bring anything along. I'm just grateful for the friendship. Book club does sound like a blast." I sighed.

"I feel like I need to warn you that book club usually has absolutely nothing to do with books, but we're all so excited to change that up and read yours!" Mae laughed.

"What are you all talking about at book club if you're not discussing books?" I asked.

"Sexy times and cock—" Mae started to say before Sloane placed her hand playfully over Mae's mouth.

"Dolly is right over there," she hissed.

"Oh, honey. Don't think I haven't heard everything there is to know about a man, or what you can do with him. Hell, you want to see Danny turn redder than a beet? Ask him what we were doing when he had his heart attack."

"Ma!" Jessie groaned.

"What? There's a reason why I ended up with five kids. I'm not just good at baking pies."

"Speaking of kids." Birdie cleared her throat, her long, blonde hair not hiding one bit of the blush that highlighted her full cheeks. "Are you feeling ready for the baby to come?"

I nodded. "Yes. So ready. And also, no. Not ready at all."

"Well, don't worry. Newborns don't require a lot of things. So if you've got a car seat, a bassinet, and some pajamas, you'll be okay."

"His room is already done," I admitted.

"Colt hasn't said anything about that." Dolly looked surprised. "I asked him the other day, and he just said the baby would be sleeping in your room with you."

"Oh, he will be. But Colt put the nursery together...years ago. He told me it was just a storage room now when I first moved back in with him, but we went in there together and he showed me. It's all done, and it's perfect."

"I had no idea," Dolly whispered.

"Are you okay with that? It wasn't too painful, was it?" Jessie asked.

"No. It was exactly what I needed to breathe a little, I think." I turned towards Sloane and Lily. "I lost several pregnancies before our divorce. The last one was...It's the reason I had to leave. I just hated seeing the pain I was causing Colt. He was meant to be a dad. And I couldn't be the thing that stood in the way of that."

"I get that." Mae gave me a sad smile, Lily reaching over to grab her hand.

"Nothing bad is going to happen this time," Lily whispered.

Mae's words finally registered. "You're expecting, too?" I asked.

Mae smiled with the rest of the women in the room as her hand went to her belly. "I am. We're trying not to let anxiety get the best of us after our miscarriage. It's such a common experience, and yet, it feels like the most isolating thing I've ever been through."

"If you ever need someone to vent to who gets it, I'm here," I offered.

"I appreciate that so much." Mae blew out her breath. "Gosh, should we get presents underway? I didn't mean to steal thunder and make that about me!"

"You didn't at all," I tried to assure her. "I'm grateful you shared that with me."

"Well, if we're doing presents, I would love to go first." Dolly stood up, grabbing a white bag with blue and pink bows on it. "I have such big dreams of spoiling this little one absolutely rotten, honey. I hope you know that. But this is something special for today. Just for you. I've been working on it nonstop since you showed up for family dinner and finished it up last night, thank the Lord." Dolly stood and brought her gift over to me.

"I already love it so much, Ma. Thank you. For still loving me. For welcoming me back."

"Violet, you never left our hearts. Not for one minute."

I smiled. Reaching into the bag in front of me, I felt the soft fabric as I pulled out the most magnificent cream colored quilt. I held it up, the fabric falling to the floor as my breath caught in my lungs. Around the border were horses with patches of violets at their feet.

"Colts and violets. I know it's silly, but I just have always had a vision for it since the two of you were engaged. That one day, you'd lay your baby on this blanket behind your house, and they'd get some sunshine while you and Colt laughed about how cute they were." Her voice caught and tears welled in my eyes. It was so thoughtful. Beyond beautiful.

"I can't believe how stunning this is. Thank you."

She nodded. "I embroidered all of our names into the blanket. If you look in the center, it's subtle, but they're there. Your mom and dad's names, too. When the baby's born, I'll just steal it back for a day and add their name."

I hugged the blanket to my chest.

"I can't even come up with the words to say how much this means to me."

"I'm glad you like it." Dolly's eyes shimmered, and I waved her over to give me a hug. In a strange way, it didn't just feel like Dolly was hugging me, but my own mother, too. We were connected through something sacred. Precious. *Motherhood.*

My new friends were so generous. Lily and her husband Gunner had gifted the most beautiful baby carrier. She swore it saved her back as her daughter grew. And Birdie had put together an entire postpartum basket for me, full of lotions and oils that smelled amazing, some teas that were good for milk supply, and even the coziest pair of slippers.

Jessie's gift had made me cry. She'd taken everyone's pictures from the family and put them in a book, with their titles underneath, so we could show the baby who their family was. Colt's picture was his official department head shot which made me laugh, and mine was from the family dinner we'd all had a few days ago. My body was half hidden by the table, but there was a hand on my belly. And although you couldn't tell who the hand belonged to, I knew it was Colt. It had all made me smile at first, but then I realized at the very end, after Dolly and Daniel, she included photos of my mom and dad from my wedding day.

That hit hard. I really did wish my dad would move back to Silver Springs. To be closer to us. To be here for his grandchild.

"Oh look, there's one more present left!" Mae giggled as she handed me the last bag.

"Thank you all again. This has been so wonderful. I just... I'm so thankful for family, old friends, and new ones, too."

I felt the hard edges of something as I reached into the bag. *Maybe a picture frame?* As soon as I pulled it out, I realized I was right. But as soon as I caught a glimpse of the edge, my mind clouded with confusion.

I had this same frame in my apartment, holding the only picture I kept out on my nightstand—from our wedding day.

Maybe I'd mentioned that to one of his brothers? Would they go out of their way to get something like that for me?

My heart sank, the sudden wave of nausea at what I was holding in my hand slamming into me so hard I almost fell out of my chair.

"Violet?" Mae's voice drifted from over my shoulder. "Oh my God."

I looked at the women surrounding me. "I don't understand." I could feel the tears prickling in my eyes.

"Let me see what that is." Dolly held out her hand.

"No," I nearly shouted at her. I held the frame close to my chest, tears now spilling down my face. I'd brought something so evil here. Something that clearly wanted to take Colt away from me again.

Mae spoke calmly while I was still trying to wrap my brain around what I was seeing. "Jessie, go get Colt. He'll want to see this."

Colt

"To becoming a dad at forty! It's truly the best sort of whirlwind there is." Hawk held up his beer, and I tapped mine against it. The fire pit was at peak blaze, steaks and chicken on the grill. My brothers—minus Lachlan, who I was pretty close to losing my shit on—were all standing here to celebrate my son.

Fuck. Hawk wasn't lying. It was exciting.

"Don't think we forgot to get you a little present." Beau smiled as he pulled a gift bag out from behind his chair.

"Wow, Beau. Did you wrap it up yourself? I never knew you had those skills," I joked.

"Nah. Jessie took care of that for us. This is from her, too, by the way. She'd brand me with the cattle iron if I forgot to tell you that."

I opened the bag, moving around some tissue paper until the edge of the present revealed itself.

A new cowboy hat.

"This is great. Thank you." My eyes worked over the details in the hat. Worn in dark leather—my favorite. My name, branded on the inside next to a word that made my chest tight.

DAD.

"We figure you've worn lots of hats over the years," Hayes said. "Son. Husband."

"Best big brother." Beau winked at Hayes, who flipped him off. "Protector."

"Friend," Hawk added.

"But this hat, we know how much this hat means to you. How badly you've wanted to wear this hat. That you've waited so many years to put it on." Hayes cleared his throat. "We're *all* so happy for you that this is finally happening. For you and for Vi."

My eyes drifted to Beau, who was nodding in agreement.

"I think—"

"I know." He held up his hand before I could finish my thought. "I need to say it to Violet, too. I'm working on it. That, and an apology."

My eyes dropped down to my hands, where my fingers were still running over the edges of the hat.

"Put it on," Hawk encouraged.

I lifted it to my head just as I heard the sliding door to my parents' deck open.

"Colt!" The worry in Jessie's voice had me spinning around to face the door. "Vi needs you."

I pushed off my chair, tossed my hat down in my place, and jogged inside. As soon as I stepped into my parents' living room, confusion slammed into me because all the women were gathered around Violet. Mae was rubbing her back, Birdie was holding her hand, and Ma was holding something that looked like a picture frame with a horrified look on her face.

"What's going on?"

Violet stood, walking towards me. "He was here, at your

parents' house," she whispered. "I'm putting everyone in danger."

Fuck. I could feel the fear rolling off of her in waves as she barreled into my chest.

I lifted my hands, cupping her cheeks. "You *did not* ask for this, Vi. This isn't your fault. Come sit back down."

We moved as one back to the sofa, and Violet curled into my side as best she could. I think if no one was around, she would have sat right on my lap, which made me want to scoop her up and take her home. But I needed to see what the hell had everyone reacting this way.

"Here." Ma handed me the picture frame.

"I'm so sorry," Lily said, her voice breaking. "I saw the present on the porch when Sloane and I got here. We thought someone couldn't make it and wanted to leave their gift."

"It's okay. We would have seen it one way or another. He always makes sure of that."

"It's from my apartment in New York," Violet whispered, not lifting her head off my shoulder. "He was in there. I mean, I knew he was, because he mentioned my cell phone in that one email, but I...I should have taken that picture with me. Why did I leave it on my dresser?"

I flipped the frame over, immediately recognizing Vi in her wedding dress. The picture was cut in half now, the side where I was once standing in tiny shreds at the bottom of the frame. And on the backing was written the same threat she'd been getting over, and over again.

MINE.

———

"Vi?" I called out her name as I kicked off my boots. I knew she'd gone upstairs after we got home, but a part of me thought she might rally after having some time to herself.

There was this itch in my stomach, like I knew I shouldn't have given her space. But she looked exhausted, and had pushed so damn hard for time on her own.

I'd gone outside, installing the car seat in the truck that had shown up two days ago. Figured being outside might make it easier if she needed to cry and didn't want me to hover.

"Vi?" I called out again as I took the stairs two at a time. Still nothing. The fucking hair on the back of my neck stood up. She would come get me, wouldn't she? If she wasn't feeling well?

I took a right at the top of the stairs, stopping as soon as I stepped over the threshold to our room. Thank God, Vi was laying in bed. She was on her left side so I couldn't see her face, but I knew that was the recommended sleeping position for this far along in the pregnancy, so I didn't give it another thought.

As quietly as I could, I made my way to the dresser. I had my watch off when the tiniest sound hit my ear. Not a sleeping sound, no. It was a sniffle. I whipped around to study her for only half a second before I saw the shake in her shoulders. Fuck. She was crying.

"Violet?" I whispered. "Hey, talk to me." My voice fucking caught in my throat as I walked around the bed and got a good look at her. She had her eyes closed, but her cheeks and her nose were cherry red. Tears were running all the way from her lashes to her chest, and her hand was pressed protectively over her belly. Christ. *Something was wrong.*

I pressed my hand to her cheek and sat on the edge of the bed, her belly bumping into my hip.

"Come on sweetheart. Was it another bad dream?"

Her eyes finally opened, but I still couldn't breathe. Because I could *feel* the fear rolling off of her.

"I haven't felt him move today."

My eyes dropped to her belly, the blood in my veins frozen at her whispered words.

"What do you mean?" My hand slid over her bump and pushed hers to the side as I pressed down, waiting for the kicks I'd laughed about so many times over the last few weeks. But there was nothing. Not a kick. Not a roll. Not a hiccup. Just... nothing.

"He was quiet this morning, but I got caught up in the baby shower and everything that happened after...I forgot to pay attention and then I realized I hadn't really felt him move." She choked out the words before more tears came. "He's not moving, Colt."

Panic crested over me like a tidal wave. I took a breath, not wanting to upset her more.

"Babies sleep. Maybe that's all this is."

Violet shook her head, her breaths shortening so fast I tried to figure out how the hell I was going to calm her down so she didn't hyperventilate.

"Don't they move less as they run out of room? I feel like that's something I heard Jessie talking about before Beckett was born..."

"No," she sniffled. God, the tears were killing me. "That's a myth. Babies should always be active and any change can mean something's wrong. I-I did this wrong. I should have told you instead of trying to do kick counts! There's only ten minutes left and I think I felt him...maybe once or twice...but I can't count that because...I...don't...know...."

I couldn't take it anymore. I was up off the side of the bed, scooping her up into my arms before I think she even took another breath.

"Colt—"

"No, baby. I'm taking you to the hospital. Have you called the doctor? Did you talk to Birdie?"

"No."

"Okay, I'll do that on the way then. But we're going to go check on him. We're going to go see that he's fine, and you can finally breathe."

Her head tucked in the space between my neck and my shoulder as her arms wrapped around my neck. The heat from her fast breaths warmed my skin. I was down the stairs twenty seconds later, grabbing my keys off the table by the door and slipping my feet into shoes before another minute passed.

"My shoes! And we need the hospital bag," Violet tried to protest, but I wasn't about to fucking let her out of my arms.

"I'm not wasting time. I'll carry you into the hospital. I'll carry you up to Labor and Delivery. I'll even carry you back to the car when we're all done and they've discharged you because he's absolutely fine. Consider me your own personal chariot. You don't need to worry about shoes."

VIOLET

This was all my fault.

I finally let myself believe I was going to get to hold my baby. I told myself no gifts, and I'd let the girls convince me to do a shower. I got cocky, flippant, and I should have known the universe would balance that. I told myself over and over again that I'd curse everything if I started to believe...How could I be so selfish? So careless?

My hand tried to come up so I could rest it on my belly, but Colt's was already there. Big, and warm, and pouring strength into me as he drove us towards the hospital in Bell Ridge. Normally a thirty minute drive, at least, Colt was going to make it there in half the time, I had no doubt. He'd turned his lights and sirens on, and wouldn't hear a word of my protests.

And I was grateful for that.

As much as I wanted to try and feel movement from anywhere I could, I settled for placing my hand on top of his. From the corner of my eye, I watched the tension bleed out of his shoulders as my touch grounded him. God, even after all this time, our presence near each other settled the rough edges of our souls. And that should scare the hell out of me.

But it only gave me hope.

"Will you...when we get there, will you call my dad? After we know what's going on. I'll need him here if..."

"Of course." Colt's jaw ticked like it did every time he was worried. It was easier to focus on my own heartbreak, to think of the ways losing our babies before had torn me apart until I couldn't recognize my own reflection. There was no way that I was strong enough to think about how much losing another baby would break him. What if I only came back into his life just to truly destroy his heart? Oh, God. My free hand reached up to brush away the tears that were spilling over my lashes. "Vi. Goddamn it, don't cry. Everything's going to be okay."

The way each word came out choppier and more raw than the last should have scared me. But it didn't. Especially those last words. Because after everything we'd been through, they only served to fuel my anger. "You don't know that. We have just one week left. One week, Colt. And it's going to happen again. Every time before, it's—"

"Every time before isn't this time, sweetheart. It's all working out. You've made it this far, all on your fucking own. You're *his mom*. You're going to hold our son in your arms. And he'll be warm, and rosy, and *breathing*. He'll be beautiful, and he'll be *alive*."

There was so much I wanted to say. Every fear, every doubt clawing up my throat and burning to escape, but I swallowed them all down.

And then a sharp gasp from Colt filled the silence. My heart stumbled in my own chest, relief flooding my entire body as I felt our son roll his bottom beneath Colt's hand.

"He moved." His voice was thick with emotion. "That was him, wasn't it? I felt him move just then."

"Yeah, he moved."

Colt grabbed my hand, lifting it to his lips. "Thank you, God."

But I knew better. One movement wasn't enough. And without a window to look in my womb, or some magic power to know what was going on in there at all times, I was left with my mind spinning every horrible, tragic ending possible.

I closed my eyes and laid my head back against the seat. Colt never took his hand off my belly, but the warmth of his touch turned cold as the claws of panic dug further and further into my body.

The truck slowed and I heard Colt slide out of the driver's side, but still, my eyes stayed glued shut. I couldn't say how much time passed, or even if we were at the hospital. All I knew was that I couldn't open my eyes.

Cold air swirled around me as Colt opened my door.

"Come on, Vi." His hands slipped around mine and squeezed before moving to my seat belt. I heard the click of the release mechanism, felt the pressure lift off my hips and chest, but I still couldn't open my eyes.

The truck rocked and I was suddenly surrounded by Colt's scent. That cologne I'd bought him for the first year we were married. Warm and spiced and in every good memory I had of our marriage together.

"Violet, just let go."

"I can't." My voice came out broken, burnt. Acrid with the pain my mind was telling me we were about to endure yet again. Only this time, I would drown.

"*Darlin'*, please. Screw it. Just cry. One minute. Scream if you have to. Hit me. I'm right here. Whatever your mind is locked in on, let it out. Because I'm going to carry you through those doors, and we're going to face whatever comes together. You got that?"

His words cracked my heart wide open. The next thing I knew, my fists were wrapped tightly in Colt's shirt as I pressed my face up against his heart. The first sob ripped from my throat and then I just couldn't stop.

"No matter what, Vi, you'll be alright. I'll make sure of it. I'm not leaving this time. I'll always make sure you're safe. I'll always make sure you're okay." He whispered reassuring words over and over again as I fell apart in the hospital parking lot. And as much as that should have been my undoing, as much as my face should have flamed hot with the heat of embarrassment, it didn't. I slowed my breathing, my chest shuddering a few times before I was actually able to see through my slowing tears.

Colt reached up and swiped his thumbs under my eyes. "Need another minute?"

"No. We need to go in and check on him."

Colt nodded, his hands slipping behind my back and under my legs.

We were inside the hospital in no time. Colt wanted to carry me up to Labor and Delivery himself, but the triage nurse in the Emergency Room wouldn't hear of it. So, down into the wheelchair I went. I grabbed onto Colt's hand, squeezing as a contraction took me by surprise.

"Vi?"

"It hurts," I groaned.

By the time we made it upstairs, I'd ridden it out, the muscles in my belly releasing their strangle hold on my breath. And ten minutes later, I was settled in a bed, scratchy hospital gown on, with wires and monitors wrapped around my belly.

Our son's heartbeat was there. They'd picked it up easily enough. And I couldn't stop staring at the screen that was tracking it. An hour passed. Then another. Watching. Waiting. Monitoring. Breathing through contractions as they came and went. Trying to get comfortable. Trying to not let my mind spiral.

"He's doing okay, Vi." Colt picked up my hand and lifted

it to my lips. The other hand already had an IV in it, hooked up to some sort of medication to reverse the effects of my blood thinners. The nurse had explained its importance, but I was so numb I hadn't really been able to absorb the information.

"He has a heartbeat," I corrected. There could be a million things that were going on inside of me, and I wouldn't be able to see any of them.

"He's going to be okay. You both are."

I shook my head. "Something is wrong, Colt. I can feel it. It's not just my anxiety. I mean...maybe it is a little. But you always told me to trust what my body was telling me. I'm listening, and it's screaming that something bad is about to happen."

"What can I do?" he asked. "How can I make it better?"

"You got us here. You're here with us."

"I'm never leaving. You couldn't pay me to leave. Probably why that bastard knows he'll have to kill me first if he wants to have you."

"No, don't say that."

"Baby, he can try. There's no way in hell I'm letting anyone take me away from you two."

I squeezed his hand, my eyes drifting back to the monitor. For the hundredth time since we'd arrived, my stomach started to feel tight.

"I think I'm having another contraction," I groaned as the pain wrapped around my back, sending throbbing jolts of electric fire down my hips and into my legs. This one was a thousand times worse than the ones I'd had earlier.

It was so bad, I barely registered the sound of an alarm going off.

COLT

"Things are going to start moving very quickly," Dr. Witten announced. He'd come into the room about a minute ago, taken one look at the baby's stats, and started ordering nurses around. I'd been so focused on Vi and the pain she was in, I couldn't comprehend the words he was saying.

"Dad, you need to take a seat?" The question from the nurse in soft pink scrubs snapped me out of my stupor. I know she told us her name, I remember her saying it, but for the life of me, I couldn't remember it now. Because everything in my body felt like it was turning off. A sick numbness slithered from my toes to the top of my head, and as soon as I looked back at Violet, I couldn't breathe.

"No," I cleared my throat as I grabbed Violet's hand, "tell us what's going on."

Dr. Witten gave me a sympathetic smile. "Violet is experiencing more frequent contractions now. Babies' heart rates can speed up and slow down during these contractions—again, completely normal—but it's important to note the length and magnitudes of these changes. Now, this is where we're getting stuck. Your little one doesn't seem to be very happy when the contractions happen, and he's starting to take longer and longer to return to his baseline. He's not coping well, so I've put in the order for an epidural and instructed the team to prepare you for a cesarean. It's time to celebrate your baby's birthday."

Violet's eyes widened to an alarming size, bouncing between my face and the nurse as she squeezed my hand tightly.

"So something *is* wrong. Take him now. Please! I want to be awake when he's born, but it's more important that he's okay when he comes out." The first tear slipped down her cheek, and I reached up to brush it away. I wanted to hop in that bed with her and hold her against me as I fell apart, too. But that wasn't my job. And from the way the nurse was aggressively eyeing me, it was clear that I had to step in and calm her down. "Why aren't people rushing in here? Colt? Shouldn't there be people rushing?"

"I don't know, Violet." I wanted to kick my own ass for how worry and dread laced every letter of her name as it came out of my mouth.

The nurse gently held Violet's arm. "I know it sounds scary, but I promise you, if there was something to be worried about, I would tell you. We've had time to get the medicine in to reverse your blood thinner, which means you can have local anesthesia instead of general. We're already cooking with gas. And I'm staying with you through the whole thing, okay? Besides, Dr. Witten is exactly who I would want handling this. In fact..." She moved around the room, pressing a button on the machine that was monitoring Violet's blood pressure. "My second baby—a stubborn boy who came out with a knack for making everything dramatic—was a c-section by Dr. Witten in a very similar situation to this. There's no one better."

Violet nodded. "My husband. He can be with us when the baby's born, can't he?"

Her *husband*. My fucking heart was in my throat.

"Of course he can. Dad, if you want to say bye to Mom right now, I'm going to take her down to the OR to get prepped. I promise a nurse will come get you when it's time to join the birthday party."

"I love you," I whispered as I dropped my head down to hers. "You're going to be fine. The baby is going to be fine."

"I won't let them start without you."

"I'm running to that operating room, Vi. The minute they tell me I can go. I'm sprinting to get back to you."

"I love you, Colt. I love you, and I'm so grateful you're here."

The side rails to Vi's bed clicked into place, and the nurse released the brakes on the wheels. She started rolling away, my hand slipping out of hers as she went.

"Oh! Your family, Colt. They should be here!"

I ran my hand over my face, falling back on to the chair. Shit. I'd been so focused on Vi...

Vi and I are at St. Clare's. The baby's coming. Heading for a c-section. She asked for you all to be here. Jessie, can you grab our bags from the closet in our room and some slippers for Vi? I have to go, but I'll text as soon as I know they're both okay.

My phone buzzed as I set it on the table next to the chair, but I didn't pick it back up. Because at the same time, a nurse came in and handed me a pile of clothes.

"Put these on over what you're wearing. As soon as you're ready, I'll take you to the OR."

I'd never gotten dressed faster in my life.

————

I swear time slowed down the second I stepped into the operating room. I'm glad Vi had reminded me to take the time to tell everyone we were at the hospital. I wanted my family there. Not just for me, but because I knew they would help ground her. If something happened to the baby...if something happened to VI...I'd fucking need them, too.

The fluorescent lights were bright, burning my eyes. I recognized the soft music she'd picked out playing over the speakers, which was a nice touch, but my heart tripped over itself in my chest when my eyes landed on her.

My wife was on the operating table, a drape pinned up over her chest. She looked like she was about to be in one of those magic acts where the magician sawed her in half. The beautiful belly I'd been so lucky to fall in love with over the last few weeks was bare, just a surgical blanket laying across her legs. It was freezing in that operating room. She had to be so cold.

I forced my legs to carry me across the room to the stool that sat by her head. Her eyes were pinned on the ceiling, but as soon as I got close enough, her face moved towards mine. Those emerald green eyes of hers pinned me in place.

"Colt..."

"Breathe, darlin'. Everything's fine. It's all going to be okay." I slipped my hand over hers, careful not to disturb the straps holding her down. *God. This was fucking medieval.*

The next few minutes went by in a blur. Dr. Witten was there, starting the operation and Violet winced, gasping when he warned her of excess pressure. I couldn't look at anything other than her. My beautiful wife. Willing to sacrifice so much to bring our son into the world.

And then I heard it. The sound of Vi's breath rushing out of her lungs in the same instant our son's first cry rang out loud and boisterously into the operating room.

"He's here." My tears flowed freely down my face as I pressed a kiss to her forehead. Dr. Witten had held him up over the curtain for a second before he was whisked off to be cleaned up by a nurse. "You are amazing, Vi. So strong. So incredible. I love you. I love you, darlin'. Forever and ever."

"He cried," she whispered.

"Yes," I laughed. "He's got some big lungs on him, doesn't he?"

"He took his first breath." Tears were now pouring out of her eyes as her body shook. I looked to the anesthesiologist who was also sitting by her head. "We did it. He's h-here and he's b-breathing."

"Shaking is normal, Dad. Don't panic," she said as if she could read my mind.

"Alright, who is ready to say hello to their beautiful baby boy?"

One of the nurses set our baby into my arms, and my knees nearly collapsed under me.

"Colt..."

The world narrowed to a singular point. *My family.* My wife and my son.

He was a perfect blend of me and Vi. Perfect. There were no other words that came to mind, everything felt so over-whelming. And then he opened his eyes and looked at me.

And I lost it all over again.

"He's beautiful, sweetheart. Look, he has your lips." I held the baby at an angle so that Vi could see his precious face. He was the cutest little chunk, and even though I'd never say it to Violet, I could see my own face in his so clearly. We'd done that. Made him all those years ago. And he was real, and warm, and finally with us.

Somewhere in the background, a monitor started beeping, but I barely registered it as Violet's smile took over her entire face.

"He's so...he's beautiful...so....dizzy."

Dizzy?

"Jackie, take dad and baby out. Now." Dr. Witten's voice left no room for argument. I felt the nurse's hand on my shoulder, but didn't want to leave Violet alone. It was only when I looked down at her face that I realized how quickly everything had changed. My beautiful wife's big emerald eyes were rolled into the back of her head. Her face had lost all of its color, and only a thin sheen of sweat covered her forehead.

"What's happening? I don't under—"

"Colt. I need you to listen to me. Violet is hemorrhaging. We're going to do everything we can, but you need to do your part, too. Come on. Let's take your son on his first walk. Okay?"

The machines in the background continued their assault on my ears as I forced myself to walk out of the operating room.

———

Forty-five minutes. That's how long I'd been sitting in our room with our son on my bare chest, waiting for some news about Violet. And yet, no update came. A nurse brought me a small bottle with formula, but I didn't dare bring it to his lips.

Violet hadn't told me what to do if she wasn't here like this. I didn't know if she would be okay with formula before she even had a chance to hold him. So it sat untouched on the table next to me. I'd ask the nurse what I should do if more time went by.

Our son's soft little coos were barely above a whisper, but they melted me. I ran my eyes over him for the millionth time. He was perfect. Had my dark hair. Vi's lips and her long, slender fingers. I'd kissed every one. And when I set his hand back down, his fingers had walked across my skin until they rested over my violet tattoo.

I fucking lost it. Staring up at the ceiling, I begged every entity in the universe to save her.

"Colt." Birdie walked into the room, her face blank.

"How is she? Do you have an update?"

"I don't. I'm sorry. I wanted to come see how you're doing. Your family is here... in the waiting room outside L and D."

"I can't see them right now. I can't leave him." I held the baby closer to my chest. "She was supposed to get to nurse him. That's all she talked about. How important it was during the golden hour."

"It is important, but it's not the most important thing. There's time. She'll have that moment."

"I can't lose her, Birdie." I felt my chin tremble as I tried to hold back the tears. "I just got her back. Our son just came into the world. I don't want to have to say goodbye to her when we just said hello to him. He needs his mom. I-I...I need my wife." The last word was nothing more than a sob.

Birdie's hand rested on my shoulder.

"I'm going to call up for an update." Fuck, I could hear the tears in her voice, too. "I'll make them tell me something. Anything. Even if I have to march into the OR myself, okay?"

"Thank you. Do you w-want to see him?"

"I'll see him once Vi is down here and has been able to enjoy his cuteness."

I nodded. It was the most cruel situation I could think of that my wife and my son weren't together in the first precious moments of his life. That I was left to capture what I could for her. My eyes drifted to my phone, propped against a box of tissues. There were only a few minutes left of storage on my phone, but I would record every last minute of this that I could for her. Maybe she'd never want to watch it. Maybe it would always be painful. But I wanted her to be able to have the memories, too, even if they were through the lens of my phone.

Birdie was gone for a few minutes. In that time, I bundled the baby back up and paced around the room with him. He was still fast asleep when she returned.

"I was able to get an update."

God, I could read her face. "Is she okay? Is she alive?"

"She's alive." Birdie nodded. "Violet had something called uterine atony. It's where the uterus doesn't start contracting down after birth, and it can cause a large amount of blood loss in a short amount of time. Luckily, Dr. Witten caught it fast, and the steps we normally take in this kind of situation were successful. They've been keeping an eye on everything, but it looks like she's stabilized beautifully."

If my son hadn't been in my arms I would have collapsed to the ground with relief. My head swam. Shit. I still might. "What does this mean for her recovery?"

"She's in the ICU right now, and they're going to monitor her closely for the next six to eight hours. If she does well, and there's not an imminent concern with her bleeding, they'll likely give the okay for her to come back here for postpartum care. She'll need to stay a few extra days for monitoring."

"Can she see the baby now? What am I supposed to do? I can't pick who I'm with..."

"Why don't you let me take the baby to the nursery. I can stay with him for a while so you can see Vi. I'm not sure if she'll be awake. If she is, she might be really confused, so just try to reassure her, okay?"

"Of course."

Birdie held out her hands to me. I pressed a kiss to my son's head and gently placed him in her arms.

"Hello, sweet boy. I'm your Aunt Birdie. We're not officially meeting right now. No, we're not. Oh, you are so handsome. Okay. We're going to have a good time getting cuddles while Daddy goes to check on Mommy. And after you've had time with her, then we can officially meet. How does that sound?"

Birdie understood without me even having to say it. It was crushing me that Vi wasn't here to have time with him before other people cradled him in their arms. I slipped my shirt back on.

"Come out to the nurses' station. I'll have someone walk up to the ICU with you."

VIOLET

Beep...Beep...Beep...Beep...

Who was making that annoying noise? It needed to stop. I was drowning in the darkness, and that noise was going to be the thing that actually broke me.

No. *Wait.*

The beeping *meant* something.

I was somewhere where that noise was important.

God, my body felt like lead. Well, the parts of it I could feel.

Wasn't I just sleeping? Why couldn't I wake up?

With every ounce of strength I had—which honestly wasn't saying much—I forced my eyes open. Only one listened to me, the space in front of me unfamiliar, dim, and blurry. But with each new blink, shapes were easier to recognize.

And then I remembered.

I was in the hospital.

The baby needed to be delivered.

Our son...*oh, God. Where was our son?*

"Baby..." I croaked, my throat so dry it felt like it might

crack in half if I tried to say another word. Colt's head snapped up off the bed.

"Vi? Oh fuck, sweetheart." His voice cracked, and I could feel his relief washing over me. "You nearly scared me to death." Fresh tears pooled in his eyes. For some reason, my vision went blurry again.

Oh, tears of my own.

"Baby..." I said again, willing him to understand. *Where was our son? Was he okay?* I couldn't wrap my mind around why I felt like a lead blanket was laying on top of me. *Why couldn't I move? Why was my body so sluggish?*

"Shh. Don't move, Vi. You're going to be in a lot of pain, and I don't want you making it worse." Colt's hand landed on my head and started moving down through my hair. "Our son is fine. He's beautiful, Violet. The most perfect little baby I've ever seen in my life."

"Where..."

"He's in the nursery. Birdie is with him. She promised she wouldn't take her eyes off of him while I was up here with you, okay? Jesus. I've been so fucking worried." His voice hitched, and I reached out to hold him. His hand. His cheek. His shoulder. Anything. I just needed to touch him. Colt clearly got the hint because in the next second, his fingers were intertwined with mine.

"I'm fine—"

Colt's eyes snapped to mine. "You are not fine. But you will be. You're going to be just fine. You have to stay, okay? You promised you wouldn't leave me again...and then I thought I was going to lose you. Please tell me you're going to stay."

Tears were cascading down my sweet husband's face. Somewhere in the back of my mind, I could feel the severity of whatever had happened to me, but it wasn't registering with my body yet.

"Don't cry," I whispered. My throat was so sore I wanted to ask for water, but just didn't have the energy to.

"Don't cry? On what was supposed to be the second happiest day of my life—because yes, marrying you is still the single best day of my life, and I will never stop saying that—you could have died. I will never get over the sight of you laying there, so fucking pale and still, I couldn't tell if you were still breathing."

My eyelids felt so heavy...I didn't want to leave him sitting there.

"Need...to see him."

"Shh, it's okay, Vi. Rest. You'll be out of here in a few hours, and you can see our son then. Just rest. Everything is okay."

I didn't want to go back to sleep, but the darkness pulled me under anyway.

———

Connor Colton Ford was the most beautiful newborn. I know nearly every mom would say that about their child, but it was true for mine. He had the biggest blue eyes, with eyelashes so long I was envious of them. His dark brown hair—a perfect match for Colt's—made the contrast with his eyes striking. The way his little nose scrunched up when he cried made me feel like I was going to melt into the ground and never walk on solid bones again. And that newborn smell? I swear that was the best medicine around.

I had to spend the first twelve hours of his life in the ICU. For most of it, I was either asleep or too out of it to really understand what was going on. But now that Connor was coming into his third day of life, I felt crushed by the weight of my guilt. For not being with him in those first hours of his life. For making Colt worry. For not being able to care for my baby.

Even now, moving was so painful. I'd been given the good pain meds while in the ICU, but as soon as they deemed I was ready to return to the postpartum floor, those had gone.

It made sense, but what didn't make sense was how I was expected to be up and moving around when every time I moved, or talked, or—God forbid—coughed, it felt like my insides were going to spill out through my incision. Jessie had been an absolute angel, ordering a support garment the second she heard I was having a c-section. At least now, it wasn't so bad. I smiled down at Connor, who was fast asleep on my breast. It wasn't easy by any means, but he'd eagerly latched on the first time I tried to nurse him and I had sobbed so hard Colt thought the baby was hurting me.

"How's my favorite patient doing today?" Birdie chirped as she walked into the room, placing her hand under the anti-septic gel dispenser. One look at the sad state I was in, and she nodded. "Right. Okay. One of the perks of having a Certified Nurse Midwife in the family is the built-in babysitter with exceptional baby caring skills! Auntie Birdie is going to take Connor to get lots and lots of cuddles as I work on some charting. Colt, I think now would be a perfect time to get Vi into the shower," she directed at him before turning back to me. "It'll do worlds of good and help you feel more human, I promise."

Colt jumped to his feet. "Is there anything I need to know about helping her? Does she need a special soap? What about washing her incision? Does that need to stay dry?"

"Love the enthusiasm," Birdie laughed. "Help her into the shower, gentleness is key. No vigorous scrubbing. Bubbles and a light touch. Just make sure the incision is fully dry before you get dressed again. And Vi? Use the shower chair in there if you start to feel tired. It actually might be great to use the chair anyway to wash your hair. Did Jessie bring you some stuff to use from home?"

I smiled. "She did. Basically dropped off all the things I'd packed and about half a convenience store more of things."

"Good." Birdie stepped closer to the bed. "I promise I'll take such good care of him while you get a little me-time, okay?"

"Why is it so hard to hand him over?" I whispered.

"Because you fought hard for this little one. For years and years. And he's so tiny, and precious, and it's pinging all of your mama bear senses. But I promise, I'll just be across the hall at the nurses' station, and if he even so much as fusses one single time, I'll bring him right back to you. How does that sound?"

"I think I can handle that."

Birdie scooped Connor out of my arms and gave us both a little wave as she ducked out of the room. My heart was suddenly pounding in my chest. I leaned back in the bed, groaning as my belly pulled. It was the weirdest sensation of pain and soreness around the incision which was still completely numb. I hated it.

"Take a deep breath, baby." Colt's hand landed on my thigh, and not a moment too soon. The contact immediately grounded me, and the panic in my chest loosened its hold.

"I'm such a mess."

"You're not even seventy-two hours out from a life changing surgery where a tiny human was extracted from your body, you lost more than a normal amount of blood, and were stitched up and walking within twelve hours. Not to mention also keeping that little human alive by feeding him milk your body is now producing."

"That is a lot, isn't it?" I asked.

"Understatement of the year, darlin'."

"Help me take a shower so we can get him back in here?"

"Absolutely."

"Lean your head back just a little bit, I'm going to try and get most of it wet without waterboarding you."

"Thanks." I chuckled. "It's been a long time since you washed my hair."

"I missed doing this."

"Taking care of me?"

"Yeah. It's the biggest honor in my life, Vi. Taking care of you. Supporting you."

I lifted my hand up, resting it on his arm. "I feel the same way. I want to throw up when I think about all the promotions I missed celebrating with you. All the birthdays. I made us miss so much." The words stuck in my throat like I'd just eaten a spoonful of peanut butter.

"None of that," he cooed as he started pouring the warm water over my hair. "It took two people making mistakes, thinking they were protecting the other person, for our divorce to happen. And we can celebrate everything we missed with Connor now. It'll be a fun way to introduce him to cake. One for each of the books you published on your own."

"One for each of your promotions."

"I love the sound of that. It wasn't celebrations missed, just celebrations delayed."

There would be so many people at those celebrations, too. It filled my heart with so much happiness to know my son was going to grow up on the ranch. With his aunt, uncles, and his cousin. His grandparents, too. Part of me wondered if I could convince my dad to move back from Arizona. I knew the house held so many special memories for him, but I also knew they were painful since my mom passed.

"What are you thinking about?" Colt asked. "You went awfully quiet."

"My dad. I was just thinking how much of Connor's life he's going to miss out on being so far away."

"That is tough." Colt massaged the shampoo into my hair, and I couldn't help the moan that escaped. He cleared his throat, and I tried not to laugh while he shifted his hips. My husband was fully clothed while I sat here naked, deflating, ripped open and sewed back together, and yet I knew without a shadow of a doubt he still would tell anyone I was the most attractive woman he'd ever seen in his life.

"We could ask him to go on the trip to New York with us."

"What trip is that?"

My eyes drifted shut. "I need to clear out the stuff in my apartment. Sublet until my lease is up."

"Or break the lease all together," Colt suggested.

I shook my head. "The penalties are too expensive. It doesn't make sense to break it when there are only fourteen months left on it."

"So, you, me, Connor, and your dad are going on this little trip?"

"If I had my way..."

"Which you absolutely will. I'll see to that." The small cup he used to wet my hair came up and dumped more warm water over my scalp, this time washing away the suds. "I actually think that could be fun."

"My small town, big-hearted, Texas gentleman thinks New York City will be fun?" I tried not to give away my surprise.

"Sure."

I squealed. "You can finally meet Ryan! And I want to take you to my favorite bagel shop. The amount of cream cheese they schmear on these things is obscene. I love their pickle and bacon cream cheese on an everything bagel. Oh, my stomach's going to growl just thinking about it!"

"Well it's not New York City, but I think we could rope someone into dropping off food from the diner today."

"I will never say no to that."

"I forgot to tell you, but while you were resting earlier, Ryan wrote."

I groaned. "Hopefully not to tell me about my deadline. I know he's been talking to my agent for me, and she's been working with the publisher, but there is just no way I'm going to make my extension deadline."

"Don't stress. It wasn't about that. But even if it was, you are more important than any deadline. He said something about needing to travel to Canada?"

"He has family up there. Goes on vacation for a few weeks every year."

Colt had switched to a bar of soap, lather now working between his fingers. His hands landed against my shoulders and I inhaled sharply. God, I hadn't thought about how this would work.

"I can do that, you know?" I muttered.

"And I can, too. Now be quiet and let me suds up my baby mama." His hands went to my back. "Can you lean forward just a little, darlin'? I'm going to get your back and then I'll rinse you off."

I nodded as I swallowed. His hands felt like heaven. I hadn't felt more grounded in my body, more present in the last few days than I did right now. And when his hands roamed over my collarbone, bringing bubbles down over my chest, I couldn't help but hiss.

"I'm sorry, Vi. Are they sore?"

"God, yes."

"I'll be gentle." And of course, he was. Colt was so meticulous, and so careful that by the time I'd been rinsed down, I felt like an entirely new person. He helped me out of the shower, moving me carefully to sit on the toilet before he started drying me off from head to toe.

"What do you want to put back on?" Colt asked as he

picked up my legs one at a time and helped me get into my fabulous and very chic diaper.

"The blue pajama set with the white piping. It's so comfortable and I just feel like I want to be cozy right now."

"You got it. Do *not* try to get up without me."

I smiled. "My boobs are hanging out, I'm bleeding, and I'm exhausted. I'm not going anywhere."

He kissed the crown of my head and shook his back and forth. "And yet somehow, you've never been more beautiful."

"You're a liar, but I'll take it."

I immediately noticed the beautiful arrangement of lilies and baby's breath that sat on the table next to my bed.

"Those are new," I groaned as Colt helped me sit back in bed. "Can you see who they're from?"

My room was filled with flowers and balloons from Colt's family and the women who had been at my baby shower. I appreciated everything, but especially the note that accompanied Lily's flowers, which told me to enjoy the flowers while I was in the hospital and to leave them behind because I didn't need the stress of figuring out what to do with them while trying to get a newborn home. I had laughed, and then immediately regretted that as the incision in my belly pulled tight. The sheriff's department, my agent, and even Ryan had sent along flowers as well. It was almost more of a flower shop than a hospital room at this point.

I watched Colt pluck the card from the holder, the smile falling from his face in an instant.

"What's wrong?" I asked.

"Nothing. Hit your call button and have Birdie bring Connor back."

"Okay." I pulled the remote over and pressed the red button, relaying the message to the nurse who answered. A minute later, Birdie popped in with Connor in her arms.

"Well, that didn't take too long. How are you feeling?"

"Better," I answered, my eyes still locked on Colt and the way his jaw muscles were flexing. *Something was wrong.* My eyes dropped to the card in his hand as Birdie handed Connor back to me.

And then it hit me.

"It's from him," I whispered. My stomach flipped, and I pulled Connor in closer to my body.

Colt nodded once. "I need to go to the gift shop and see if they can tell me who sent this. I don't want to leave you two alone."

Birdie squared her shoulders. "I'll stay as long as I can. On your way out, explain what's going on to the security guard at the nurses' station. Don is working today, he'll be more than happy to stand outside the door until you come back."

COLT

I was going to kill him. Whoever this sick fuck was, I was going to take him out before he got within a hundred yards of my family again.

Now that the bastard's here, you can finally be mine. See you soon, Amore Mio.

The words played over and over and over again in my mind. Sick prick. Violet wasn't his love. She was *mine*. And I was at the point in this disgusting cat and mouse game where I wanted him to come for her. Because I'd end things, once and for all.

I knew the sign-off was a clue. Smug. Pompous. Overly confident that I wouldn't be able to figure it out. But I did. I knew.

Because only one character in all of Violet's books used that term of endearment. The answers would be in that book.

The elevator chimed and opened out on the first floor of the hospital. I hadn't been down here in days. Not since I brought Vi in.

A tall, lanky kid stood behind the register of the gift shop. "How can I help you today, sir?"

"A flower arrangement was just delivered to my wife's hospital room. I'm wondering if you can tell me who sent it?" I slid the card from the flowers across the counter to him.

The kid shook his head. "It looks like they didn't leave a name to put on the card, and it is our business policy to not give out that information."

"Alright. Thanks." I pocketed the card, knowing it was just another piece of evidence that would be added to Vi's case file. But something in my gut told me this is where we were going to catch him.

"Hey, what are you doing down here?" I turned, Hayes strolling in through the double doors with a large paper bag in his hand and a shit-eating grin on his face. "Got so hungry you couldn't wait for me to bring up food for lunch? Had to meet me here?"

I shook my head. "Didn't even know you were on your way over."

"Well, yeah. Told the guys at the firehouse I'd give their congratulations to you and Vi in person. Wait...why do you look like you're about to kick someone's ass?"

I groaned. "Is that fried chicken?"

"Uh, yeah?"

"Let's go. Vi deserves to eat it while it's still hot."

My brother clapped his hand on my shoulder, and we walked in silence until I was facing the elevators again.

"So, what's going on? It's not Vi or Connor, is it? They're both still okay?"

"Yeah, physically, they're good. But Vi's stalker sent her flowers."

Hayes' eyes went wide as the elevator opened, and four people filed out between us. Luckily, we were the only ones to get back on. I pressed the button for the third floor.

"He knows she's here?"

I nodded.

"How? How the fuck is that possible? How does he know her room number?"

"I don't know. I finally had a fucking minute to get back to Gage. I had him tracking an email the bastard sent, but I guess the signal was bounced through a VPN. He was able to get me the name used to register the email account, but it was a dead end."

"Shit."

"Yeah. But I think this guy finally messed up. He called her a nickname. The same one Vi used in her very first book."

"So your book theory holds up."

I nodded. "I need to get my hands on a copy of it. I think the wild goose chase through all the clues in different stories was just for his amusement. The real answer is going to be in that book."

COLT

It was going to be a beautiful day, sunshine and bright blue skies. Violet and I had been home for nearly two weeks with Connor, and things had been calm. Aside from the extra security I had Hawk install before we even made it home from the hospital and the way my family continued to monitor things on the ranch, Vi and I had been left to our happy bubble.

And God, how happy it was. Every day felt like a goddamn dream. We were tired zombies, at the mercy of our littlest family member, and yet even the late night feedings and endless diaper changes were bliss to me.

Now at the kitchen table, I rocked a very sleepy Connor in my arm, my free hand scrolling through the report Hank had just sent me. I'd already had the conversation with him about not leaving Vi until this stalker situation was sorted. Thankfully, he agreed, but I was ready to type up my resignation letter and hand deliver it myself if he had other thoughts about where my priorities should be.

And while life with a newborn and a postpartum wife were bliss, an eerie calm had settled over everything, too.

Because there hadn't been any more deliveries since the flowers in the hospital. No more ominous notes. No more threats, veiled or not.

Violet had been struggling. She was trying to be so strong for me, but I heard the gasps that came in the middle of the night when her mind convinced her the person behind all this was there to take her away.

And I fucking hated it. Because I found nothing in her book. No clue. No idea what the hell this sick person was planning next.

My eyes went back to the report. It only took a few days for the warrant to come through for the flowers at the gift shop. And just like I'd thought, we pulled a name from the receipt. *Alexander Bishop.* The billionaire finance mogul who swept Arianna Valentine off her feet in Violet's first book. *Amore Mio.* The asshole had made his purchase with one of those prepaid gift cards that acted like a credit card, which unfortunately meant our trail ended there.

I couldn't understand why he hadn't popped back up since then. Surely, while we were distracted with Connor, it would be the perfect time to try something?

My brother's picture popped up on the screen over the file, and I swiped to accept the call.

"Hey, what's going on?"

"I need you to talk to Lach." Hayes' voice was firm. He probably wanted to kick my ass a little for dropping family things as Vi and I settled into being new parents.

"You want me to leave my newborn baby and freshly postpartum wife to talk to our brother? The brother who couldn't bother coming to the hospital when Vi almost died? Couldn't bother driving to my house to meet Conner when we came home? He didn't even fucking respond to my text when I invited him over. What's Jessie doing? She could always get through to him before."

"She's tried. Look, we fucking all have. I wouldn't be interrupting this time for you and Violet if I thought there was any other option. He's not doing well, Colt. It's gotten bad over the last few weeks." Hayes cleared his throat. "He stopped talking to Mom and Dad. Won't let them bring him over food. Won't let them in to spend time with him. You know they don't want to push, but I just barged in there...It's not good."

I ran my hand over my fucking unshaven face. I knew my time in our happy little family bubble was about to burst.

"Fine. Vi is sleeping, and I'm not missing out on bath time. I'll go this afternoon when Connor is down for another nap and I'll try to knock some sense into him. You have to come over here, though. Someone needs to be here for Vi and Connor, to keep them safe."

"Fuck. I wish I could. You know I love them both, but I got called in for a shift tonight. I'm leaving in ten minutes."

"Got it. I'll ask Beau."

"Good luck. Let me know how it goes with Lach."

"Yeah. Stay safe tonight."

"Always do."

I chuckled, then groaned as I hung up the call with Hayes and watched Violet walk into the room.

"What's wrong?" My gorgeous redhead, still so curvy and absolutely glowing although the dark circles under her eyes showed just how exhausting these last few weeks had been for her, walked over to me. Vi's arms wrapped over my shoulders and crossed over my chest as her lips found mine the second I turned towards her.

I knew a lot of guys who said bringing home their first child put a wedge in their marriage. But the second we brought Connor into the house, it was like every last fear we'd been holding onto, every last little wire that had been holding us apart, dissolved. I hadn't asked Vi, but for me, the energy between the two of us felt the same—bubbly, electric, *alive*—as it had the day after we were married.

That's why one morning, I'd pulled her wedding rings back out and placed them on the dresser. She'd given them back to me the day of our divorce, even though I tried to tell her she could keep them. I didn't want to pressure her, so I just slipped my own ring back on, came downstairs and waited.

And when she walked into the kitchen in her sleep shorts and nursing bra, hair pulled up into a messy bun with her wedding band and engagement ring back in place, I nearly fell to my knees and sobbed. It might not be official on paper, but Vi and I knew nothing would ever tear us apart again.

"I have to go see Lachlan. Hayes called…said he's not in a good head space. I won't be long, though. It's going to be a beautiful day if you want to bundle Connor up later and take him for a short walk. Might be our only chance over the next few days. There's a cold front moving in; storms are coming."

She sucked in a sharp breath. "How bad is it supposed to get?"

My hand slid around her wrist, letting my thumb put some gentle pressure on the pulse point there. "Can't be as bad as that crazy storm we made it through when we were in tenth grade."

That storm front had spawned ten tornadoes across six states.

"Remember how the winds uprooted that tree right in front of the school?" she asked as her thumb dusted across my beard.

"Yeah, I remember," I chuckled. "I remember Hayes climbing all over it, too, and the principal calling Mom and Dad down to the office over it."

"You Ford boys sure were a handful."

"I think *were* is being a little too generous."

"Yeah, but you're the law now. You have to behave."

My fingers gently massaged her side and she laughed. Brilliant. Loud. Free. Her hair spilled out of the soft, silk tie she'd pulled it back with, the red tendrils dancing across my face as retribution for tickling her.

"Careful," Vi giggled, "I'm not sure I won't pee on you."

"Shit. Sorry." I placed my hand over her soft belly, wincing. "Did I hurt you?"

"Not at all." She rolled her eyes. "I'm not that easy to break. Tell me about Lach. Want me to cancel my visit with Ryan and bundle up Connor so we can go with you?"

"God. Yes. I would love that." I set my forehead on the space between her shoulder and her neck. "But I think Lach needs some tough brotherly love right now. I feel like there are going to be a lot of swear words said."

Violet held up her hand. "I get it. Besides, I think it'd be a little unfair to Ryan, flying all this way to see me. Can't really tell him no now, he's up in the air."

"I told Hayes it would have to wait until after Connor's bath. I'm not missing that. And I won't be gone long."

"Take as much time as you need. And don't feel bad for wanting to check in on your brother. I want to know that he's okay, too. You have to go."

"I don't want you here on your own while I'm gone." I ran my hands through my hair.

Violet sighed as Connor cooed from his bassinet. Both our eyes went to him, but he quieted right down and stayed asleep. "Ryan is only here for like an hour before he has to fly back out. I've got to make sure I understand the breach of contract and he can walk me through whatever backlash there is going to be from missing my deadline. And he wants to meet Connor, which he should, seeing as how he is going to be his godparent."

"Shouldn't I have some say in who our child's godparent is?"

"You do. You can pick whoever you want as your person. I'm picking Ryan." Violet kissed me, then pressed against my chest as she stood. She scooped up Connor, bringing him to me. "He's been the only friend I've had since I left here. And he's always had my back on all my publishing stuff. I trust him."

"Hey, buddy," I cooed. "I can't believe they won't give you some leeway for his birth."

"That's just how it works in these situations, Colt. I don't blame the publisher for holding to the contract. I mean, they've already given me an extension. I can't just keep taking advantage of that. And with everything from the books...this person...I'm not sure I want to keep writing anyway."

"Vi, you can't let him take that from you."

"I'm not. Those stories...those worlds...they were all built on a well of pain I no longer have access to. Or, maybe I do still have access to it, but I don't want to live in that pain all day every day just to have the creativity there. I'm happy just being Connor's mom right now."

"And what about being my wife?"

She smiled. "I'm wearing my rings, aren't I?"

Her hand lifted and she wiggled her fingers towards me. I snatched them quickly, pressing my lips over the jewelry. "Still, I don't like the idea of you being upset over anything right now."

"I'm not. I promise. How could I be when I have him... and I have you."

"Love you." I squeezed her thigh.

"Love you, too."

I cleared my throat. "Oh, before I forget, I'm going to ask Beau to come over."

She groaned. "I can take care of our baby by myself."

"You're three weeks out from having a c-section. It's not about if you can take care of yourself or not. I know you *can.* But I don't want you to have to. I would ask Jessie—"

"No, don't bother her. She has Beckett to worry about."

"Okay. So that leaves you either heading over to be with my parents, or having my parents or Beau come be here."

"Colt."

"I know you trust Ryan, but I've never met him, Vi. I want my brother here. My parents would protect you with their lives, I know, but I trust Beau to pick up on anything weird going on."

"Fine. Beau can come over, only if it's not a problem for him."

"It won't be." I know full well he'll be hell bent on getting the ranch ready for the storm with the ranch hands, but he can delegate and get his ass over to be with my family.

Balancing Connor in one arm, I pulled my phone from my pocket, ready to shoot off a text to Beau.

> Hey. I need you to come over to the house. Got to go kick the shit out of Lach. Need you to be with Vi and Connor.

BEAU:

> Give me twenty. I'll be there.

VIOLET

I smoothed my hands over my shirt for the fifteenth time.

"Chill, Vi. You're so nervous it's giving me the jitters."

I rolled my eyes. Beau was sitting on the couch in the living room, scrolling on his phone.

"What's so entertaining over there?"

"Just tracking Birdie's flight. She was nervous…"

"I didn't realize she was heading out of town." His nerves now made sense. I swear, I hadn't seen him without Birdie by his side since I came back.

"She's going to some midwifery conference in Colorado. Won't be back for a week."

"That's gotta be tough."

"For her, yeah. She doesn't like being away from her sister. Lainey can be a real piece of work. I'm sure Birdie is worried about her."

"I meant for you," I admitted.

"Why would it be tough for me?" he asked, a look of true confusion settling across his face.

"No reason," I laughed. "Sorry you got stuck on babysitting duty. I told Colt I'd be fine, but—"

"No. I'm happy I'm here. Colt's right. Keeping you and Connor safe is what matters." His hand ran along the backside of his neck. "Look, I know I said it to you at the hospital after Connor was born, but I am really sorry for how I treated you when you came back."

"And like I said, I appreciated the apology, but it wasn't necessary. You were protecting Colt. Something I thought I was doing too all those years ago. Family stumbles sometimes, Beau. Doesn't mean I don't love ya like the pain in my ass little brother that you are."

"I love you, too. Like a much older, not-much-wiser sister." He winked at me. "And I'm happy everything's worked out for you both."

I was just about to deliver a zinger of a comeback when I saw a flash of black pull into the driveway, and the conversation with Beau died on the tip of my tongue.

"Ryan." I smiled as I opened the door, my business manager standing on the other side in a crisp suit. I don't think I've ever seen the man in a t-shirt and jeans, and that was just the type of guy he was. Type-A to a T.

"Well, well. If it isn't my favorite romance author. Gone off to a sleepy little town and fallen back in love with her ex-husband. Instead of art imitating life, I see we're letting our life imitate our art now."

I wrapped my fingers around his outstretched hand and smiled as he gently squeezed me back.

"Come in. I'm sorry you had to drive out all this way. I know it was a trek, but with the baby, I just can't really go anywhere yet."

"An hour drive from the airport is nothing. I hit worse traffic at LaGuardia all the time. The weather's getting a little tricky out, though." He chuckled as I held out my hand to take his jacket. "And I swear it's already dropped fifteen degrees out there. I miss New York. This is for you." He set a brown paper bag in my hand.

"Thank you?" I had no idea what could be inside, but it was sweet of him to bring something for me.

"It's that tea you were always drinking from your favorite little place around the corner from your apartment. Oh, this must be the infamous once-an-ex-but-an-ex-no-more husband?"

Beau laughed as he stepped forward, holding out his hand.

"I'm definitely *not* the husband."

"He's my ex-husband's brother," I explained. "Colt's taking care of a family matter, but I know he's going to try to get back here before you leave so he can meet you. Beau is here just to make sure Connor and I are..."

Ryan nodded. "Protected. I get it. It's crazy to me that they haven't caught the creep yet."

"Yeah." I shivered. I hadn't had a single night yet where I hadn't woken up breathless, convinced he was there, ready to snatch me away from my family.

"And this little goober must be Connor?" Ryan's question pulled me back. I could feel Beau's questioning gaze on me, but I didn't have the energy to reassure him that I was fine.

"That's him. The sweetest little blessing there ever was. Why don't we go sit at the table? If you want to hold him, just wash up in the sink first."

"Of course. You're such a natural mom. I love it." I knew he was teasing, but a warmth spread through my chest. "When is your dad coming to meet him?"

"In a couple of weeks. He'll most likely stay over the holidays."

"Oh, so he isn't out here yet?"

"Nope, not yet. I wanted to have time with just the three of us. It was important to me."

"And that's why I'm here now, ready to talk over your breach of contract." He winked, but suddenly my stomach clenched. "Lucy said if we had any questions to give her a call and she could hop on a video with us, but I told her this was all pretty standard stuff that I'd been through with another client of mine recently. So if you felt comfortable with me walking you through the matter, then we would only reach out if we absolutely had to."

My agent was the best, but I couldn't stand to see the disappointment in her face. And I knew she'd try to hide it, but I really did feel like I was letting everyone on my team down. Probably because I was.

I fiddled for a bit in the kitchen, getting two cups down from the cupboard. I filled Ryan's with coffee and excitedly poured hot water into mine, grabbing one of the teabags he gifted me.

"You know I don't want to be insensitive, but we promised the publisher the manuscript would be ready last week. That was a firm deadline."

"They liked the manuscript I sent."

Ryan nodded. "They liked the direction the manuscript you sent was going in, but without your completed manuscript or any edits, they can't move forward, and you know how slow this industry moves sometimes. It's the author's job to hit their deadlines. The publishers can change whatever they'd like to on their end, but you can't."

"That seems predatory," Beau mumbled from behind his phone.

"That's just how this business works." Ryan shrugged his shoulders, his eyes momentarily dropping to his watch before returning to me.

"Listen," I said, "I don't blame them at all. I already was granted the extension and I blew it on this one. I might bow out and take a break for a while. Just while Connor is young, until I get my feet back under me."

"They want their advance back, Callie. And I think that's a fair trade. The rights to the book would revert to you, so if in the future you want to publish it yourself, then you could."

I nodded. It was fair.

"What did he just call you?" Beau choked out as his eyes went wide. He'd seen Hayes make the mistake of calling me that the first time I visited the ranch. God, we were all just babies back then. But that didn't matter. Because I'd kicked him in the shin and Colt had howled with laughter while Hayes took off limping back to the barn.

"It's my pen name—Callie Ford. I don't use Violet Murphy for my writing."

"He doesn't know that?" Beau asked.

"Of course Ryan knows my real name, but we just keep it all the same so he doesn't give out my legal name to anyone by accident."

"Mm." Beau went back to his phone.

"I get that this puts you in a tough spot, but I just had Connor a few weeks ago. It was traumatic, and I'm still getting my footing—"

Ryan held up his hand, making me choke on my excuses.

"I know, and I understand. Really, I do. I get it. And that's why I'm going to tell you I want you to do what's right for you. I've already told Lucy I was pretty sure this was the way you'd feel. That we wouldn't be looking to try and negotiate."

My head swam as I took another sip of the rose hip tea. Swirling the liquid in the cup, I realized it didn't look quite the same as all those cups I had at the small cafe by my apartment.

"You said you picked this up at Kathy's?"

"Yep. Right on the corner of Jefferson. That's the one you

like, right? The girl behind the counter mentioned missing you the last few weeks."

"That's the one. This just…I don't know. Doesn't taste the same."

"Probably the change in atmosphere. Like having lobster ravioli out on the range."

I laughed. "No one says 'out on the range' here. It's not the eighteen hundreds."

He crossed his arms and leaned back in the chair. "I don't know. I'm pretty sure I passed a chuck wagon advertising passage on the Oregon Trail."

There was no way I could hold back the colossal eye roll I had after hearing that. "I love Texas. I'm happy this is going to be home."

Ryan coughed. "What do you mean? Aren't you coming back to New York?"

"No. Colt and I have talked about coming up to clear out my apartment, but I want to be here. This is where my family is. This is where I want to raise my son."

"Callie…just don't…don't make any crazy decisions now. I know it might feel like you need to because of the baby and this contract dissolving, but we'll find another home for your book if that's why you don't want to go back. It'll sell, and you'll be able to keep things going in New York."

"Hey, Ryan?" Beau called from the couch.

Ryan turned his head towards Beau as I stood up and checked on Connor who was still fast asleep in the bassinet. Gosh, I was feeling so exhausted, I might need to take a nap before Colt got back. After the meeting. Once Ryan was safely back on his way to the airport, I'd take the baby and head to our room.

"What flight did you say you came in on?" Beau asked.

"Avalon 216, out of Newark. Don't tell me they're canceling flights. I swear I never book through them, but they were the only ones with a red eye I could snag back to New York on short notice."

"No. They haven't started canceling flights yet, but the storms coming in aren't going to be a joke."

"Colt said they wouldn't hit until later. Why are you asking him about his flight?" I asked.

Beau was acting weird. He tucked his phone back in his pocket, standing before taking two steps towards me.

"Because, there wasn't a flight in from Newark through Avalon today."

My eyebrows pulled together.

"What?" There had to be. How else had Ryan made it into Dallas before driving here?

"There wasn't a flight today, was there, Ryan?"

"Look, man, I don't know what you're getting at, but I was definitely on an airplane today."

Beau shook his head. "I don't think you were." He took another step towards me. "I thought it was weird that you said it only took you an hour to get here from the airport. Because yeah, sure, if you looked it up on the internet, they would tell you that's the time it takes. But there is major construction going on between here and there. That adds at least twenty-five minutes. And with the storms we had last week, there's a detour around the main road you'd take to get to the ranch. So that's another twenty minutes of detour just to get out here."

Ryan shrugged. "Didn't think I had to report traffic patterns to you."

"But that's not what really struck me as odd. Because Violet has been buzzing all day with excitement about you being here. Going on and on about how you are the best business manager, and how she loves you to pieces. How you love and appreciate her. There were literally tears in her eyes when I showed up because Colt was going to miss meeting you. That's how much you mean to her."

"She means so much to me too. Callie, babe, I don't get what this is about?"

"Beau?" I asked.

He stepped in front of me, his back blocking my view of Ryan. "I know for a fact, any man who loved Vi would not dismiss the weird shit that was happening to her in New York. He wouldn't get mad at her coming home, or deciding to stay where she felt safe. He wouldn't try to sell her on moving back and leaving her family behind again."

I moved back from Beau, a step towards Connor, still fast asleep in his bassinet. The floor felt like it was melting, and I blinked trying to understand why I was feeling so funny.

"I do love Callie. I'm not mad at her for choosing this. I just want to make sure she's making the right decision for her."

"Beau?" I called my brother-in-law's name, hoping he would hear the urgency in my voice. Because I could no longer stop my body from swaying. I took a step forward, but the vertigo pitched me farther than I'd meant to lean. My body was falling, and I couldn't stop it.

"Vi?" His hands stopped me. "Hey, what's wrong? Vi? Shit. I'm going to carry you to the couch, okay?"

"That's why I had to do what I've done. Because she's not meant to spend her life in this dinky little town. She's not meant to live a mediocre life as a wife and a mother." Ryan's voice droned on, but Beau didn't pick me up. A little clarity came back, some of the tingling in my arms and legs fading.

"Beau?"

"He's holding Connor," he whispered.

My eyes snapped to Ryan, who was in fact holding my baby. *Why?*

"Ryan?" I questioned.

"I don't want to hurt this baby, Callie. I know you think it's your son, but it's not. I'm happy to leave him here, unharmed, for your ex-husband to take care of. But you have to come with me. Now."

"She's not going anywhere with you." Beau's fists clenched by his side, but he and I both knew nothing could be done while Ryan held onto Connor. My sweet baby wiggled, a startled cry coming out as he began to wake.

I needed to stall. I needed to do whatever I could to give us enough time for Colt to come back. "I'll need to nurse him soon. Colt won't be home for a while. Can we wait? I-I'll tell him I want to go back to New York. Just the two of us."

"No, Callie. I know what you're doing. It's why I had to slip a little something to help you relax into your drink. You'll come with me now. You were meant to be mine. You were meant to have that with me."

Ryan placed Connor back into his bassinet, running his finger over my son's cheek before walking towards me. Then he lifted his sweater, and I saw the gun on his hip. I wanted to scream. I wanted to gouge his eyes out. I wanted to fight him with everything I had in me, but my body just wouldn't listen. Everything felt too loose. Too far away. I knew I needed to focus, but I couldn't.

Beau stepped in front of me as Ryan approached. I hated that Beau wasn't standing in front of Connor. He needed protection. He was so little. So fragile. Who knew what Ryan would do if we upset him? That's why I forced myself to stand. I walked on shaking legs, taking two small steps before Beau caught me.

"Violet, no." His voice was deep, commanding, but it didn't have the same effect on me as Colt.

"Stay here. Watch over him, okay? Make sure he's safe. There's some milk in the fridge and a canister of formula we haven't opened on the counter."

"Vi..."

"Tell him I love him, okay? Both of them. Tell them this was me choosing them."

"Or, you could tell him the truth," Ryan sneered. "That Callie is finally going to be happy. Finally going to be free. With me."

His hand wrapped around my arm the second I got within reach of him. Beau took a step towards us, but Ryan tsked, pulling the hand that wasn't holding onto me out of his pocket. He was wearing a pair of brass knuckles.

Beau's eyes dropped to Ryan's hand for a split second while I silently begged him not to do anything stupid. But if there was one thing I knew about Colt's brothers, without a doubt, whether they were still upset with me or not, they would protect me.

Beau lunged. Ryan held onto me as he stepped towards Beau, pulling his hand back before slamming the brass knuckles at full force into Beau's jaw. I watched in an instant as he fell to the floor.

"Beau!" I dropped to my knees, my entire belly hurting from the sudden movements. Oh God. He wasn't moving. He wasn't groaning. I...I couldn't tell if he was breathing. He needed help. I had to get him help.

"Come on. We need to get going." Ryan's hand wrapped around my arm, grasping so tightly I winced.

"Connor...I need..." The words burned in my throat. "I need to say goodbye."

His eyes blazed, but he nodded. "Two minutes, Cal."

I got up to my feet, ignoring the burning pain, and scooped Connor up. "Come on, sweetheart." My voice wavered as I walked towards the stairs.

"Callie?"

"He needs to go in his crib, where he'll be safe until Colt comes back. Please. Then I'll go. I promise."

Ryan followed me upstairs. I wished there was something I

could have used as a weapon. I wished my arms and legs didn't feel like they were dead weight. I was terrified I was about to drop the baby or trip with him in my arms.

But I made it to his room. I made it to the crib. And I gave my beautiful boy one last kiss as I laid him down.

My legs gave out, knees hitting the floor with a loud thud. Ryan pulled me to my feet, shoving me towards the door.

The last thing I heard before I was dragged down the hall was the soft cooing of my newborn baby.

COLT

I stormed up the front steps of my brother's house, the sun warm on my back. I thought about just walking right in, but stopped short of the door, knocking twice while swearing under my breath.

It only took a minute for my brother to answer the door. I looked him over, same sandy-blonde hair he'd had since we were all kids, a scruffy beard that he'd grown in the months after his accident. He was dressed in a white shirt, jeans, and had a flannel on. What the hell was Hayes' problem? Lachlan looked fine!

"Uh, what's going on? And since when are you just out and about? Vi finally get sick of you hovering and kick you out?"

"No. Hayes called me. Said something was going on with you and I needed to talk some sense into your head. Feel like inviting me in?"

"That's a hard pass. Thanks for stopping by."

Lachlan moved to close the door, but I was faster. I stopped the movement with my palm, sliding in past him. His cane slipped out, slapping across my thighs.

"Don't take another step in here without taking your boots off," he demanded.

"Fine." I slipped my boots off. Normally, I'd just leave them right where they landed—I wouldn't be staying long anyway—but I noticed how his shoes were all lined up and facing the wall. I'd never seen him do that before.

"Come on. I have some coffee brewing. Feel like having a cup since you fucking barged in here?"

"Yeah," I answered, still looking around. "That sounds great."

Listen, my brother wasn't a messy person, but he also was never super clean. Hell, as a mechanic, he used to come home covered in grease and who the hell knows what else. It covered his clothes. His skin. But as I walked through his inexplicably clean house, I heard the water turn on in the kitchen. He was washing his hands. The water turned off as I walked in. But a second later, he was back to washing his hands.

"Lach?"

He sighed, shaking his head. I thought he'd turn off the water and come sit at the table with me, but he didn't. I watched my brother turn off the water, wipe his hands off on the towel next to the sink, and brace his arms on the counter.

I saw what Hayes did. I saw the pain radiating off our brother.

"I have to wash them again."

"What? Why?" I asked.

"Because you interrupted the counting and I need to know that I got to twenty-eight. Don't ask why twenty-eight, Colt. Just let me fucking get there so I can come sit down."

I didn't speak. I dropped my eyes to the table and didn't dare move. Again, the water turned on. I heard my brother scrub his hands. And finally, the water turned off. Lachlan muttered something under his breath, but a second later I could hear the clanking of mugs on the counter and the steady stream of coffee being poured.

He set one cup down in front of me, taking the other to the opposite side of his table where he joined me.

"Want to tell me what's going on?"

"No."

"Hayes said you weren't letting Mom and Dad come over here anymore, and I thought for a second maybe you were struggling and had let the place go. But, fuck, it's never looked better. But that's just it...isn't it?"

"What?"

"When was the last time you left your house?"

"Doesn't matter," he mumbled.

"When was the last time you drove your truck?"

My brother's eyes met mine, the challenge there.

"Fuck, Lach. I'm so goddamn sorry."

"You ain't got nothing to be sorry for. I'm fine."

"So fine you have to count how long you wash your hands for, and if it isn't perfect you have to start over? How long were you stuck at that sink? Because you didn't mean I interrupted you with speaking, did you? I interrupted you by coming here."

"It's fine."

I slammed my hand onto the table. "It's not fine, I don't want to fucking hear that word again. Everyone in this family loves you and is worried about you. Tell. Me."

"Damn, man. I didn't mean aim for the heart."

"I don't have time to be gentle, Lach. You're fucking struggling. Everyone sees it. Everyone feels it. You got Mom crying every time your name comes up. Dad swearing under his breath about getting you into therapy. Even Jessie won't stop texting us all about getting you help. I should have been over here sooner. Should have kicked your ass into asking for help faster."

"I don't need help," he griped. "It's just my goddamn leg."

"I thought it was better. After the last surgery, the physical therapy was supposed to help you get rid of that thing." I nodded towards his cane.

The screech of Lachlan's chair across his flooring filled the air. "It would have, if I could make myself go there. You want to know how long I've been trapped in this house, Colt? Three months. Since the day my surgeon said I didn't have to go back to their office for more bullshit. I've been in this house all day, every day for three months. And that's not the worst part. I'm fucking trapped in here." He limped as he put weight on his leg without having the cane in his hand. I wanted to jump up, to offer some sort of assistance, but I knew that wouldn't help.

"You don't want to leave? Or you *can't* leave?" I asked. My phone buzzed on the table, but the distress on my brother's face was too much, I couldn't pull back. I couldn't let this go with him. Somewhere deep inside I knew what it cost him to open up like he had, and I couldn't lose that connection with him.

"My mind won't fucking let me leave! I can't even go on the porch without feeling like my breath is being stolen away from me. I fucking tried last week. I forced myself out there, and by the time my foot hit the top step of my stairs, I was shaking so bad I thought I was going to pass the fuck out. I'm not this pathetic person! I'm not scared of what lives out there. The type of shit that my best fucking friend got caught up in and the kind of shit I paid the price for. That car falling off the lift and crushing my leg broke something inside my damn head. And I don't know how to get out of the hole it put me in. So I sit in my house. And I do all the things my mind tells me will keep me safe, keep everyone I love safe, and try to make it another day."

I nodded, running my hand over the stubble on my chin.

"We will help you. We will get you help." It wasn't a suggestion. It was nonnegotiable.

"I don't want to deal with a shrink," he spit back at me.

"You don't get a fucking say at this point. You just said out loud the fucking words I have nightmares about when I think about how close we were to losing you."

"I can't leave." His eyes sparkled with tears. My baby brother was hurting so deeply, and I didn't even see it until now. I didn't see it until it was almost too late.

"You won't need to. We'll find someone who can do tele-health first if that's what needs to happen. And we'll all come around more. You *will* let us in. Mom and Dad, too."

"They don't deserve to see me like this. Broken. Needing to be coddled."

I stood, my hand landing on his shoulder. "You are not broken. This is part of healing. You've done everything possible to get your leg healed. Now it's time to heal from everything that injury took from you."

I didn't ask, or wait for him to be ready. I simply wrapped my arms around my brother's shoulders and squeezed. My favorite thing about being the oldest was the way my siblings looked up to me. It had always been an honor to watch the way they would follow me around, emulating the way I did things. My heart fucking shattered knowing I'd let Lachlan down. I had been so wrapped up in my own life that I wasn't able to see how desperate of a situation things had become.

Lach pulled back from our embrace, clearing his throat and turning away from me to wipe his eyes. Fuck, I needed to wipe mine, too.

I sat back at the table, opening the message waiting for me.

Beau:

> There's something weird about this Ryan guy. You need to get back here. Now.

Fuck. He'd sent that message ten minutes ago. I jumped up from the table, sending my cup of coffee crashing to the ground. Lachlan cursed behind me, but I was out the front door before he even had a chance to ask what was happening.

As soon as I sat in my truck, the alarm chimed on my phone. Violet had armed the security system with the alternate code.

Something was wrong.

VIOLET

"We're almost to the barn, Callie. We'll get inside and I can figure out what's next. You won't be so cold if I can get you inside." Ryan's hand grasped painfully around my wrist. Thank God he hadn't wanted to take Connor with us. The temperature outside was dropping alarmingly fast, wind whipping small droplets of rain against me so harshly it felt like my skin was being sliced open.

Beau needed to be okay. He needed to wake up.

And even if he didn't wake up—Lord, the thought made my stomach heave—Colt would be rushing back. I'd used the silent alarm code at the house.

The wind kicked up, light rain turning heavier as we walked on the edge of the woods towards the barn. Ryan clearly didn't want to be seen, but I was still holding onto hope that someone would be securing something on the ranch. Maybe Danny or one of the ranch hands would be checking on the horses? Jessie might be taking in clothes off her clothes line. Someone, anyone, that I could signal to get help.

My incision pulled tightly as Ryan jerked me closer to him.

"I don't understand." My voice wavered, and I wanted to scream. The last thing I wanted was to be weak. Because weakness was just going to slow me down. But the bitter cold from the storm front and the adrenaline dumping into my bloodstream were making my body shake. Physically, I *was* weak.

And then I saw it. Colt's truck racing across the far field. The one that led from our house to Lachlan's. He'd gotten the alert. Connor would be okay.

"Inside. Now." Ryan shoved me into the barn, tracking Colt's vehicle over my shoulder. My eyes frantically searched the building, but there was no movement. The rain crashed harder, somehow feeling more harsh hearing its echoes on the roof than it had slamming into my skin outside.

Ryan paced in front of me, looking over the items on the table to our right.

"This wasn't how it was supposed to be. This wasn't how it was supposed to go," he mumbled to himself, his hands combing through his hair.

"Can you take a minute just to explain what's happening right now?" I asked.

"We don't have a minute! I need to get you there. To the house. Yes, the house. I wasn't supposed to be in there before, but I couldn't wait. I had to be near you. I had to smell you. I needed that release so badly, Cal. I'm sorry. I'm so sorry. I should have waited for the right time. That's now. That's right now."

"Ryan, you need to slow down. None of this makes sense?!"

"He was trying to take you from me. And he can't. He can't have you." Ryan's hand touched my cheek, and I recoiled back. He shook his head, little droplets of water spraying down as he ran his fingers through his hair. "I knew what you were doing from that very first novel. You were writing to me. Hiding messages in your story line that only I could see. I loved it. Our own little game. I was so nervous to reach out to you that first time. But then you were excited to hear from me, and it gave me a whole new purpose. We'd work together to build the life we were meant to have together."

"I...I don't understand. I didn't write you messages in my books."

"You DID!" His eyes were wild. I shrank back, wishing like hell the Fords kept their branding irons on the wall behind me. But there was nothing. Nothing to reach for. Nothing to grab. No one to call out to for help. "It was so clear that you were Arianna, and I was always meant to be your Alexander."

Shit. Shit. Shit. *Shit.* Colt was right. This was some delusion spurred on by my stories. Ryan reached out to me after *A Thousand Starless Nights* was published, and that's how we connected.

God, I was so stupid. How could I let this happen? He'd been in my life, plotting this for five years? Thinking I was writing love stories for him when they were my soul calling out to Colt...

"Okay, okay," I replied, holding out my hands. "You're right. I'm so glad you found those messages."

I felt repulsed by the words I was saying, but calming Ryan down was my first priority.

"Why do you want to take me to the house?"

"Because, that's where it all started for us." I must have looked confused, because he shook his head and sighed. "The house that Arianna inherits after her parents die. We need to get back there before the storm really starts. Otherwise, it won't be perfect."

"That cabin is a long way from here, Ryan. I can't walk that far. I need to be back with Connor. He's going to be scared. He's just a baby."

"I'm fucking sick of hearing about that baby, Callie! I let you put him up in his crib, safe and sound. That wasted time! You said goodbye. It was never supposed to be *his* baby. It was always supposed to be you and me. Just the two of us! And then you had to go off and do this. It was a fucking mistake. That baby is a fucking mistake." His pacing became more frantic until his face snapped towards mine. In two steps, his hands were on my shoulders. "It's okay. I'm not mad at you for wanting to know what motherhood could be. But the baby is his now. *Colt's.* We have the chance to start over. Forget about your mistake. Forget about that baby. It's just the two of us from here on out. Come on."

His fingers traced down my arms as he pressed his face closer to mine. I turned just in time for his lips to press against my cheek.

"Ryan, please." I squirmed, trying to get out of his hold. Instead of being mad, or backing away, he smiled. His hand cupped my cheek and he nodded.

"You're right. I need to save our first kiss for when we are surrounded by candles and flower petals, just like you planned." His eyes went to the rafters of the barn. "The rain is picking up. We're going to have to make a run for it."

"I can't run. The incision from my c-section isn't fully healed."

His face darkened as he looked down at me. "Then I'll just have to carry you."

The thought of him touching me more made acid churn painfully in my stomach. "No. I-I'll try. Okay? I'll try to keep up with you. And if I can't, then you can carry me. I want to show you how strong I can be."

He nodded, a smile crossing his face. "I knew you'd see. This is all going to work out, Callie. I promise. We're going to make it perfect."

Every cell in my body ached. But I hadn't complained. Not when the skies opened up and drenched us. Not when I stumbled and tripped over fallen branches and roots in the woods between the ranch and my parents' house. Not when my insides felt like they might fall out through my incision. I used to know this area like the back of my hand. Colt would meet me out here, and we'd sneak off to the springs.

I tried to think of how to use that to my advantage. If I could bring him somewhere that would trap him and give me time to get away. But there was nothing. And more than that, Ryan seemed to know exactly where he was going. *Is this how he was watching me? In the woods? Lurking in the shadows?*

The thought sent a shiver through my body just as the house came into view through the thick trees.

"You'll have to clear the security alarm when we go in," he said. His hand slipped up to my elbow as my knees started to buckle. God! My belly ached from all the movement. "Careful. We're almost there. We'll get nice and dry, and I'll warm you up in front of the fireplace."

I wracked my mind for what significance the fireplace had in my story. And then I remembered. The fight. The storm.

Ari had run out of Alex's place in the middle of a snow storm. He'd found her collapsed, covered in snow...and taken her back to her house because it was closer.

He peeled off her clothes, warmed her by the fireplace...and it was the first time they were intimate together.

Oh no. *Oh fuck, no.*

A key appeared in Ryan's hand, and he quickly unlocked the door. The *door open* alert started chirping, and I knew we had twenty seconds before the alarm would sound. I thought about it. For a second. Just letting the alarm sound and praying that he would run. As if he could sense what I was thinking, Ryan stepped closer to me, running his hand along the small of my back. No. There was no way he would run. I knew what I needed to do.

I move towards the panel. 0525. The day Colt and I were married.

The alert stopped chirping, and Ryan smiled.

"Good girl."

Ew. There was only one man in the world that could say that to me without me wanting to gouge his eyes out. And Ryan was not him. "I need to use the bathroom."

"I'll come with you." He started to walk towards the stairs, but I reached out, setting my hand on his arm.

"No! Please, Ryan. I need some privacy. I need...I need to dry myself off and I'd like to make myself presentable. I must look like an absolute mess right now. Why don't you..." My eyes drifted to the kitchen. "Boil some water? I have tea or hot cocoa in the cabinets. That would be perfect if you want to start a fire in the fireplace."

He nodded. "That does sound cozy. Don't take too long, or I'll have to come looking for you."

"I promise, I'll be quick."

God, my legs were trembling, but I forced myself to stay upright as I climbed the stairs. Whatever he'd put in that tea was still making me feel so weak. But I wouldn't let it win. I had to get back to Connor. To Colt.

I made it into my bedroom and marched straight through the door leading to the bathroom. I closed the door, trying my hardest not to make a sound as I slid the lock in place.

Colt was coming. I could feel it in my bones. The code would work. He'd get here. He'd stop this.

He'd save me.

Colt

My truck pulled up outside our house, and I didn't even bother turning the engine off. I trusted Beau. And the fact that he wasn't answering his phone scared the shit out of me. Vi had used our panic alarm code in the security system. Our wedding date. She needed help. A car I didn't recognize was parked in the driveway.

Taking the steps two at a time, I burst in through the front door. I half expected Violet's shocked face to greet me, but there was only silence.

"Vi?" I headed towards the kitchen where I expected to find them. I needed to hear her voice. I needed someone to goddamn answer me. "Beau? What the hell is going on?"

Just as I stepped around the cabinets, my foot hit something solid. Dropping my gaze, my knees gave out and I fell to the floor.

"Beau?" My brother groaned, a bruise and swelling visible on his jaw. "Beau...wake up. Christ. Where the fuck is Vi? The baby! Beau..."

"He wanted her," my brother groaned, his eyes opening but not focusing on me.

I didn't wait for anything more. I ran. *Where the fuck was Connor?* Did that bastard take them both? My phone was out and I was on the line with dispatch before I hit the stairs. Taking them two at a time, I barked orders over the line, rattling off every piece of information I knew about Ryan before taking a breath, waiting for the instructions to be repeated back to me. As soon as I knew help was on the way, I slipped my phone back into my pocket and ran to the nursery.

Throwing the door open, my knees buckled at the sight of our son, swaddled tight with rosy cheeks, fast asleep in his crib. I needed to get someone over to the house as fast as I could.

My hands shook as I stepped out of the nursery.

"Hey, how's Vi?" my sister asked as she answered her phone. "I was going to ask if she would be good with me dropping off some freezer meals, but the weather is really changing—"

"Jess," I cut her off. "I need you and Hawk to come over here and look after Connor. Vi's missing. I need to search the ranch. But Beau's hurt and I can't leave Connor here alone."

"Hawk and I are coming right now, Colt. Okay? We're at the main house, so we're close. Beckett's going to stay with Mom and we'll come get Connor."

"Thank you." Those last two words burned as I said them. I ended the call, slipping the phone back into my pocket as I moved around the nursery. Violet had to be the one who laid him down here, I knew that in my heart. She'd kept him safe from Ryan. My eyes searched for any clues, but there were none that I could decipher.

She must have been so scared. Fuck, I needed to get to her. I grabbed the baby monitor and turned it on, breathing for a moment at the sight of our son so peaceful in the crib Violet had picked out a decade ago.

My feet felt heavy as I walked down the stairs. Beau was

sitting up, grabbing his head as his back leaned against the cabinets.

"I'm so sorry, Colt. *Fuck.* I'm so sorry."

I walked to the freezer and grabbed a bag of frozen vegetables. "It's not your fault. I got your message and came back as soon as I did. I should have been here."

Beau hissed as I pressed the cold bag against his face. "Ow."

"I had dispatch roll an ambulance out here."

"I don't fucking need—"

"You had your bell rung and you were out cold. Yes, you do. And you'll be heading to the hospital to make sure nothing is broken in your face. I'm already dealing with one stubborn brother who wouldn't ask for help. You're taking it even if I have to force you, too."

Beau closed his eyes. "Connor?"

"He's fine. Upstairs, asleep. Jess is on her way."

As if summoned by my words, my sister and her husband burst through the door.

"We're here! Oh my God, Beau!!" Jessie's voice was frantic.

"What can I do to help?" Hawk immediately asked.

"Just keep Connor safe. I don't think he should go out in this weather, and I don't think Ryan will come back here, so everyone here should be okay. Just hunker down as best you can through the storm, okay?"

"Christ, your jaw looks awful." Jessie stormed to the freezer, grabbing more bags of frozen vegetables and tossing them to Beau.

"I'm coming with you," he groaned as he pressed the cold makeshift ice pack against his skin.

"Absolutely not."

"I am. She was my responsibility, and I fucked everything up. You two losing each other the first time was your own goddamn mess, but I'm not being responsible for you losing her again."

"You need to be here to tell the deputies who respond what happened. They're on foot, Beau. I have a chance of catching them if they went deeper on the ranch."

"Colt, I know you want to go after them right now, but it might be a smarter play to wait for backup. He's unhinged. There's no saying what kind of weapons he could have."

Hawk had a point—but I couldn't just do nothing. I couldn't sit in our house, thinking of all the horrible things that sick bastard could be doing to her, without taking some sort of action.

"You're right. I don't want to get her hurt, or worse, if he's truly unhinged."

———

Living far outside the limits of Silver Springs was a blessing in many ways. The time it took for help to show up was not one of them.

I fucking paced back and forth with the baby monitor in my hand for what seemed like an eternity before the patrol cars and ambulance filled my front yard. I tossed the monitor to Jessie and was out the fucking door before anyone could say my name.

The rain poured down as my porch filled up with my coworkers.

"Ford, tell us what the fuck is going on?" Jonesy stood in front of me, his eyes wide with worry. The paramedics moved past us, heading straight into the house to deal with Beau.

"Demco, Mcallister, Langley. I want you on this house. My son is in there, and no one who isn't already inside should step foot in there until I'm back with my wife. One on the inside, two on the outside."

My phone chirped in my hand. As soon as I flipped up the screen to look at the alert coming in, I pointed to Nate and ran down the stairs towards his patrol car.

"Give me the keys!" I yelled over the wind and rain.

He dug into his pocket and tossed them over the hood. We were both inside the vehicle in a flash, his door not even closed as I started backing out of my yard.

"Where the fuck are we going?" he asked, grabbing the oh-shit handle above his head.

"I know where he took her. We're going to get my wife back."

VIOLET

"Callie?"

Shit. Shit. *Shit.* That monster was calling my name from the bottom of the stairs. I'd only been up here for a minute. One freaking minute! I needed something...anything...to give me a chance at getting away. I frantically pulled out the drawers in the bathroom as quietly as I could, ignoring the burning from my incision. God, I'd been so numb trying to keep up with him on the walk over here...I couldn't focus on what damage had been done there. I needed to survive whatever the hell he had planned.

His footsteps were loud on the staircase, drumming in half-time to how fast my heart was fluttering. I opened the last drawer, praying there was something more than a few old hair pins and soap bars. Something metallic caught my eye.

Scissors.

Sliding them into my still wet nursing bra, I quickly closed the drawers and pulled the fresh shirt I'd grabbed out of the dresser and walked out of the bathroom. Ryan was standing in the doorway, rage rolling off of him—until he saw me. Then it turned into something worse. Something so much darker.

Lust.

Trying not to recoil at his gaze, I walked as steadily as I could manage. I forced myself to smile the closer I got to him.

"Ryan, you came up here so fast! Did the water boil already? I think I'm getting a sore throat from being out in the rain like we were. I'd really love some tea."

His hand came up, stroking my wet hair, his fingers tangling awkwardly in the strands.

"You didn't have time to dry this while you were up here?" he asked.

"I didn't have anything to dry it with," I answered, sliding past him in the doorway. *Come on, Colt. Where are you?*

I walked down the stairs, holding my belly against the jostling motion of each step, only to freeze when I saw what he'd done. The living room was set up exactly like the night Alex and Arianna spent together. The couch throw pillows were down on the floor, blankets were spread around, and matches were by the fireplace, ready to start a fire.

"Do you like it?" Ryan's hot breath on my neck made my stomach roll. But I pushed down the nausea and nodded, using my speechlessness to project nervous excitement instead of complete dread.

He pulled my arm back so fast I couldn't react. I spun, his hand cupping my breast, and I yelped. Ryan's brows pulled together as his fingers skated over the rough outline of the scissors.

"Are you hiding something in there?"

I shook my head. My eyes dropped to his waist. *Where the hell was the gun?!*

"You are. Take it out. Now," he growled. "Let me see, Callie."

I pulled the scissors out, biting the inside of my cheek so I wouldn't cry.

"What were you going to use these for?" His eyes went

wide when I didn't answer. "Ah. You want to hold a weapon against me? I'm such an *awful man* that you feel the need to protect yourself from me, when all I was trying to do—all I've ever been trying to do—is protect you? Keep you safe from the world and *love you*? That's a crime?"

He threw the scissors to the floor and stormed into the kitchen. My parents had two knife blocks, and he grabbed the biggest, longest blade from the block closest to us.

"Ryan..." I held my hands up, my eyes never leaving the knife in his hand.

"Callie. I love you. If you tell me you don't feel the same, you might as well carve my heart out right now. Take the knife." The veins in his neck bulged. "TAKE IT!" He thrust the knife at me, my scream cutting through the air.

A split second later, the front door exploded inward. Ryan turned, knife still in his hand, lunging for Colt as he burst through the doorway.

Colt's weapon was drawn on Ryan in the next heartbeat.

"DROP YOUR WEAPON!" he shouted. Ryan stopped advancing, but held onto the knife. Colt's eyes flicked to me for one second—but that's all it took for Ryan to move again.

A second figure was in the doorway, and the bang of a gun going off filled the house. I screamed, covering my ears as I fell to the ground. Hands roamed over my back, down my arms, trying to pry my hands away from my face.

"It's okay, Vi. You're okay. I've got you. You're safe."

My eyes flew open at the sound of his voice. "Are you okay?" I cried.

"I'm fine."

"Oh, God. Ryan..."

"Jones had every right to fire on him, Vi. He wasn't going to stop."

I heard Nate talking into his radio as he held pressure on

Ryan's stomach. The knife was somehow across the floor; he must have kicked it after Ryan was shot.

"I need...I can't be here anymore," I gasped. My lungs burned. The place where our son had been cut from my body felt like it was on fire. Every inch of my body shook and I felt like I was going to fall into a million pieces. "C-Colt?"

"I've got you baby. It's just the adrenaline. Take some deep breaths."

"Connor?" I cried.

"He's fine. Hawk and Jessie are with him."

"Beau?"

"He's good, too. Stubborn as always, but hopefully on his way to the hospital to get his head checked out."

"Birdie's not h-here. He n-needs someone."

"Let's just make sure you're okay? How about we focus on that for a minute."

———

An ambulance came and took Ryan to the hospital—with about twenty-five deputies who each assured me one hundred times that he would be handcuffed to the bed the entire time he was in there, and promptly charged with a flurry of words I didn't quite comprehend. Colt was giving his statement to someone from the sheriff's department, while I sat huddled on the couch under a pile of blankets.

I just wanted to get home to my baby, but I knew we needed to take a trip to the hospital, too. He'd slipped something in my drink to make me weak, and I wouldn't risk nursing our son and exposing him until I knew what it was, and that it was no longer in my body.

Nate walked back into the house, his hand coming up to clap Colt's shoulder a few times before he turned towards me.

"Hey, apple-anche. You good?"

I nodded my head. "Thank you, for having Colt's back. He was distracted. He looked at me, and I distracted him. Ryan was so close. If you hadn't...I'm so sorry you had to..."

"No." Nate sat next to me, his hand resting on my arm. "I did what I was trained to do. I discharged my weapon to protect another officer from potentially fatal harm. He had a chance to stop. Colt told him to drop the weapon, and he chose his fate. And I'd do it again, Violet. It was the right call."

I nodded. "Are you going to be in trouble?"

"I'll have my badge and weapon taken until internal affairs completes their investigation. It's standard in things like this."

"So, you'll be stuck on front desk duty?" I smiled.

"Yeah, I guess I probably will be. But knowing you and Colt are safe...it's worth it."

Colt turned from the deputy taking his statement and walked over to me.

"Ready to head home?"

"Yes. More than ever. We just have one stop to make before we can."

"What?" His face scrunched up. "Where?"

"The hospital," I said, groaning as I stood. My body felt like it was filled with wet sand. Colt's hands were on me in a flash, Nate jumping up beside me.

"What do you mean the *hospital*?" Colt grumbled. "I thought you said you were okay?"

"I am. Ryan slipped something in my drink earlier. I don't feel as weak as I did immediately after I sipped it, but I'm worried about nursing Connor."

Colt bent down, one arm going behind my knees as the other slid behind my back.

"Oh God!" I yelped. My arms wrapped around my husband's neck. "You don't have to carry me."

"Yes, I do. Nate, get a ride back to the station with one of the other deputies. I'm taking your vehicle."

Nate chuckled from somewhere over my shoulder. "Sure thing."

"Don't do that to me, Vi." Colt's voice was filled with emotion as he set me in the passenger seat of the patrol car. "Don't downplay something serious. I need to know. I could have had you at the hospital already."

"I'm okay."

"Promise me. I almost..." He pressed his forehead against mine. "You are the most important person in my life, and I almost lost you tonight. Forever. I can't..."

"Hey," I said, pulling back so my hands could frame his face. "You found me. You came for me. And you saved me. I'm okay because of you."

I pressed my lips against his.

"I'm okay because of you," I repeated, knowing he desperately needed to hear those words and much as I needed to say them.

COLT

Three weeks later...

I heard Violet before I saw her; sleep rumpled and stretching as she came around the corner into the kitchen.

"Morning, darlin'." I smiled as I adjusted Connor in my arms. "How did you sleep?"

The nightmares hadn't quite left her yet—Ryan, prowling in the night, taking her away from our family—but every time they came, I quickly wrapped her up in my arms and kissed away the last tendrils of the fear that tried to swallow her whole.

"Sleep was pretty great. I had a mild heart attack when you both weren't in the room with me when I woke up, though." A book landed softly on the table in front of me.

"Sorry," I winced, "I thought I might be able to sneak down here and let you get some actually restful sleep."

"I'm fine. You let me sleep in yesterday, too." She leaned down and kissed me while my hand rested on our son's chest.

"I thought maybe this morning you'd want to talk over wedding details." I wasn't trying to push. But officially making Violet mine was the last piece of protection I could put in place for her.

"Really chomping at the bit, aren't you?" she asked as she took a sip from my coffee cup.

"It's important to me," I admitted. "Connor and I have the same last name. It's important to me that you do, too." My eyes dropped to the book she was nervously tapping her fingers on. It wasn't her usual style of cover, rather a leather one with deep ridges that formed what looked like an abstract ocean wave.

"What's that?"

"Oh," she smiled, "just a little gift for you."

"For me? What is it?"

Violet slid the book closer to me, but kept her hand in place so I couldn't open it.

"This is everything, Colt. Everything from the years we were apart. I want to start with a fresh slate, and I don't want there to be any secrets between us. These are my memories, but I want them to be yours, too. Before I give you it, can I have your phone?"

"Of course you can." My brows pulled together. "Why?"

"I think, while you take some time to read through this, I'd like to watch the video of you bonding with our son while I was in the ICU. I'd like to put those memories in my heart."

I typed Vi's birthday into my phone—yes, that was my lock code—and pulled up the video.

"Hand Connor over. I think I'm going to need to snuggle him as I watch this," she said.

Violet's arms were steady as she cradled Connor to her

chest. She gave me a quick kiss before disappearing back upstairs.

A minute later, I sat out on the back porch, the cold bite to the wind a welcome contrast to the way the direct sunlight was making me squint. My ass was firmly planted in the spot Vi spent so much time in all those years ago. The place I sat in when I was missing her over the years.

I held the book in my hands, contemplating if I was strong enough to read what I knew was going to be Vi's heart poured out onto paper. But she'd given it to me for a reason, and I wanted to honor that.

I flipped through the front, and the dates at the top of the pages made me gasp. Letters to me, starting from the night before our divorce was finalized.

Colt,

Tomorrow is a day I've been dreading since the words first fell out of my mouth. I don't want to leave you. I don't want to go. But I know I have to, for you to have a chance at happiness. Your eyes used to light up every time you saw me walk into the same room. But now, they are just filled with worry. And I can't keep doing that to you. Making you worry. Making you hold me while I break down. While I hurt. And scream. And try to find a reason to be here anymore. I'm not who I was when we got married. I'm a shell of that woman. Of the person you fell in love with. And I hate that for you. You deserve so much more. I don't want to let you go, but I'm going to. Please let

me. Fall in love again. Have babies. Let laughter
and joy back into your life.

I can't give that to you, but I can give you the
chance at it with someone else.

My vision blurred and I swallowed past the pain in my
throat. *Goddammit, Vi.* I should have seen what she was
doing. I should have known...

Turning a few pages, I saw another date I recognized. Her
mother's funeral.

Colt,

You were there today. Like an answer to my
prayers. How many times over the last few months
have I cried myself to sleep whispering your name?
And you were there. Like you heard and had to
come to me. Because you knew I was hurting. I'm
so grateful for that. For you. I don't think I would
have been able to get through today without you
being there. And I need you to know, if only on
this piece of paper and never in any other capacity,
that I still love you. So completely. With every
fiber of my being.

I want to come home. I want to fall asleep in
your arms and wake up early enough to send you
off to work with lunch and a kiss, like we did
before. I miss you more than I've ever missed
anyone in my life.

I'm leaving for New York next week, and

something in my heart is screaming at me to just go back to Silver Springs instead. Because what if I was strong enough to admit that this was all a mistake? And then I realize that's just being strong for something I want. I'm selfish. And you don't deserve that.

Fuck! I should have stayed. I should have been able to hear her say all of that to my face, because I would have set the record straight so fucking fast. A splash hit the page, smudging some of the ink. I looked up at the sky, brilliantly blue with not a cloud to be seen. I wiped my face, realizing my own tears were the culprit.

A red ribbon caught my attention. I flipped past nearly the entire middle part of the book. I would go back. I would devour and commit to memory every single word she wrote to me over the years. But I knew Violet. She'd flagged this part for a reason.

Colt,

I'm going to do it. One last chance to become a mom. And I'm using our embryo. I don't even know if you remember that it's in storage, or if you even care at this point. But it felt weird to not tell you. God, I'm so hopeful. Hopeful that it will work. That by some miracle, this baby will be the one to stay. And I'm so sorry that I can't tell you I'm doing this. I just can't risk breaking your heart again. I want so badly for you to be there. Helping me with the God awful injections. Holding my

hand when the embryo is placed in my womb. I
know I don't deserve that...

I scanned through the entries, my hands shaking even
though I knew what was coming.

> Colt,
> I'm pregnant! I can't believe it...

> Colt,
> I made it to thirteen weeks! I'm sitting here
> sobbing just praying for viability now...

> Colt,
> I felt him move...

> Colt,
> I made it to twenty-four weeks. He's viable.
> We finally made it to viability...

> Colt,
> I have a reader who's being weird. I don't
> know if it's the pregnancy that is making me feel
> so anxious about it, but things are starting to esca-
> late and I'm afraid...

> Colt,
> I'm coming back to Silver Springs and I'm
> scared you're going to hate me forever for not

telling you about the baby sooner. I couldn't. But he's almost here and I know you'll keep him safe. If I can't. If something happens. You'll keep our son safe.

Colt,

I haven't written in here since the day I left New York. But I want you to know...The baby's here. He was born, and you were there. You held our son before I did. You're holding our son right now in your arms, and I can't look away because I'm scared this is just a dream...

I couldn't continue. I was crying so hard that I had to close my eyes and take deep, gasping breaths. Feeling her grapple with the weight of every decision, knowing the depth that she struggled going back and forth on when it was safe to tell me about the baby, my heart broke for her.

I would come back to the book. I would read everything in detail. But right now, I needed to hold my wife.

I walked into the house, struck by the silence. I couldn't remember the last time it was quiet during the day. And I loved that. Because Violet and Connor made this house a home.

At the top of the stairs, I heard the water running, and my heart dropped. As soon as I walked into the bedroom, I could see a huddled figure sitting in the shower.

I checked on Connor, fast asleep in the bassinet by our bed, cheeks rosy and all snuggled in a swaddle. My clothes came off, left in a pile by my dresser. I'd deal with them later. Vi was most important right now.

Her cries were muffled, but I could still hear them. Fuck.

Steam billowed out as I opened the shower door, trying to make enough noise not to scare her, but gentle enough that she would feel safe telling me what was going on.

"Vi?" I sat down on the tile floor, my legs bracketing her hips. Her only response was more tears.

"Violet. What's wrong? Are you upset about the video? Hey, talk to me."

She twisted, sitting up on her knees, her arms flying around my neck. The momentum nearly bowled me over, but I caught her and steadied us both before I toppled over.

"I love you so much. I'm so sorry you thought I was going to leave you again after he was born. I had no control over that but I promise, nothing—*nothing*—could ever make me leave. I love you."

"I love you, too." I pressed a kiss to her forehead.

"I'm ready, Colt."

"Ready?"

She nodded. "To be married...Again."

BEAU

Four months later...

I cracked open the cold bottle of beer, sipping the overflow of foam as I leaned back in the old wicker chair on my front porch. Summer was just around the corner, and I was already feeling run into the ground managing the ranch.

The weather the past few days had us scrambling. Nothing new; just a harsh line of storms that didn't pass through as quickly as we were anticipating. Had our cattle out in a far pasture and needed to drive them into a closer field in order to keep them safe. Sure, they weathered the storm just fine once we got them where they needed to be, but it was an oversight I was ready to get chewed out for.

My dad was pushing me hard to take over our family's ranch. The Silver Ridge Ranch had been ours for over a hundred and fifty years, and keeping its legacy alive fell squarely on my shoulders. Lucky for me, I loved ranching. You wouldn't catch me ever trying to be a deputy like my brother Colt. Or a firefighter like my brother Hayes. Nope. Leave the chaos of humans to them. I was happy with the cattle.

A car started driving up the long road to my house. I could tell you every detail about that damn car just from the sound of its engine. I'd been listening to it drive to my place for the last fifteen years. And I could tell you every last detail about the blonde-haired, sun-kissed, probably absolutely exhausted woman behind the steering wheel.

Birdie's car spun up dirt that danced in the lowering sunlight like glitter. Fitting, because my best friend was all sunshine and rainbows. She'd been that way the first day I met her in kindergarten.

And as much as I enjoyed being a black cloud, pretending nothing could move or shake me, that couldn't be further from the truth. Because in quiet moments like this, when I could sit here and watch my best friend drive towards my house after a day that felt like it might never end, it was easy to whisper the truth for only my lonely ears to hear.

I loved her.

Not a new revelation for me. No. Instead, it was one I'd thought about over and over a million different times throughout our friendship. My family was so goddamn pushy about it, I'm still surprised she hasn't run away from their constant comments about us. And yes, fuck. I'd meant to make a move. To shift us from the friend zone into something more. But the weight of the world was always on Birdie's shoulders. She'd basically raised her sister on her own after her dad took off. Her mom was—and let's be honest, still is— flighty at best. Probably why she nicknamed her daughter 'Birdie'.

The car came to a stop right next to my truck, and out she stepped, looking absolutely dead on her feet. I wanted to run out and scoop her up. Tell her I was running her a bath and that her plate for supper was being kept warm in the oven. But I wouldn't.

I couldn't risk everything falling apart. Because if I only

ever got to experience this woman in this way, it was more than I fucking deserved. I wouldn't let anything break us. Not even my hope that something more might have once been in the cards for us.

"Hey, cowboy. You waiting out here for little ol' me?" she teased. Her hair was sticking out of the braid she had draped over her shoulder. I'd learned a long time ago when Birdie first started working at the hospital that the messier her hair was at the end of a shift, the more chaotic it had been for her.

I chuckled, bringing the bottle back to my lips. The amber liquid went down, cooling the fire in my belly.

"Hey, chickadee. Rough shift?"

She ran her fingers over her hair as she walked up the steps towards me. I thought maybe she'd head right inside and go get changed, but instead, she stopped two steps away from me, took the bottle out of my hand, and drained it.

"I'll take that as a yes?" I asked as she handed the bottle back to me. "You look exhausted."

"Wow. Thanks. You know just how to charm the ladies, don't you?" Birdie chirped at me.

I reached out, taking hold of her hand. She squeezed against my hold playfully. "I just meant you shouldn't have driven all the way out here if you were so wiped out."

"Yeah. I know there's no scientific data to support this, but I swear low pressure systems send everyone into labor. I delivered three babies during the storm. Dr. Witten delivered five over the last two shifts, including a set of twins. It's just madness there right now."

"I wasn't sure if you were going to head to your place or come out here, but I did save you some steak and a baked potato. Feel up to eating?"

Sometimes, after a long shift, she wouldn't eat until after she slept.

Her hand patted against my chest, and I knew what her answer was before she even opened her mouth.

"Okay." I chuckled. "I'll put it in the fridge for when you wake up tomorrow. Go on. Head upstairs."

Her smile was blinding, and my heart tripped over itself in my chest.

"Are you tired?" she asked, yawning as she looked over her shoulder out across the fields. "You have to move the herd before the storm rolled through?"

"Yes, to both of your questions. But I'll take the couch tonight. Just gotta jump in the shower and then I'll get out of your hair."

"It's your bedroom, Beau."

"I don't think I'm responsible for the fancy, ice cold sheets on the bed, or the frilly lace curtains that got put up, though. You might as well enjoy them. And I'm not sure how it happened, but my bottom drawer is filled with your pajamas..." I teased.

"You're always getting the short stick in this deal. I feel bad."

"Are you kidding me? Knowing you're upstairs...knowing you're safe in my house. That's the fucking dream, Birdie. I'll sleep like a king on the couch. Always do. Come on." I slid my hand against the small of her back, gently pushing her inside after I'd opened the door.

She took off up the stairs while I made my way to the kitchen, taking her supper out of the oven and dumping it into a container to keep it fresh until tomorrow when she could reheat it. There was a little more cleaning up to do from cooking, but it could wait until the morning. I didn't want to keep her up with running the shower too late.

Right as I walked in the room, she was stepping out of the bathroom. *In my shirt* and a pair of her sleep shorts. Fuck.

"Bathroom's all yours." She smiled as she pulled back the comforter and got into bed.

"Right." I cleared my throat, grabbing some clean clothes out of my closet. One five minute shower set on the fucking coldest temperature I could get it to, and I was towel drying off my hair as I opened the bathroom door, expecting to see her fast asleep in bed.

But she wasn't. She had every part of her body tucked into the blankets. Except for her eyes. As soon as her gaze met mine, I couldn't help but chuckle.

"Shouldn't you be sleeping?" I asked.

"Maybe you could..." Her eyes closed for a second, and I could feel the apprehension pouring off of her. Tossing my towel in the hamper, I padded towards the bed.

"What?" I tugged at the blanket covering her face.

"Can you stay? Can we snuggle?"

She had a tough day. A really tough day, if she was asking me to stay. "Of course I can stay. You want to talk about it?"

"About your cuddles?" she deflected.

"Birdie..."

"No. I don't want to talk about it. Because you're going to get all growly and protective, and I'm sleepy and just want to forget about what happened."

The temperature in the room dropped twenty degrees. Something *bad* had happened. "I don't like the sound of that."

"I'll tell you about it in the morning. Tonight, I just want to feel safe. I just want to know I'm safe. Please, cowboy?"

"Alright. But in the morning, first thing, we'll talk about what happened. Promise?"

"Promise."

I slipped into bed behind her. This was nothing new; we cuddled from time to time. Usually after something upset one of us, but sometimes there was no reason at all. Other than the need to be close to each other. No matter the reason, every time we ended up like that, it felt so fucking special. I was her safe place. And holding her tight, feeling her relax against me, it just served as a reminder that she was mine, too.

My arm moved under her back, an attempt to get her to roll towards me. But as soon as I touched her side, Birdie gasped.

"What the fuck?" The words, drowning in concern, raced out of me. "You're hurt! Did someone hurt you?"

"It's nothing," she whispered, rolling towards me to press her face into my chest.

"Chickadee, you're crying. It doesn't feel like nothing. Tell me. What happened?"

"In the morning. Remember? I just need...I just need some sleep. I promise this reaction isn't because I'm hurt. I'm not. I'm sore, but good. I'm just really tired."

"Am I going to see a bruise on your side in the morning?" I asked, letting my chin rest on her head.

"Probably," she mumbled, already sounding like she was slipping towards sleep. "Don't be grumpy. Sleep."

Like that was going to fucking happen. I needed to know how she got hurt. I needed to know if there was someone I needed to hurt in return.

A loud banging noise came from downstairs.

"Someone's knocking on the door," Birdie whispered.

"Probably just one of my brothers. They can fuck off until morning."

"Beau. They wouldn't just show up if it wasn't something serious. Go check."

"I don't want to leave you—"

"I'm fine." She yawned before rolling away from me. "I'll probably be asleep by the time you come back up here."

I nodded, not that she could see. As gently as I could, I moved off the bed, mentally running through the list of curse words I was about to unleash on whichever dumb ass brother of mine had ruined this moment for me.

The shock of a lifetime came when I opened the door, and instead of being greeted with one of my brothers, a petite woman in a pantsuit greeted me. A woman *with a baby.*

"Uh, hello. Can I help you?"

The woman looked up from the baby in the car seat and smiled. "Are you Beau Lindsay Ford?"

Christ. *The full government name.* I hadn't heard anyone mention my middle name since Hayes let it slip last year when we went to Austin together. What the hell did this lady want?

"Careful with that middle name, please. I haven't advertised that since it got out in fourth grade, and I got the shit kicked out of me on the playground. But, yes. I am. Who are you?"

"My name is Annabell Slater. I'm with Child Protective Services. May I come inside?"

Child Protective Services? What the hell was someone from there—someone with an infant in a car seat—doing on my doorstep?

"No children live here, Ms. Slater. I'm confused on why you would need to come inside."

Her brows furrowed. "Mr. Ford. Are you acquainted with a Ms. Rosa Monaco?"

My mind went blank before flooding with images of that night out with my brother.

Fuck. The woman I slept with last year...the one night stand from Austin. I'd made a mistake. *Her name was Rosa.* I fucking made a mistake, and buried that night down so deep because of the guilt I felt every time I looked at Birdie. My eyes dropped to the baby in the car seat. Bright blue eyes stared back at me. The same as *my* bright blue eyes.

"Yes." My throat felt like it was swelling. I couldn't breathe. "Is she okay?"

"Can I please come inside, Mr. Ford?"

"Beau. Mr. Ford is my dad. I'm just Beau."

Her face softened. "Beau. Can I please come inside?"

Soft footsteps sounded behind me. "Hey," Birdie greeted. "Is everything okay?"

Her eyes moved from me, to the woman, and then to the baby. "Oh my goodness, who do we have here?"

"Maybe it's best if we talked in private?"

"This is my best friend." The words squeaked past my scratchy throat. *Jesus.* Could you go into anaphylactic shock at the realization you had a fucking kid you knew nothing about? "She can stay."

Ms. Slater nodded. I pointed to the sofa, walking to it on shaking legs. Birdie sat next to me, her eyes glued to the baby the entire time. This woman was about to tell me I was a dad. I could feel it in my bones.

"Beau, I'm very sorry to have to tell you this, but Rosa passed away three days ago."

"Rosa?" Birdie questioned. *Fuck. Oh holy shit. My life was imploding in front of my very eyes. I'd fucked up and Birdie... God. This was going to hurt her. I was going to fucking hurt her.*

My hand dragged across my face, the stubble of a beard I should have shaved days ago scratching against my calloused skin. I couldn't feel it. I couldn't feel anything. Except shame, knowing I had to admit to something I wasn't proud of. "I slept with her when I went out to Austin for that rodeo weekend with Hayes, what? A year ago?"

"Juniper is four months old," Ms. Slater announced. The timeline matched. And then it hit me. She'd said the baby's name.

"Juniper..." I whispered. My heart squeezed. My daughter's name was Juniper. Something kicked inside my chest, a weird tightness as I let the idea of having a daughter take root. But maybe I shouldn't. Maybe I was getting ahead of myself.

"You're named on her birth certificate as her father. It's our first step when one biological parent, the primary care-giver, passes away, to locate the other biological parent."

Birdie sucked in a sharp breath next to me, but I just nodded. She had my eyes. Of course she was mine. Ms. Slater worked on getting the straps of the car seat loosened while I turned to face Birdie. All the color had drained from her face, and it wasn't just exhaustion that lined her red-rimmed eyes.

"You're a dad," she whispered, and I nodded.

"I didn't know. Can I hold her?" I croaked as the baby... *Juniper*...was freed from the seat.

"Of course."

She fussed as Ms. Slater transferred her into my hold. It should have been easy for my mind to deny it. For the loudest part of my brain to lash out in denial. But looking at her, looking at this little baby that fit perfectly into my arms and settled in my embrace, I knew there was no use denying it. I'd been a dad for four months, and hadn't even known it.

What the hell was I supposed to do now?

How will the news of Beau's unexpected fatherhood shift his —and Birdie's—whole world? Read their story in Sudden Summer, Book 2 in the Silver Ridge Ranch series!

ALSO BY TILLY H. COLSON

MEN OF CLARENCE COUNTY:

Hank

Jackson

Sebastian

Johnathan

Samuel

SILVER SPRINGS SERIES:

Silver Linings

Silver Secrets

Silver Sanctuary

Silver Shadows

Silver Sunrise

SILVER RIDGE RANCH:

Blue Norther

Sudden Summer

Derecho

Firestorm